BLIND
LUCK

Scott Carter

Cover design by Emma Dolan

We acknowledge the support of the Canada Council for the Arts for our publishing program. We acknowledge the financial support of the Government of Canada through the Book Publishing Industry Development Program (BPIDP) for our publishing activities.

Darkstar Fiction
an imprint of Napoleon & Company
Toronto, Ontario, Canada
www.napoleonandcompany.com

Printed in Canada

14 13 12 11 10   5 4 3 2 1

Mixed Sources
Product group from well-managed forests and other controlled sources
www.fsc.org Cert no. SW-COC-000952
© 1996 Forest Stewardship Council

FSC

Library and Archives Canada Cataloguing in Publication

Carter, Scott, 1975-
        Blind luck / Scott Carter.

ISBN 978-1-926607-00-9

        I. Title.

PS8605.A7779B55 2010   C813'.6   C2010-900891-X

to Keri and Harlow

One

When Dave Bolden's eyes finally opened that morning, it took him a moment to remember the night before. He had eaten a sushi dinner, drunk tequila, played pool, had more tequila, and kissed a redhead with high cheekbones and a perfect smile. He worked past the dull ache pulsating up his neck, through his brain and into his eyes, which felt so dehydrated, they hurt until his memory admitted it: a redhead with jowls and crooked teeth. The cab ride home was even less reliable. He remembered the smell of coffee, the glowing ember of a cigarette, swearing, small talk, honking and a driver named Jim, James or Ju Hee. All the names seemed possible, and whatever his name was, the driver hadn't looked anything like the identification mug shot of the cab owner on the back of the headrest that framed him as a fifty-something black man with receding hair and dark eyes that belonged in Hollywood. Or was that someone at a booth in the bar who'd drunk wine with a plate of mussels? Mornings were like that for Dave. He struggled to assemble a series of moments memorable enough to create a spark, but with details as elusive as a dream.

This was the true punishment of too much booze. Left with a body that begged for rest and a mind forced to stay awake, it was as if his brain had decided that if he did this voluntarily, then he was too stupid to deserve the peace of rest. He ran his swollen tongue across the roof of his mouth as he turned his head towards the clock to see that it was eight fifteen. *Eight fifteen?* Adrenaline shot through his system and forced him upright. *I slept through the alarm. Did I set the alarm?* The cold floor on his bare feet helped to pull him out of the world of sleep.

He grabbed a towel from the back of the door and was on his way to the bathroom when his right baby toe smashed into the wooden leg of a cabinet.

A burning sensation ran up his leg, harsh enough that his neck reared back and his eyes winced in pain. The blow stopped him. He didn't hop, scream or swear. He just wondered whether or not the toe was broken, until the fear of showing up late for work forced him into the shower. He turned both water handles to see a drizzle that meant one of the downstairs neighbours was also in the shower. His fingers tested the water, but the cool result just heightened his frustration, so he turned the handles off and on three times between prayers that each twist would result in a surge of water pressure.

He was about to give up when the pipes hissed and released a steady stream of warm water. Unfortunately, there was no time to enjoy. A quick scrub under each arm, a soapy water wipe of the groin, and he reached for a towel. He thought of the look of disappointment Mr. Richter would wear if he showed up late. It wasn't Richter's style to grandstand or yell. The look was more than enough, the one that proved you should know better, work harder, and embrace the opportunity to be employed there.

Dave had pressed the elevator button five times, as though that would make it come faster, when he realized he'd left his wallet on his dresser. It was tempting to just press on, but he needed money for a cab, so as the elevator doors opened, he pivoted hard on the carpet. He forgot things most mornings. Some days he forgot his cell phone and others his wallet. He'd tried a lot of things, but nothing seemed to help. Leaving sticky notes didn't work, leaving messages on the inside of the front door had proved futile, and leaving himself messages on his voicemail just annoyed him. Mornings were simply forgettable for Dave.

With his wallet in one hand, he adjusted his tie with the

other while doing his best not to focus on the drained reflection looking back at him in the elevator mirror.

He knew no morning should start like this, but no one should drink six pints and three tequila shots on a work night either. He never planned to stay out late; some nights he just felt compelled to go out, and whether he had a meeting the next day or a routine nine to six, he would leave his apartment and deal with the next day when it came.

The cool air helped his head, so he took a series of deep breaths through his nose. He hadn't reached the corner of his street when he heard someone say his name.

"Dave Bolden?"

He looked up to see a face that registered in his memory, although not strong enough to produce a full name. Grade Eleven math, or was it geography? He was an annoying kid who always asked about parties. Jimmy something.

"Jimmy Kerrigan, man. You don't recognize me, do you?"

"Sure I do. My mind was just on something else." Dave extended his hand while his eyes scanned for a cab. "How are you?"

"Good. I'm good. Jeez, I haven't seen you in years, Bolden."

Years weren't long enough for Dave. Jimmy was the kind of guy you never want to see after high school. A vivid reminder of a time when going to the right party formed the pillars of self-esteem, he was desperate and awkward.

"So what are you doing with yourself these days? Where are you working?"

Dave's eyes dropped to his watch. "I'm an accountant."

"An accountant? You're kidding me?"

"No."

"I never would have guessed that, man. What with all the…" Jimmy's fingers rose to his lips in an exaggerated joint-smoking gesture.

"Well, that was a long time ago."

"Yeah. Good times though, right?"

Dave couldn't even feign a smile.

"I'm working security right now. The hours are great, and I'm pretty much my own boss."

"Sounds good. Listen, I'd love to talk, but I've got to get to work."

"Okay. We should get together for a drink some time."

"Sure."

"Are you on Facebook?"

Dave nodded, even though he wasn't.

"Cool. I'll let you know when I'm going out."

Dave gave Jimmy's hand a quick shake, walked to the corner and hustled across the street to face traffic. He stepped out to hail down a cab, but it already had a passenger. The urge to swear forced him to squeeze the handle of his workbag. He didn't want other people to hear his frustration or how angry he was with himself. Two more cabs passed. He wasn't the only one cutting it close, but he felt like the only one not making forward progress. The urge to keep moving led him a few blocks down the street. Every couple of steps, he swivelled his neck to check for an oncoming cab, until one finally pulled over.

"Thank you so much," Dave said, dropping into the back seat.

"You must be late," the driver smiled. He spoke with a cigarette gripped tight in the left corner of his mouth and talk radio ranting about housing prices loud enough to be noticed.

"Dufferin and Dundas, please."

"No problem."

The stress intensified Dave's headache, which now felt like someone was tugging on his brain from a rope attached to the core with fishhooks. The smoke made him nauseous, so he rolled down the window to let in a blast of cool air.

"Smoke bothering you?" the driver asked.

"I'm a little hung over."

"Fair enough." The driver dropped his cigarette into the ashtray and crushed it with a large finger. "You're not going to barf in the cab, are you?"

Dave shook his head. "It's not that bad."

"You look like it is. You should have called in sick."

Just hearing the words bothered Dave. He'd watched his father call in sick too often growing up, and listening to the obvious lies and watching the look of guilt on the man's face had made him swear never to take a sick day. You take a few cough drops, hug a box of tissue and throw up in a wastebasket if you have to, but you do it at work.

He arched his neck on the headrest to look out the rear window and into the blue sky. *Thirty-five-year-olds should be married. Thirty-five-year-olds should make breakfast for their families and drop their children off at daycare. Thirty-five-year-olds should not be scrambling to get to work with one of the worst hangovers in history.*

"Right here is fine." Dave gestured to a newspaper box on the corner across the street from his work. The clock on the dash read eight fifty-six, but his watch read eight fifty-seven. "Thanks again, you saved me." He passed the driver a twenty.

"Thank you for holding your stomach in my car."

The driver extended the change, but Dave waved it off. He waited for a break in traffic with his eyes locked on the name RICHTER ACCOUNTING in block letters on the window of the boutique accounting firm. Positioned between a photocopy centre and a used record store that reeked of marijuana, this was clearly not the city's business core. The driver of an SUV flashed Dave the middle finger as he jogged past the vehicle to the sidewalk, but he didn't have the time or energy to respond.

The familiar jingle of the same bells he heard every workday greeted him, but in his hung-over state they clanged like the sound of church bells at noon. He reached for his temples and did his best to smile for his colleagues. The office was well decorated but small. With sturdy furniture from the seventies, generic colours, and more wood than plastic, the place was a throwback. This was where Dave spent fifty-something hours a week. He'd never envisioned a place like this when his dad had told him as an undergrad that he had never met an accountant without money.

Four cubicles and a front reception desk made up the visible working space. Shannon, a thirty-something receptionist in black pants and a black top just barely acceptable for the workplace, raised her eyes from a flat screen.

"Good morning," she said in a tone far too sexy for the office.

They'd bonded after they'd stayed later than anyone at the Christmas party, shared stories about university and made out until she'd panicked about being intimate with someone from work.

Mr. Richter turned from the water cooler, glanced up to the clock then returned his eyes to Dave. Neither his boring suit nor shaggy grey hair fit his wealth, but money didn't matter to Richter the way it did to most people in the accounting business.

Richter loved the work. He valued the interaction with the clients, the trust, and the responsibility. Many sixty-six-year-olds with that much money retire, but Richter never mentioned the word.

"You look tired." He gestured at Dave with his cup of water.

Dave offered a meek nod while walking past the boss to a pot of coffee adjacent to Irene's desk. Dave had never figured out why Richter had hired Irene. She was in her mid-twenties, full of energy, and chose play over work every time. She talked on the phone to friends, took numerous cigarette breaks, surfed the Net, and kept eBay on her desktop. She pressed hold on her phone, lowered her headset and spun her chair towards Dave.

"Out late last night?"

He raised his mug of coffee as if toasting success. "Very."

She opened the top drawer of her desk, and the white tips of her French manicure stood out against the black surface.

"Headache?"

"I'm feeling the burn."

She removed a bottle of Aspirin from her desk and held it up as he passed so he could take it from her without breaking stride.

"You're the best."

"I know."

Dave wished he'd made out with *her* at the Christmas party. Irene was someone with panache. He scolded himself while he walked past Todd, who smelled like hot dogs. The man didn't even raise his eyes from a document long enough for a perfunctory exchange, but Dave liked it better that way. Todd was so bland, so overweight, such a shell of who he wanted to be, that all he did was remind Dave of the ultimate futility of life as a number cruncher.

Dave stepped into the washroom, opened the first stall door and stepped away with disgust when he saw a toilet full of shit. He thought of Todd's heavy frame hunched over, with his cheeks flushed and his podgy fingers flexed around his newspaper.

"Christ."

He wanted to say more, to open up the door, drag Todd back into the washroom and yell, *Is this any way to leave a toilet?* But he couldn't. Todd wasn't the one who was almost late and already on a bathroom break.

He entered the next stall, removed a few strips of toilet paper to cover the seat and sat down. In a smooth motion, as he had done many times before, he tapped two Aspirin into his right hand and chased them with coffee before putting the coffee cup and Aspirin bottle on top of the toilet paper dispenser. Bent over, with his hands cupped on his head, as if by stabilizing it he could stop the pounding, he pleaded for a clear thought, until a loud rumble warned that he should look up.

This was the type of noise he knew shouldn't be happening. Too random and violent to be deliberate, it was the type of chaos that instinctively provokes fear.

He listened carefully to assess the situation, but an explosive sound followed the rumble, so he put a hand on each side of the stall in anticipation of the ceiling caving in.

He waited for paint chips, then plaster chips, or the entire second floor. The sound of glass shattering and metal crumpling filled the room as his arms flexed, but the ceiling never fell. He raised his eyes with caution to the lights above him to see that there wasn't even a crack in the surrounding paint, then it became that clear the noise had come from the main room. Two deep breaths and he pulled up his pants from his ankles, exited the stall and walked towards the main room, unsure whether or not he wanted to see what awaited him.

The washroom door creaked as he opened it, so he pushed it hard to get it over with and stepped into the main room to see two-thirds of an eighteen-wheel big-rig truck filling the space. Steam blew from the grill, making everything hazy, but Dave could still make out the tail end of the truck on the sidewalk and road, which made it clear that the vehicle had blown through the business's front windows.

He scanned the room, but it took a moment for the details to work past the shock. Shannon's legs stuck out from the debris, Mr. Richter lay face down beside her, and Todd's back and broken arms were visible beneath the truck's side. Dave had expected more noise, but the room was remarkably quiet except for the faint sound of plaster dust, glass and metal settling. The quiet confused him, as if this were all a bizarre nightmare, until he looked across the room to where Irene lay partially covered by rubble.

A human-sized dent in the wall above her body provided evidence that the truck's impact had propelled her into the plaster. The room looked surreal, but everything about the pool of blood around Irene's head was real. The colour, the mess and the finality were all vivid enough to force Dave to admit that this was really happening. He wanted to rush over to all of them and help somehow, but he couldn't move.

The truck had destroyed the building and killed everyone he worked with. Shock defied his will, so he stood there absorbing the unbelievable until the sound of approaching sirens tore through the quiet with increasing intensity.

Two

Ruby Bolden looked at her husband like she wanted to shake him. "The front lawn really needs cutting, Jack. The neighbours are starting to stare."

Jack was too engrossed in the pages he held to hear anything beyond the possibilities running through his head. In the previous minutes, he had completed more math than he had in four years of high school. Number of races, multiplied by the horse's odds, multiplied by the wager. If only the rest of life was so linear.

"Do you think you'll get to it today?" Ruby persisted.

Jack still didn't respond, so she put both hands on the table where he sat and leaned forward so that only a glass bowl of marbles separated them. "I said, are you going to get to it today?"

Jack looked up, and the nerves above his right eye twitched so strongly, he had to rub the socket. "Get to what?"

"The lawn. The neighbours are starting to stare."

"So let them cut it."

His eyes returned to the pages. Number of races, multiplied by the horse's odds, multiplied by the wager.

"For Christ's sake, Jack. It'll only take you fifteen minutes."

Jack looked up again, folded the pages and rose from the seat. "I'm joking. I'll do it after Dave's game."

He kissed her on the cheek and stepped towards the living room, where Dave played with a collection of miniature cars in front of a T.V. tuned into a game show.

"You ready, buddy?"

Dave hopped to his feet, nodded and grabbed his baseball

glove from the couch. Ruby hadn't said a word since Jack had risen from the table.

"Wish him luck," Jack said, kissing her again.

"Good luck, David. Have fun."

"Thanks, Mom."

Jack didn't say much during the drive to the ballpark. Sports talk radio debated whether or not taxpayers should have to contribute to a new stadium while Jack waited for injury reports and odds.

Number of games, multiplied by the odds of each team winning, multiplied by the wager. A station wagon cut in front of them on the way into the parking lot, prompting Jack to lean on the horn, drop the window and fire a middle finger into the air.

Eight-year-olds only play six innings. By the bottom of the fifth, Dave had ten strikeouts in a one-nil game for his team. Jack leaned into the heavy-set man beside him. With a thick red beard and a protruding brow, the man looked almost primitive.

"Your son playing?" Jack asked.

The man turned his head. "What's that?"

"What number is your son?"

"Fifteen," he said, pointing to a kid a good thirty pounds heavier than anyone else sitting in the dugout. "What about yours?"

"Mine's the pitcher."

"The kid's got a good arm. He must have half a dozen strikeouts."

"Ten."

"Ten?"

"Yep. And I've got a fifty that says he's at a dozen by the end of the inning."

"No way. Ritchie's up soon, and there's no way he whiffs again. He's leading the league in home runs, you know?"

"So let's make it a hundred."

"Two more strikeouts by the end of the inning?"

Jack extended his hand. "Guaranteed."

"You're on."

The man with the red beard cursed Dave's next four pitches, but after opening with a ball, he fired two strikes past the batter. His next pitch was a fastball that left the batter swinging for air and sent the crowd into a loud series of oohs. Jack didn't even smile. This was his son. He had watched Dave many times before and knew he didn't pitch like an eight-year-old.

Dave almost hit the next batter with a curveball that sailed high enough that the boy dropped his bat and headed for the dugout. The coach tried to steer him back to the plate, but the kid shook his head until snickering from his teammates forced him back into Dave's line of fire. The kid couldn't keep his bat steady as Dave reared back for the next pitch, and when the ball came, he closed his eyes as he swung. He must have surprised himself by making contact, because as the weak grounder rolled towards the shortstop, he remained at the plate. After his coach screamed him into the moment, he got about three steps towards first before the shortstop threw him out. Jack stirred in his seat while the man beside him with the red beard clapped awkwardly.

Jack wanted to cheer for Dave, but all he saw were the mistakes the kid had made with the last two pitches. *Keep your head down; drive the pitch with your lead leg; stop looking at the homeless guy picking through the garbage can beside the stands.*

The man with the red beard rose to his feet as his son Ritchie approached the plate from the batter's box.

"Let's go, Ritchie. It's your field, son."

Ritchie looked even bigger close up. With large hands, chubby cheeks, accentuated by the helmet pressing against them, and feet the size of many men's, he looked more like a ten or eleven-year-old.

Dave's first pitch bounced into the gravel before the catcher secured the ball.

The man with the red beard shook his head. "That's right kid, you don't want to put it anywhere near the strike zone with my boy."

The second pitch avoided the ground, but it still landed too far away from the strike zone. Frustration surged through Jack's arms until his fingers wrapped around the bottom of the bench. *Eyes up, snap your wrist.*

Dave raised the peak of his cap and wiped his face with his forearm. He looked over at the homeless man, who was only visible from the waist down as the rest of him stretched for something he wanted at the bottom of the can. Dave pivoted towards Ritchie, cocked back and fired a fastball right across the plate. Ritchie swung so hard, he fell to one knee. The crowd and both teams chuckled.

"The kid's got a rocket for an arm," a man with a ponytail sitting behind home plate repeated to anyone that would listen.

Dave chose a slider for the next pitch, and Ritchie caught enough of the ball to send it spinning three feet backward into the cage. The man with the red beard rose to his feet again.

"He's catching up with it. Attaboy, Ritchie. You've got a beat on it now."

Jack didn't hear a word of the trash talk. He never did. What he saw was Dave focussing on everything but the next pitch. The boy heard his teammates screaming his name, his opponents cursing him, and he was watching the catcher's mother—a woman of no more than thirty wearing a pink top that struggled to contain oversized breasts. *This boy's got to learn to focus.*

Dave exhaled, reared back and side-armed a curveball too low for the strike zone, but Ritchie didn't see a curve. He guessed a fastball and swung another full-weight swing as the pitch zipped past him.

"Strike three," the umpire yelled.

The man with the red beard dropped to his seat. Jack nodded while tapping the empty wood between them. The hundred dollars felt like a hundred thousand. The next inning the coach decided to sit Dave, and the closer allowed four runs in a four to one loss.

"How about some ice cream?" Jack asked in the car. "You've earned it."

Dave didn't respond.

"I don't want you feeling bad about the loss. You threw twelve strikeouts. That's more than one for every year you've been on the planet. You've got nothing to feel bad about."

"We lost."

"*They* lost. You pitched twelve strikeouts and went two for three with a double and an RBI."

The words didn't remove the frustration from Dave's face. His eyes narrowed to form the look that accompanies all eight-year-olds learning the humility of defeat, but Jack gave the horn a honk anyway.

"Hell, let's make it an ice cream cake then. I'll teach you how to celebrate before the day's done."

He honked the horn again and poked Dave under the armpit in his most ticklish spot. Dave tried to look angry, but within seconds he broke into a smile.

Three

Dave waited in the detective's office for twenty minutes, and he replayed finding his dead colleagues twenty times. Instead of the soft rock on the office radio, he heard the crumpling of metal that had accompanied the destruction. An image of the eighteen-wheeler looking as out of place in the office as a fully functioning reception desk would look in the centre of the road shadowed every thought, and flashes of his colleagues' broken, limp bodies haunted him.

A detective's office was the last place he wanted to be, but they had questions, and he understood they needed answers. He thought of his bed, the covers pulled tight over his head; his father's nursing home, and any bar with a thick, cold pint, when Detective Naves entered the room. Sitting across from Dave, Naves looked like the archetype of how actors chose to portray detectives on T.V. shows. He wore a forgettable suit, had a strong build and ran a finger over a moustache that would make most people think of Halloween. But it was clear he didn't see himself that way. His forty-something eyes were proud, and everything about his manner and comfort in the environment suggested he had been doing the job for years. He looked at Dave long enough to make him feel uncomfortable before saying anything.

"Do you want another coffee?"

"No thanks."

"Then I'm going to get started, if that's okay with you."

Dave nodded.

"How long did you work at Richter Accounting?"

"This is my seventh year."

"And what is your official job title?"

"Accountant."

"How many employees worked at the office?"

Dave thought of their broken bodies. "Art Richter owned the business, and there were four others including me."

"Do you remember who entered the building last that day?"

"Yeah, me. A couple of minutes before nine."

"And the accident happened at six minutes after nine?"

"Best I can tell."

"Did anyone leave the office after you arrived?"

"Not that I know of. But if they did, it couldn't have been for long."

"And you were in the washroom when the truck made impact?"

"Sitting down in the washroom."

Detective Naves paused for a moment to scratch behind his ear with the pen. "How much time passed between you going to the washroom and the incident?"

"I'm not sure, maybe two minutes."

"Was anyone alive when you entered the main room?"

"There's no way anyone was alive."

Detective Naves picked up his pad of paper. "You must have an angel on your shoulder, Mr. Bolden."

He looked at Dave for a moment the way detectives do. He absorbed every detail and worked to make connections. What he likely saw was a man who realized for the first time in his life that horrible things can happen to him.

The realization was different than the painful scares of a broken bone or setbacks like being dumped by a girlfriend or passed over for a promotion, because he had to accept the finality.

Detective Naves rose from his seat. "There's a psychologist here who would like to speak with you."

Dave shut his eyes. He just wanted to go home, take a shower and let everything settle in. He didn't want to talk about how he felt; he didn't know himself yet.

"I've seen a lot of tragedies in my years here, Mr. Bolden," Detective Naves said. "And I can tell you that people who speak to someone are better off for doing so."

Dave nodded. It was easier to agree. A part of him wanted to say, *I don't give a fuck how many tragedies you've seen, you haven't seen my friends mangled under an eighteen-wheel truck.*

But that required energy, and he barely had enough to stay conscious.

A woman with short red hair, a sprinkle of freckles on both cheeks and pistachio eyes entered the room as Detective Naves left. A visitors' pass dangled from a clip on her suit jacket: Dr. McMillan.

"I'm Mia," she said, extending her hand. Dave was surprised to find it colder and sweatier than his. She sat down and sipped from a large styrofoam cup of coffee. "I'm a trauma councillor, Dave. I work with cases like yours, cases with incidents where there are few survivors."

Her voice felt an inch away from his face. He wanted to drag her back to the office, back to the smell of fried wires, back to the look of crushed bodies and dare her to speak with that tone then.

"Look, I appreciate your offer, but I don't want to talk any more. I've already been here for awhile, and I just want to go home."

"Do you live with anyone, Dave?"

It took him a moment to accept that she had ignored his wishes. "No."

"Is there anyone you can stay with for a few days?"

"I just want to go home."

"Or maybe someone could stay with you."

"I don't want anyone to stay with me."

Half frustrated by his ignorance and half-inspired by his defiance, she looked at Dave like she knew something he didn't. She took another mouthful of coffee before continuing. "You're going to have a lot on your mind; it'll be best to have someone to talk to."

"I just want to get home."

"It's important that you don't blame yourself for what happened." Dave looked at her like she was crazy, and not crazy in an intellectually-weird sense, but shit-in-your-hand, preach-on-the-subway crazy. "These type of horrors tend to be so overwhelming," she added without pausing, "so far away from the common experience that the mind copes by ascribing meaning."

"I'm not doing that."

"Not yet. But if you find yourself looking for a reason why this happened, or thinking in any way that you had something to do with people dying or living, I want you to call me."

She slid a business card across the table. Dave noticed she wasn't wearing a wedding ring.

"Fair enough."

"Will you do me a favour before you go?"

Dave made eye contact. Her eyes swirled with an intensity that confused him, and he wasn't sure whether she was stimulated by her job or if she genuinely cared. He didn't respond, but his look suggested she could go on.

"Take ten minutes and write down every detail you remember about what you saw."

"I know what I saw; I can't get it out of my head."

"Today you can't. But the odds of you distorting those memories as the days go by are very high, and the odds of you distorting those memories to fit the theories you'll develop to explain why you lived and your coworkers died are even higher. What you write down now will protect you from yourself later."

Shut the fuck up, he thought. *Protect me from myself? I don't need protection from myself. I need protection from eighteen-wheel trucks.* He picked up her business card before rising from his seat.

"I'm leaving now. Thank you for your...words."

She didn't try to stop him. In fact, nobody spoke to him as he entered the precinct lobby to wait for an elevator.

What Dave didn't know was that Grayson Leonard was watching him from a bench, where he sipped on a white mocha. Grayson wore an Armani suit and looked at Dave with eyes that capitalized on details.

He found the tiny differences most people didn't notice—the differences that separated the poor, middle-class and rich. He joined Dave by the elevators.

People walking past looked a moment longer at Grayson than they did anyone else in the lobby. They watched him like he might be a famous lawyer, detective or Mafia Don. Nothing about him was average or forgettable. At almost forty-five, his physique looked ten years younger. Even in a suit, it was obvious his body was strong, and his cleanly-shaved head, swarthy skin and warm eyes belonged more in a movie than the muck of the downtown core. He stepped into the elevator behind Dave, waited for the doors to close to ensure privacy, then turned towards him.

"Mr. Bolden?" Dave looked up. "My name is Grayson Leonard. I'm from SBT Global Investors. We were scheduled to meet this afternoon."

Dave shook the extended hand as a reflex, but he didn't get past the word "meeting". Surely the man hadn't tracked him down at the police station to remind him of a meeting. He didn't know whether to ignore Grayson or punch him.

"I imagine your head's spinning," Grayson said.

Dave chose to ignore him.

"My heart goes out to your colleagues and their families. I tracked you down here because the owner of our company, Mr. Thorrin, wants to meet with you. He has an offer he believes can make some good of this tragedy."

Dave made eye contact for the first time. As much as he wanted to confront Grayson, the tone of the man's voice was disarming. Equal parts enthusiastic, honest and engaging, he reminded Dave of a politician.

"An offer that's for you only."

The elevator stopped, and they stepped out into a crowded lobby. Dave deliberately stayed quiet until he led them outside and into the much needed fresh air.

"This guy you're talking about…"

"Mr. Thorrin."

"Mr. Thorrin. He realizes what happened today, right?"

"He does, but he feels it's in your best interest to focus on the future." Grayson extended a card. "This has my work extension and two cell phones. Give me a call and let me know when you'd like to meet with Mr. Thorrin. Within the next twenty-four hours is best, as he's anxious to get this process under way."

Dave looked at him like he was crazy. There had to be a catch to this, but Dave felt too exhausted to figure it out. Maybe the man was crazy, or maybe he was actually a journalist working hard to get a story no one else had, or an insurance shark looking to angle his way into details about the crash. Grayson's extended hand held position in front of Dave for a moment before he noticed.

"It was a pleasure to meet you, Mr. Bolden."

They shook hands, but when Dave pulled away, Grayson held on. It wasn't the type of hold that had any sexual connotation, but a firm grasp that waited to see what might happen if he held it a little longer. Dave finally freed his hand, and they exchanged a long look before heading in opposite directions. Grayson didn't wash his hand for the rest of the day.

Four

When Dave was nine, his father left him overnight at a stranger's house. Only, he hadn't planned to, especially not when he woke his son up that morning.

"Let's go. We've got a big day ahead of us," he said, pulling on Dave's feet.

Dave opened his eyes to see his father hovering over him and almost screamed until he noticed the index finger shushing him to be quiet.

"Where are we going?"

"It's a surprise."

"Is Mom coming?"

"No, we're going to let her sleep." Two day's stubble ran thick on Jack's face. Purple bags shaded his eyes a sickly colour, but he was smiling. "Let's go have some fun."

Bob Dylan played loudly on the car's speakers while Jack's lips mouthed the words. Dave didn't say anything until the car pulled into Bubba's Burgers.

"You ready for a burger?" Jack asked.

"For breakfast?"

"I'm starving, but you can have whatever you want; it's going to be that kind of day."

Dave thought of the week before, when he'd asked for French fries after Saturday morning baseball practice. *No way you put that garbage in you this early.* Dave seized the moment, ordered a burger, fries and onion rings, and finished off with a strawberry sundae.

Jack wrote on a small notepad as he ate behind the wheel. He put the burger on one thigh and the notepad on the other. Dave couldn't see what he was writing, and between the burger, rings and ice cream, he really didn't care either. All he knew was that his dad hadn't stopped smiling since the day started.

"Okay," Jack said, gathering up the wrappers. "Now we can get down to business. Any guesses where we're going?"

Dave shook his head.

"We're going to buy action figures. Plural. Not *a* G.I. Joe. G.I. *Joes*. As many as you can fit in your arms."

Dave visualized it. He figured he could hold at least seven, eight if he held one between his teeth; maybe even nine if he hopped with one between his knees. The thoughts set off a wave of excitement that combined with the sugar breakfast to make him bounce-in-his-seat hyper. Dave was watching his dad get out of the car to throw out the garbage when a man approached with his hat held out for change. Even at his young age, Dave could tell that a different man lived somewhere beneath the bushy beard, skin distorted by veins too close to the surface, and eyes glazed with unrest. Jack did better than change, he stuffed a twenty in the man's cup.

They'd pulled into the toy store parking lot when Jack's pager started to buzz. Before he could reach it, the vibrations sent it across the dashboard until it fell into Dave's lap. He passed it to his dad.

"The vultures always come to the prey, buddy."

Dave was used to his dad uttering bizarre phrases, metaphors or clichés insinuating something at least a step away from his nine-year-old mind.

Jack had misled Dave when he said he could have as many action figures as he could carry. He ended up buying more. Dave inched his way to the cash with a figure between his legs and one pinched in each armpit while Jack sauntered behind him with five more. The total cashed out at $155. Jack paid the high schooler behind the counter $170 and met her return of the change with hand palm up.

"No, no, no. That's for you."

They weren't out of the parking lot before Dave pulled an action figure from the bag.

"Can I open one now?"

"Of course you can. In fact, you owe it to the guy. Think how long he's been waiting to get out of there."

Dave thought of toymakers, soldiers and what it would be like to be trapped in plastic. His father looked over at him at the next stop light.

"You know we can't tell Mom about this, right?"

"Why?"

"Well…she doesn't believe in spoiling you."

"Why's she so mean?"

"Don't say that. She's not mean, she just wants what's best for you. She doesn't want you to take things for granted."

"I don't."

"I know. Just keep this one under the radar."

"How?"

Jack looked at the overflowing bag. "I'll get them up to your room for you."

The pager vibrated again. This time Jack picked it up immediately. He looked at the number before turning his head to Dave.

"We've got to make a stop before we go home, buddy. I have to drop by my friend Tom's house. He's got a son a year older than you. Johnny. He's a cool kid."

Fifteen minutes later, Dave sat in a living room where everything was orange, thinking that Johnny was anything but cool. Johnny's black hair hung over his head in every direction except for a four-inch strip across his forehead that was cut straight, so he could see. He didn't turn from the T.V. after saying hello. On his knees, with a miniature baseball bat in his left hand, he watched a game show with gaudy lights like it was the most interesting thing he had ever seen.

"We're just going to go into the kitchen for a drink. You want anything?" Jack asked.

Dave thought of his unopened G.I. Joes in the car, but he knew his dad just wanted to leave the room, so he shook his head. He was glad that Tom left too. Tom was a huge man, all fat and as big as the wrestlers Dave watched on T.V. Something about his face made Dave uneasy. His eyes were too small for his head, his cheeks were so fleshy they seemed to smother his face, and he had a spotty beard that was thinner but longer than Dave's dad's. Dave was wondering whether he should say anything to the back of Johnny's head when a woman teetered into the room in knee-high boots and hugged him before he could respond.

"Oh my god, you must be Jack's boy."

The woman smelled of a mixture of sweet perfume and cigarettes. The hug felt good. "You are adorable," she said, tickling his cheeks with press-on nails.

That felt good too. "I'm sorry Johnny's no fun, sweetie, but he loves his T.V. Don't you, baby?" She bent down to kiss the top of Johnny's head. For a moment, Dave thought she was going to fall, until she steadied the wobble. He had never seen heels so tall.

Jack re-entered the room without Tom. He squeezed the woman's hand before she kissed him on the cheek.

"Tom and I have to go out for a bit. Can I leave Dave with you?"

"Of course. We'll have a good time together."

Dave's heart began to race.

"I've got to go out with Tom for awhile, so you're going to stay here with Linda."

"Can't you take me home first?"

"I'm afraid not, buddy. I've got to leave right now, but I'll be back before you notice. Watch some T.V., have a snack, and I'll be back before you're done."

Three hours later, he was still gone. Linda sauntered into the living room with a tray of drinks in tall glasses. Dave was afraid to move from his position on the couch.

"Here's yours, Johnny, and yours, sweetie," she said, leaning down to kiss Dave on the cheek. "And Mommy's." She brought the straw to her lips and pulled until her cheeks sucked inward. Dave took a sip of his. The drink consisted of fruit juice and crushed ice with a wedge of orange cut into the shape of the sun. He was surprised that it tasted so good. He was about to thank Linda when she started to dance.

"Come on, Johnny, dance with your mother."

"I'm watching T.V."

"How about you, cutie?" She pointed at Dave with a long nail. He was afraid to say anything, so he just sat there until she took him by the hands and led him to the carpet.

"Let's go, move those hips, little one."

Dave moved like a robot. One foot in front of the other, he rocked without hip movement. Linda couldn't stop laughing. She didn't stop moving either. The Stories' "Brother Louie" led her in every direction as her hair swirled and her hips swayed. Dave watched in amazement until the sound of a phone ringing interrupted the moment. Linda answered, short of breath. Her voice was raspier now.

Within seconds she went to the hall, and a beat after that, she yelled into the phone as her heels stomped their way up the stairs. Dave stopped the music, and Johnny turned from the television.

"Do you want to have a hamster race?"

"What?" Dave wasn't sure he heard him correctly.

"Do you want to have a hamster race?"

"Sure," Dave whispered. He was afraid to say no.

"Cool."

Johnny opened the cage, dug into an excessive amount of wood shavings and removed two of the fattest hamsters Dave had ever seen.

"Which one do you want?" Johnny asked, holding them out for Dave's inspection.

"I don't know."

"It's an important choice, because the loser gets this." He put a foot on the ruler-sized baseball bat.

"What do you mean?"

"I mean if yours wins, you get to kill mine, and if mine wins, I get to kill yours."

"But they're both yours."

"Only because you haven't picked one. Now which one do you want?"

The hamsters suddenly looked much cuter. The fat appeared fluffy, and the teeth seemed to form a smile.

"Let's go," Johnny pushed.

Dave pointed to the hamster with a white tuft of hair almost like a mohawk.

"Good choice," Johnny said, waving the hamster through the air like a toy airplane. "He's a little younger." He gripped both hamsters tight as he knelt on the floor, where the oversized daisies patterning the carpet made a ridiculous racetrack. "First one to the wall wins."

Dave felt faint. He wanted to run, to tackle Johnny, to scream for Linda and return the hamsters back to the safety of the cage. But he didn't do anything.

"Ready...set...go."

Johnny released the hamsters, but neither of them moved forward. Dave's tried to make it back to the cage until Johnny's leg stopped it. Johnny's didn't fare any better. After a series of circles, he just stopped moving, but the absurdity didn't deter Johnny's enthusiasm.

"Go, go," he screamed as he bounced on his knees.

As if on cue, or perhaps because they feared Johnny's high-pitch, both hamsters headed for the wall at once. The speed of their humpy bodies surprised Dave.

He thought of grabbing the bat from the floor to seize control, but the thought didn't last long. Johnny was a year older, which to a nine-year-old might as well have been a decade. He was in Grade Four, he was taller than Dave, and he wore a silver chain.

Johnny's hamster bumped into the wall first.

"Yes," he cried.

Dave didn't blink twice before Johnny picked up the bat in one hand and the hamster with the white tuft of hair in the other.

"Where's your bathroom?" Dave asked.

"Upstairs, end of the hall. Why?"

"I need to go."

Johnny raised the bat. "You don't want to see this, do you?"

Dave shook his head.

"Fag."

Dave exited the room with thoughts of the hamster being clubbed, but they disappeared as soon as he saw how dark the rest of the house looked. An uncovered red bulb gave the stairwell a little light, and it seemed like there were a thousand steps. He was tempted to sprint up them in order to avoid the eerie creak of each stair, but the darkness waiting for him kept him to one at a time. The higher up he got, the more he thought he saw a shadow waiting at the top, so he locked his eyes on the next step ahead.

His heart beat so fast that he reached the hallway believing he could see the boogeyman, ghosts, vampires or a serial killer. He took a deep breath, stepped forward into the darkness and stumbled on something. His momentum took him into a wall with a thud, and fear sucked the air from his chest. He felt the wall frantically for a light switch, and a series of gasps escaped his lips until his finger touched a dimmer. He turned the dimmer and saw that he had stumbled over one of Linda's boots. The other boot sat upright against the wall. He looked down the hall to see a door slightly ajar illuminated by the light on the other side. The door wasn't more than fifteen steps from where he stood, but he moved almost in slow motion.

The thought of Linda stumbling out of one of the rooms and making him feel more uncomfortable than he already was scared him as much as the dark. The house was narrow, so he couldn't do more than spread his arms before he touched both walls, and that's how he inched down the hallway, with his fingertips leading every step.

He stopped moving in front of the door to take a series of deep breaths, when a creak from behind sparked him into pushing the door fully open. The need for light superseded the fear of embarrassing someone. Everything looked normal. Ugly drapes covered the window, a chipped mirror hung over the sink, and low-wattage lighting gave the room a yellow tinge. Just seeing the toilet made his bladder relax enough that he almost started peeing right there. He had shuffled a few steps forward when something he saw out of the corner of his eyes stopped him on the spot. For a moment, he wondered if his mind had deceived him. Most of him wanted to run, but he knew he couldn't, so he turned to see Linda fully submerged in the bathtub. Dave had no idea what this meant, but he knew enough to pull her head from the water. She was heavier than he expected. Slick with bath soap, her body looked an unusual colour.

With his arms around her shoulders, hands clasped, he pulled her up until her weight pulled them both down. Linda's upper body now hung over the lip of the tub, and her fingers dangled towards the floor as water dripped from her hair.

Dave scrambled to his feet, slipped on the wet tile and fell into the wall before getting back up and running downstairs to find a phone to call 911.

His dad came back to the house twenty minutes after the ambulance arrived. But that's not what Dave remembered about the night. What he remembered for decades after is that if his dad had not left him, no one would have found Linda in time to save her.

Five

The clock marked his twenty-fourth hour without sleep as it turned to eight thirty, and Dave stared at it with spite. Every cell in his body wanted rest, but his mind wouldn't stop running through details: the size of the truck, the smell of shit in the toilet stall, the hangover that saved his life. The equation plagued him. If he hadn't slept in, he would have been behind his desk when the truck hit—a desk that the truck had hit right after the reception desk. Twelve hours slipped by fast in the current of those thoughts.

The more he thought of the truck, the more anything seemed possible. The ceiling lamp he stared up at could fall and crush his face, a brain aneurysm could kill him in seconds, and he could shut his eyes only to never wake up. An article he'd read a few days before told of a man who'd bled to death from a nosebleed. The journalist used the phrase "bleeding out". The possibility of dying from something so common had seemed shocking when he'd read the article, but now it felt probable. *If you can think it,* he thought, *then it can happen. And if it can happen, then in a long enough timespan, it will happen to you.*

A stiffness in his lower back begged him to massage it as he lifted himself from the bed and put on a T-shirt. He didn't want to spend another second alone. He felt trapped in his brain, and a sudden urge to tell somebody about the tragedy surged through him with an undeniable force, as if sharing what happened would make it more real or less real. He wasn't sure what he wanted more, but what became clear was that he needed someone else's perspective, and while every instinct warned him that it was a bad idea, he felt compelled to tell his dad.

"Morning." A neighbour from a few apartments down nodded, stepping out of the elevator as Dave stepped in. This man had no idea that Dave had almost died just twenty-four hours before, and no idea that Dave had seen the dead bodies of his colleagues. It occurred to Dave that there were at least thirty people living on his floor, yet none of them knew that he had narrowly escaped a tragedy. Somehow, the anonymity felt entirely inappropriate.

A cab dropped him off in the drive-up of 29 Palson Road. Dave preferred the euphemism "29 Palson Road" instead of Senior Citizen's Home.

Two elderly women chatted on a bench just outside the front doors. Since his dad's first day living there, Dave had developed a habit of imagining what the older people he saw were like when they were his age. He envisioned what they used to do for a living, and whether or not they were attractive. Something about the images he conjured made him uneasy, so he tried not to do it, but it had become a mental reflex. This time he saw two people who would have been friends if they'd met decades earlier. The one on the left had been vain in her time, which was surprising for someone who sat before him with a bit of breakfast's dried egg on her face. But he could see that she'd been beautiful once. With high cheekbones, mischievous eyes and full, pouting lips, she must have been uniquely beautiful in her prime. The thought of her working at a library or organizing charity events didn't do her justice. If she had been born twenty-five years later, she would have been an architect or fashion designer.

The one on the right had never been attractive. He guessed the hair on her lip hadn't come with old age, and her sharp tone and thick frown lines suggested a lot of children without a lot of money. Both women wore wedding bands, despite the reality that their residence was a drop-off for widows. He hoped to be that loyal one day.

A young orderly Dave knew only as Chris walked towards his

dad's room. Chris had worked at the home since Mr. Bolden had moved in. He looked in his early twenties, but a few comments during his brief exchanges with Dave suggested he was closer to thirty. Nothing about his look framed him for a career in gerontology. Thick blond stubble covered his shaved head, a bushy goatee accented his superhero jaw, and everything about his word choice and delivery made Dave think of ski bums. Chris adjusted a pair of headphones dangling from his neck.

"You picked the right time to come, he's in a good mood today." He stopped before Mr. Bolden's room. "Let me know if you need anything."

Dave took a moment before opening the door. The lack of sleep made the hum of overhead lighting, the smell of cleaning products, and the faint sound of talk radio coming from every room more depressing than during his usual visits. He stepped forward to see his dad sitting with his back and head propped up by pillows on his single bed. A soccer game played on a T.V. screen he didn't take his eyes from.

He sat on top of his covers with a pair of beige cords riding too high at the ankles and a green cardigan buttoned tight around his chest. Despite thinning white hair and heavy wrinkles, blue eyes and a symmetrical face suggested he'd been handsome in his prime. An oxygen mask dangled from his neck, and an oxygen tank rested on a stand beside the bed. Dave hugged him tighter than he had in months.

"How are you today?"

Jack pushed off the hug like a kid embarrassed by his father's affection. "Enough of that sissy shit. The Leafs won by two goals; that's three to one you owe me."

Dave removed a blanket from a wooden chair before pulling it closer to the bed so he could sit beside his dad. "I need you to listen to me, Pop, this is really important."

"Don't try that snake tongue with me or I'll cut it off. I want my money."

"Look at me. Look at me."

Jack's eyes widened while his voice mocked in an affected tone. "*Look at me, look at me.*" He pulled his hand away from Dave's. "I'm looking at you, you bloody fool."

"I need you to focus today, I need you to see me, okay? I'm your son, Dave, not your bookie, Alex. Your son. Dave, not Alex."

Jack shifted uncomfortably before his eyes locked back on the T.V. screen, where a Scottish mid-fielder had received a yellow card for tripping. Dave tapped his dad's closest knee.

"Are you listening?"

"Yeah, yeah. Stop poking at me, for Christ's sake."

Dave couldn't speak fast enough. He didn't care that his dad watched the soccer game, and he didn't care that Jack probably wouldn't remember the conversation.

"There was an accident at work. A truck crashed into the building and killed everybody I work with. I probably would have died too, but I went to the washroom. If I went ten minutes earlier or ten minutes later, I'd be dead. If I decided to check my email or chat a little longer, I'd be dead. Fuck, if it took me five minutes longer to get a cab that morning, I'd be dead. But it didn't. Everything happened the way it did, and I'm alive."

Jack turned his head towards his son. He stared at Dave for a beat to ensure their eyes locked before he spoke. "I want my money. The Leafs won by two, and you owe me three to one."

Dave couldn't' remember exactly when his dad had started forgetting things. The doctors were so concerned with his emphysema, they hadn't paid attention to his inconsistencies. But Dave had noticed his dad's random assignment of names, the way he'd called a Honda a Hyundai or a Hyundai a Harley, and his love of dialogue from *The Dirty Dozen*, even though the words he quoted were from *Spartacus*. People used to joke about his dad's funny way of saying things, until it progressed into such random misinformation that conversations were ruined.

Dave stepped outside 29 Palson Road to see Grayson standing in front of a black stretched Mercedes limo. His overcoat matched the vehicle's grey piping.

"Hello, Dave," he said, stepping forward.

Grayson was the last person he expected to see outside of his dad's building. He considered walking past the man, but before he could react, Grayson stepped forward.

"My apologies for intruding upon your personal life, but Mr. Thorrin is concerned that I was too vague when we first met."

Dave examined him for a moment to be sure he hadn't hallucinated the character in the muck of his sleep-deprived mind. "Look, I'm exhausted. I haven't slept in…"

"He wants you to understand the benefits of meeting with him, so we feel it's best to be direct. Mr. Thorrin believes you're lucky."

"Lucky?"

"Yes."

"Why?"

"Because you survived."

"Four friends of mine died, he calls that lucky?"

"Where were you when the truck hit?"

"The washroom."

Grayson stepped closer to him as if letting him in on a secret. "Do you know the variables involved in you being out of the room when the truck entered the office? Because I deal with numbers for a living, and I can tell you that something was working in your favour."

The close talk felt uncomfortable, so Dave took a step to the side. "That's not luck."

"Well, this is. Mr. Thorrin is in the limo, and he's willing to pay you five thousand dollars to talk while we drive around the block a few times."

"Five thousand?"

"That's correct."

"You're lying. For all I know you're crazy."

"Have a look at the car, Mr. Bolden. This isn't a wedding-day special."

He was right. The six-door Mercedes looked fresh off the lot.

"What's the name of your company again?"

"SBT Global Investors."

"Five thousand in cash?"

"If you like."

"Then let's do it."

Grayson smiled, nodded and reached for a door while using the other arm to wave Dave inside. Dave ducked his head and sat down on a cream leather high-back at one end of a horseshoe couch. A quick glance around proved it had all the amenities—a bar with drinking glasses and decanters displayed, a flat-screen T.V., DVD player and fibreoptic lighting. Thorrin sat at the other end of the couch. He extended a hand while Grayson made his way past Dave to the next seat.

"It's a pleasure to meet you, Dave."

Though he looked to be in his fifties, nothing about Thorrin looked past his prime. With full hair, a defined frame and eyes alive with intensity, his body seemed to shun aging. The air smelled of leather, but he smelled of sweet cologne. He wiped at his upper lip, where a small scar in the shape of a half-moon ran down to the right corner of his mouth. Dave wondered whether it had come from sport, an accident or a fight.

Thorrin passed Dave a wooden case.

"What's this?"

"It's for those you lost; some things are too important to insult with words."

Dave opened the case to find a twenty-year-old bottle of scotch. "I don't understand why you're doing this," he said as he closed the case.

Thorrin spread both arms over their respective rests. He

probably drove around so much in this limo that it was more a living room than a luxury automobile.

"I know about loss, Dave, and I can tell you that the only thing that moves past the sorrow is the pursuit of gain."

He picked up an envelope from the seat beside him, tapped it twice on a knee and extended it to Dave. "You earned this just by showing up, but this is tip money compared to what you're capable of. I think you're blessed with the power of luck. I've made millions anticipating new trends in the marketplace, cultivating new resources, and you, you are a new resource. You can't buy luck."

Dave shifted in his seat, and his eyes darted between the two men before settling on Thorrin. "You think I'm lucky because I survived an accident? Hundreds of people survive accidents, probably thousands."

"Not tragedies as odd as yours, they don't. Do you know the odds involved in this happening on the day I was scheduled for a meeting?"

"Tragedies happen every day."

"Maybe, but a look at your profile suggests this isn't a one-off."

"My profile?"

"Research is key to any investment. You had a twin brother who died at birth, correct?"

"So you're saying it's lucky that my brother died?"

"No, I'm saying it's lucky that you lived." Thorrin spoke without notes or prompts, which made Dave look at Grayson to see if he would reveal an explanation.

"You've never had a serious illness, you avoided all common childhood diseases like chicken pox and the measles, and there's really no mention of injury at all in your medical history."

"How did you get information about my medical history?"

"I paid for it."

"Well, you didn't pay enough. I broke my arm the spring of sixth grade in the middle of baseball season. There's no luck in that."

"No, but there was luck in breaking it falling from a school apparatus. Didn't you use the twelve thousand dollar settlement your mom sued for to buy your first car while most of your classmates were still cramming into buses?"

The limo hit a series of potholes, causing everybody to bob in their seats. Dave leaned forward for the first time.

"I don't understand what you think I can do for you."

Thorrin held up a folded newspaper, which he unfolded to the business section. "I want you to select stocks. The return on your selections will be fifteen per cent, just like a good agent."

The analogy pried a smug smile from Grayson, who sat with his hands in his lap.

"Stocks?" Dave asked.

"That's right."

"You don't want me to pick stocks. I don't know anything about the market."

"It won't be the knowledge that makes us money."

Dave knew enough about risking money not to be blinded by the lure of possibility. "And what happens when I lose your money?"

"You won't." Thorrin passed him the newspaper with his business card clipped to the top. "Take a night to absorb what I said, then pick a stock. Any one you want." He dug into his suit jacket, removed another envelope and tossed it into Dave's hands. "There's another five thousand in there. Consider it an advance on your selection."

"This isn't a good idea."

The limo stopped back in front of 29 Palson.

"Go out for a nice meal, get yourself in a good mood and come by my office tomorrow afternoon with your selection."

Before Dave could respond, a driver opened the door. Dave wanted to return the envelope, but five grand has a way of deflecting instincts. Grayson extended his hand.

"Good day, Mr. Bolden."

For the second time, he held the shake longer than he should've, until Thorrin's look suggested that he wanted Dave out of the vehicle. Dave stepped onto the sidewalk, unsure of what to say next.

"I'll see you tomorrow, Dave," Thorrin said.

Dave stood on the corner for a few minutes without moving before raising the newspaper to eye level. He hadn't picked a stock since a high school business project.

Six

Dave went to his first funeral when he was eleven. In the morning, he stood beside his mother as she poured a cup of tea.

"Maybe Dad wants a cup," he said.

"I don't think so, dear."

She stirred in the sugar without looking up. Her eyes were defeated and devoid of any spark. Dave thought it was at least the third day in a row she had worn her green sweater, and he hated seeing her so dishevelled.

"Can I ask Dad if he wants breakfast?"

"You shouldn't go in there."

"I can make him banana pancakes."

"You shouldn't go in there."

His dad had been in bed for two days, the drapes were drawn, and he hadn't come out for any meals, to watch the Leaf game or to take Dave to baseball practice.

"Mom?"

"Yes?"

"Is Dad sick?"

She didn't answer the question. Her silence told Dave his dad *was* sick, which increased his anxiety. She was supposed to say he was just tired or that he had been working too hard, but the silence felt worse than specifics.

His mother turned to face him. "Dave, I want you to look at me."

He locked eyes with his mother's.

"I don't want you going into your father's room. Do you understand me?"

Dave didn't blink.

"It's very important you give him space right now. I don't want you to see him like this."

Dave looked at her like he didn't want to see her worried, disappointed, or ashamed. He promised himself he would never look that way. The weight of that promise held his thoughts as he picked at a bowl of bran cereal until he heard the T.V. in the living room. The sound of the deep-voiced newscaster meant his mother wouldn't be moving for an hour, so he crept down the hall and up the stairs, confident that he had some time.

He ran the bathroom tap for a minute to make sure the water was cold before filling a cup. Entering the room with something to offer relaxed him. His dad was sleeping in the fetal position with his large back facing the door and layers of blankets covering most of his head. Dave knocked on the now-open door.

"Excuse me, Dad, I don't want to bother you, but I thought you might be thirsty, so I brought you some water."

Every second that passed made him more nervous, so he waited a moment. Two deep breaths led him to take two steps closer to the bed.

"Also, I'm going to make breakfast, so if you want some banana pancakes, I can do that."

There was still no response, so he reached out to touch his Dad's back. Suddenly the man spun around with a monstrous growl, grabbed him by the arm and tossed him into the bed, which sent the water splashing over the covers. Dave released a primal scream. His dad then moved to the boy's ribcage, where tickling fingers and a more playful growl freed Dave from shock.

"I got you there, didn't I?" Jack said.

Dave mouthed "yeah" as he caught his breath.

"You should see the look on your face."

"You're not sick?" Dave asked.

"No, I'm not sick. I just needed to refuel, and there's no

better time to get back up and going than when my boy offers to make me breakfast."

"Are you going to get up?"

Jack tapped him on the shoulder. "I certainly am. And you're coming with me."

"Where?"

"You'll see. But right now I need you to do two things. I need you to go downstairs and get me the sports section, then I need you to change into your suit."

"My church suit?"

"That's the one."

Dave hopped out of the bed to see his mother standing in the doorway.

"With all the noise you made, I thought you hurt yourself."

Dave knew better than to respond. She stepped into the bedroom as Dave slipped by her. Jack now lay on his back.

"Did I hear you say you'll be joining the waking world today?"

"I am," he said as he sat up. "I'm going to take Dave out this afternoon, but when I get back, we should go shopping."

"Where are you going?"

"Boy's stuff."

"I told Dave not to come in here."

"It's okay, I'm glad he did."

They were in the car ten minutes before his dad said a word. Dave knew this wasn't going to be an ordinary outing. He hadn't worn his suit since the previous Christmas, and he hoped he looked as cool as his dad—businesslike, powerful, someone people listened to.

"We're going to my friend's funeral," Jack said as he lit a cigarette. "His name is, was, Conner Drake. You never met him, but he was a good guy. A loyal guy." He rolled the window down a pinch to let out some of the smoke.

Dave wondered what all kids wonder when they hear the word "funeral". "How did he die?"

"Heart attack."

Dave and his dad were the only guests at the funeral. The sun broke through a pack of clouds as they made their way through damp grass to the grave site, and Dave's heart began to race.

He had never seen an open grave, and the mound of fresh dirt made it difficult for him to focus on the priest's words. The thought of being buried terrified him, and suddenly this wasn't about a man's funeral, this was about him. He tried to rationalize that he would be dead, so it wouldn't matter, but the thought of being trapped in a box under all that dirt won. Tears welled up in his eyes, but they weren't tears of sympathy. He cried because he was terrified that one day he was going to be buried, eaten by maggots and reduced to bones. His eyes dropped to the ground too late to avoid detection, and tears wet his cheeks. He never wanted to go to a funeral again. The thought of his dad dead, under all that dirt, made him want to scream, until his dad's hand wrapped tight around his.

After his dad thanked and hugged the priest, they took their time walking back to the car. Every few steps, Jack bent down, found something to throw and chucked it as far forward as he could. Dave waited for him to bend down again.

"How come we were the only people at his funeral?"

Jack looked up at him for a moment from his knees before rising. "He didn't have any family or friends, and he didn't have a job, not one you go to everyday anyway."

"What about a wife?"

"Not even a girlfriend."

Dave didn't have the nerve to ask what was really on his mind. Why do people have to die? What happens to people after death?

And if he died somehow before his dad, would his dad promise to come to the funeral as a guarantee that somebody would be there?

Jack smoked three consecutive cigarettes as they drove. Dave watched the way his dad held the tip of the filter in his teeth, and he noticed the way his index finger curled over to meet the thumb as he drew deep on the cigarette until his lungs filled with smoke. There was something calming about watching his dad smoke like this.

But the funeral had shaken him. He didn't want his father to die alone like Conner, so he made himself a promise that no matter where on the planet he would be when his father died, he would attend the funeral.

"You know what we need?" Jack said, tossing a butt out the window. "We need burgers."

"Yeah?"

"Maybe two."

When his dad was in this type of mood, there were no exaggerations. He ordered two bacon burgers for himself and two junior burgers with everything on them for Dave. They wanted a booth, but the place was crowded, so Dave sat down beside a large man hunched over his food. His dad sat across from him. Dave wasn't two bites into his first burger before he noticed his dad staring at the large man. And for good reason too. The man had four burgers in front of him, one in his hand and another wrapper crumpled up on the tray made six in total.

Dave did his best to examine the man out of the corner of his eyes without getting caught staring. Huge did not do this guy justice. A black cable-knit sweater with the sleeves rolled halfway up his forearms looked like it might burst at any moment, the way it stretched over his frame. His face was stubbly, and a smear of mayonnaise stood out on the corner of his right lip as he chewed as much of the burger as he could fit into his mouth. This was not a handsome man.

Jack sat up straight in his chair and turned slightly towards the large man so that they made eye contact.

"That's a lot of burgers," he said, gesturing to the man's tray. The man looked up at him, and his tongue probed at a chunk of food in the pouch of his cheek. He didn't respond, so Jack continued. "What's the most burgers you've ever eaten in one sitting?"

"Ever?"

"Yeah."

"Ten."

The man put down his burgers as if the question warranted his full attention. Jack leaned in closer. "Ten? Ten of these burgers?"

"A few times."

Jack tapped the table with an index finger. "I've got a hundred that says you can't eat ten today."

"A hundred?"

"Yep. If you don't eat ten, you owe me a hundred. But if you do, I give you a hundred and pay for your burgers."

"How much time do I get?"

"As much as you need."

The man wiped sauce from his hands before extending his podgy finger. "You're on."

They shook. Five minutes later, Jack had four more burgers in front of the man. In the first ten minutes, he finished two more burgers, bringing the total to four. He dabbed a heavy sweat from his brow with a napkin before unwrapping another burger. Dave moved from the seat beside the man to one that opened up behind them. The more the man ate, the more he sweated, and the more he sweated, the more he swelled. Nothing had tested Dave's gag reflex like that before. Burger, ketchup, processed cheese, relish, special sauce and burp mixed with the sweat. Jack didn't move at all. He just sat back, sipped on his drink and watched the big man go.

Thirty-two minutes later, on his eighth burger, the mouthfuls turned to nibbles, and he thoroughly soaked each piece in his Sprite to make swallowing easier. His eyes bulged like someone had pumped them up with air, while sweat stained both sides of his shirt. Another bite, and his Adam's apple jumped with a harsh gag.

"That doesn't sound good," Jack said. He removed two fifties from his wallet and placed them on the table. "Maybe a little visual incentive will help."

The man's eyebrows narrowed like he wanted to swear, reach across the table and strike Jack, but his stomach couldn't handle the jostling, so he pulled a handful of money from his pants pocket and put it on the table.

"I'm done, you fucking sadist." He gestured to an ATM. "I'll be back with the rest."

The man waddled to a machine near the front doors while Jack pumped his fist in the air.

At the first stoplight, Jack passed Dave twenty dollars. Dave didn't know how to respond, so his dad prodded him with a wink. "Just don't show your mother."

"How did you know he couldn't eat the burgers? That guy was huge."

"Because people always exaggerate. That's the curse of pride. You paid fifty for a pair of jeans, you say thirty-five, you make fifty-grand a year, you say sixty, you can eat eight burgers, you say ten."

Dave looked at the twenty with thoughts of baseball cards. The day marked a series of significant moments in his life. He'd attended his first funeral, and he'd watched his first proposition bet.

Seven

Dave stared at Shannon's freshly covered grave after the ceremony ended, with thoughts filling his head of their perfunctory exchanges, morning greetings and lunches. They'd shared an unspoken bond, relied on each other to make every day of work more bearable, and as a result, more meaningful. Most of the people in attendance made their way to the parking lot, but Dave felt someone standing behind him. He pivoted to see a handsome man he guessed to be in his late thirties. With an overcoat, dress pants and a square jaw that centred under a thick mane of hair, his exterior appeared healthy at first glance, but a closer look revealed the man's eyes were too dry, and the flesh beneath them hollow and drained.

"Dave, right?"

Dave took a moment before nodding. The man extended a large hand.

"I'm Shannon's husband, Tim. We met at that dinner thing for Christmas."

"Of course, yeah."

"Do you know when the other funerals are?"

Dave saw the fog in his eyes. He saw the dam of denial that compelled Tim to ask expected, clichéd questions so he wouldn't throw himself in front of the closest moving car. Dave knew he had to play along. "I haven't heard."

Tim surveyed him from head to toe before focussing on his face with the type of awe autograph seekers show celebrities. "How did you survive?"

The question stunned Dave. The right thing to do was to be

nice and help the man with his shock, but the words shook him. "I was in the washroom."

"You definitely picked the right time." Tim patted him on the shoulder. "Take care."

Dave got in a cab and headed for Thorrin's office. He pulled the second envelope Thorrin had given him from the inside pocket of his jacket, as if by holding it he was closer to giving it back. The thought of writing down a few stocks from a newspaper to give Thorrin what he wanted crossed his mind, but in the end he didn't want to deal with the ramifications of losing the man's money. The risk simply wasn't worth the daunting odds of a return. He wanted to give back the money, excuse himself politely and forget they'd ever met.

A converted warehouse space in the city's west end framed Thorrin's daily business. The location worked because it was close enough to downtown to be a minute away from the action but just far enough outside the city's core that a ridiculous amount of space came at a reasonable price. The lobby's speckled floor and the wooden banisters on the staircase made Dave think of Seventies cop movies. A woman in her fifties with a large nose and far too much eye make-up pointed at him with a pen.

"Who are you here to see, sir?"

"Uh, Mr. Thorrin. My name's Dave Bolden."

"Take a seat, Mr. Bolden. I'll let him know you're here."

A seat meant the gorgeous black leather couch flanked on either side by silver stand-up ashtrays. Dave felt the leather hug his back as he sat down.

He was wondering whether he could swing an accounting gig from Thorrin's interest in him when he looked up to see Grayson standing beside him.

"Did you get here easy enough?"

"Yeah."

"Good. We were going to send a car, but we thought it best to give you your space." Grayson spread his arms to draw attention to the surroundings. "Let me give you a tour."

They stepped into an elevator that couldn't fit more than four people. The tight dimensions made Dave feel claustrophobic for the first time in his life, until the elevator stopped at the fifth floor, where the doors opened to reveal a huge, open office. At first glance Dave guessed it was about five thousand square feet. He followed Grayson through the space, where white veils circled office stations, pool tables sat throughout, and trees in cement blocks painted white ran two lines through the middle of the room.

Dave couldn't take his eyes off of a bed that was suspended a foot off the ground by four chains hanging from the ceiling and veiled by a see-through white curtain.

"What is this place?"

"It's a think tank. Minimal employees, client wining and dining, a merger of work and play." Grayson pointed to a door at the end of the room flanked by two horseshoe pits. "That's Mr. Thorrin's office down there."

They passed a bar area elevated six inches from the rest of the floor. Everything about the place was dreamy. The bar's floor was aqua, the white seats formed buckets like giant ice cream scoopers, and a series of circular lights were built into the floor.

Grayson led the way past a woman with short, slicked back hair talking on a headset as she pecked at a laptop before they reached Thorrin's office. Grayson pointed to an L-shaped cream couch.

"Have a seat, and I'll tell Mr. Thorrin that you're here."

Dave waited for Grayson to disappear behind the door before he sat down. A woman behind a see-through curtain that circled her office space caught his attention. He stared to see if she would acknowledge him, but she never did. A model with buck teeth on the cover of a fashion magazine lying on a side table caught his attention until Grayson reappeared from behind the door.

"Follow me," he said, holding the door open with one hand.

Thorrin's office was equally opulent. With a stainless steel fridge, stove and two mahogany tables, it looked more like a living space. They passed a half-moon of suede couches before turning a corner to find Thorrin sitting behind a desk. He rose with an extended hand while Grayson left the room.

"It's good to see you again, Dave." His hands clasped together as he leaned forward on the desk. "How do you like the place?"

"It's different. You're an investment company, right?"

"Not *an* investment company—outside of the banks, we are *the* investment company in this country. We have over a hundred professionals and other offices in Montreal, Vancouver, Calgary, Boston and New York."

"Why was a guy like you going to a boutique accounting firm like Mr. Richter's?"

"He'd been handling a section of my finances for thirty years. Before he had his own place, and long before I started this company." He sat down and traced his jawline with a thumb. "So, what do you have for me?"

Dave put the envelope of money in front of him. "Just this. I came to return your money."

Thorrin sat upright again. "Why?"

"Because I'm not a good luck charm. Trust me, if you knew more about my life than the facts you've pulled out, you'd believe me."

"I knew enough to know you need this money. I know you have a father in an expensive senior's home, and I know you borrow money from less than reputable people to keep him there."

Dave's face flushed. He wanted to leap across the table and hit Thorrin until he stopped moving, but even anger knew that wasn't a good idea.

"I don't know what you think you're going to get out of me by digging into my personal life, but let me save you the trouble—I'm not worth it."

"I disagree."

"Think about it, if I was really as lucky as you say I am, why would I need to be in debt to anybody?"

"Because you don't know you're lucky."

Dave shifted his weight to one side of the chair and back again. "Look, you can talk your way around this all you want, but the truth is, I'm just another guy."

"You don't believe, do you?"

"Not at all."

"Maybe I shouldn't either." Thorrin rose from his seat. He looked broader through the chest and longer of limb standing up. "Come with me."

Thorrin walked around the desk and past Dave into a connecting room, where Grayson sat on a couch watching stock tickers on two flat screens. Thorrin removed a pack of playing cards from a shelf filled mostly with books before gesturing to Dave. "Take a seat."

Thorrin sat down in a chair closest to the windows so that the three of them formed a half-moon around a glass coffee table with a ying/yang sculpture the size of a candy dish in its centre. He removed the cards from the package and shuffled the deck three times. Each shuffle made Dave more uncomfortable.

"What we need is a concrete demonstration of your capabilities. Grayson, can you choose a card for me, please?"

Grayson turned his attention from the screens for the first time and responded as if he'd been waiting for the question. "Ace of spades."

"Of course. The ace of spades it is." Thorrin fanned the cards in his hands and extended them to Dave. "Pull me out the ace of spades."

Dave looked at the cards for a moment. The stupidity of the request annoyed him as much as the situation unnerved him. "It's not going to happen."

"Choose a card."

"We can do this a hundred times, and it won't happen."

"Choose a card."

"Okay, to stop this insanity, gladly." Dave picked the third card from the left, smiled and flipped it towards Thorrin and Grayson to reveal the six of hearts. "You see? No magic. I'm just like anyone else you put a deck in front of."

Thorrin nodded at Grayson, who got up to walk over to Dave's far side. Thorrin pointed the cards at Dave. "Don't confuse luck for chance; there's nothing random about you. For luck to kick in, you need to have something at stake."

Grayson removed a gun from somewhere in his suit jacket. It wasn't the first time Dave had seen a gun, but it was the first time a barrel had hovered inches from his head.

"Something to gain or lose," Thorrin continued.

"What the fuck are you doing?"

Thorrin fanned the cards before extending them again. "Now, choose a card."

"You're going to kill me over this?"

"Choose a card."

"Because that's what's going to happen. I'm not what you think I am, and I don't want to get killed over it."

Grayson cocked the gun's trigger and pressed the barrel's cold steel against Dave's temple. "Choose a card."

Dave snatched a card to get it over with, looked at it with disbelief and turned it slowly towards Thorrin to reveal the ace of spades. Thorrin smiled the universal smile of being right. "There we go."

Grayson took a few steps back with a sly grin before opening the revolver to reveal the gun as a starter's pistol.

Thorrin unfolded a stock sheet and spread it out on the table. "Now you can choose a stock."

Sweat beaded on Dave's face. The room seemed too bright. Each breath felt filtered, and only his disbelief kept him from passing out or running for the door. "I don't know what you did to the cards, or how you fixed the outcome, but that wasn't luck."

Thorrin tapped the sheet. "Enjoy your gift, Dave, pick a stock."

The moment overwhelmed him. He was trying to figure out how they set the cards up when Thorrin raised his voice. "Pick a stock."

"It's your money. You want me to pick a stock, you're willing to stick a gun to my head, I'll pick a stock."

With closed his eyes, he fired an index finger to the page. Thorrin circled the name Dave pointed to with a blue Sharpie.

"Thank you."

"Can I leave now?"

"Absolutely. Grayson will take you wherever you like. I hope you understand I would've been doing you a disservice not to show you what you possess."

Dave's face showed no expression. In any other surroundings, Thorrin's words would be dismissed as crazy, but when you own five thousand square feet decorated with leather, mahogany and the finest technology, the words pass as business.

In Grayson's car, Dave looked out the passenger window in an effort to create as much distance as possible. Advanced Japanese lessons played on the stereo. Grayson mouthed the words for 'Would you like to stay the night?' then turned to Dave. "Why so quiet?"

The question surprised Dave. "You pointed a gun at me."

"It was a starter's pistol."

"You sure about that?"

"You were never in danger, you just had to believe you were."

"I almost pissed myself."

"It's unfortunate we had to startle you, but you needed to see for yourself."

"All I saw were two crazy people capable of a cheap card trick."

"Your selection had nothing to do with us."

Dave turned his head back to the window until he pointed

at a low-rise apartment building up ahead. "This is me up here. The corner is fine."

Grayson pulled the car to the curb before shutting off the engine. He turned off the Japanese lessons and locked those intense eyes on him. "I have another offer for you."

"I pass."

"Do you have any brothers or sisters?"

"No."

"Well, I do, and my sister, she's wonderful, but she has to have the worst luck on the planet. I want you to spend an hour with her so she can absorb some of yours."

"Do you hear yourself?"

"Your hour is worth two thousand dollars to me."

Dave wanted to get out of the car, but two thousand dollars triggered the learned response. He had senior's home payments and loan payments, and he wanted a trip to the Bahamas.

"She must be in bad shape if you're willing to pay me two grand for an hour."

"I wouldn't take her to Vegas with me. You won't repeat a word of this, but you need the context to appreciate her situation. She's divorced, suffered four miscarriages, developed a wheat intolerance in her twenties; she's on her eleventh broken bone, and she's colour blind."

Dave didn't listen past the miscarriages. "That's no fun."

"No, it isn't."

"Save your money, though, hanging out with me won't do anything for her."

"I disagree." Grayson removed a thick envelope with an address written on the front. "There's half the money and her address."

Dave knew it was risky, but loan shark interest and unemployment made resisting the size of the envelope impossible.

"Meet me there tomorrow at four."

"What do you want me to say to her?"

"It doesn't matter. Just be around her for an hour."

Dave stepped out of the car. He considered handing the money back until Grayson leaned across the passenger seat. "Thank you."

Dave shut the car door and watched Grayson drive away. Dave knew what it felt like to wish change for a family member, and if it was as easy as paying someone two grand to fix his dad's problems, he would have done it years ago.

Eight

Dave saw a gun for the first time when he was thirteen. That night he'd dreamed of track and field day at school. His relay team positioned him lead off, but when the starter's pistol fired, he couldn't move, no matter how hard he tried. All he could do was watch the other runners get smaller down the track. The part of him that observed the dream play out as if he were God knew that it was an anxiety dream. This part of him was most frustrated, because he couldn't will any movement.

A school bell rang loud as he tried to move, until everyone on the track surged en masse towards the school. He wanted to scream, to beg for another chance to race, but the moment passed. He stood alone on the track and prayed for the bell to stop ringing until a part of him recognized that the noise came from the waking world. His mind rushed from sleeping, to groggy, to terrified. The doorbell should never ring at two in the morning. He thought of his mother, who was full of enough sleeping pills she would sleep through a car crash, let alone a doorbell. Two weeks earlier, he'd broken a picture while wrestling with his friend Marlon, and she hadn't woken up—not when it smashed to the floor, not when they swept up the glass, and not when they giggled while doing a pathetic job of staying quiet.

The doorbell cut through the silence again. Ding-dong. The sound was far too friendly a noise for someone at the door at six minutes after two. The bell sent shivers down every limb. He considered staying put and hoped to avoid going to the door, but there was no way it was a salesperson at two a.m., so he decided he had to answer. Someone might be lost or hurt.

But then it occurred to him that maybe the person was checking to see if anyone was home. At that moment, he decided it was better to answer the ring than to wait and see if the next step was for someone to break into the house.

A quick glance through the door's half-moon of small windows revealed that the porch light was out. His mother never turned the porch light off until daylight, so he flicked the switch up and down a few times, but still no light. Ding-dong. The sound made his fingers tingle. Fear made his hands stiff, but he didn't want his mother to deal with whoever stood on the other side of the door, so he turned the deadbolt fast, and the loud click of metal on metal broke through the silence.

He could hear the sound of shoes or boots moving on the porch, so he grabbed the doorknob and pulled in one motion the way people remove band-aids to get the pain over with. A rush of cold air came through the gap between the door opening and the safety chain, and his heart pounded harder than he ever imagined possible as he peered into the darkness, until a face appeared in the gap. He drew his head back. Reaction told him to scream, but no sound came out.

"Relax," the face said. "I'm a friend of your father's. Is he home?"

Dave looked at the stubbly face. The man's eyes were a striking hazel that looked too soft for the shaved scalp and stubble they centred. Dave shook his head.

"He's not home?"

Dave shook his head again. His dad hadn't been home for two days. His mom said he was at his friend Craig's, but he knew better than to offer that information.

"I need you to open the door for me, kid."

Dave saw another man beside the first. This guy was shorter, and parts of his blond hair showed beneath the toque fitting tightly on his head. Dave smelled something like smoke wafting from the men, only sweeter. The smell made Dave think of incense.

"Are you listening to me, kid? I need you to open the door."

"I can't do that."

Dave's words sparked the man with the toque. He positioned himself in front of the gap so that Dave could see him from the waist up and lifted his jacket to reveal a gun tucked into his pants.

"Do you see this? This will be in your mouth if you don't open that door."

The other man pushed the man with the toque to the side, saying, "Are you retarded? Put your fucking jacket down and lower your voice." He turned back to Dave. "I understand why you don't want to let us in, but you've got to understand, your father owes me money. Money he hasn't paid me, and I need to clear that up."

"My dad's not home."

"I understand that. And I know your mom probably is, and I know that scares you, so I'll let you know up front that we're not here for her. Now you've got two choices here, kid. You either let me in, I'm gone in fifteen minutes, and your mother never has to see me, or I kick in the door, wake your mother, and things might get a lot crazier. That make sense to you?"

Dave nodded. He lifted the chain and waited for the door to burst open, but that didn't happen. The man gave Dave a moment to step back before coming inside.

Both men wore dark jackets and jeans. The man who did most of the talking maintained eye contact with Dave while the other one lit a cigarette.

"Here's how it's going to work. Your father, the piece of shit that he is, owes me two thousand dollars. Two thousand that he refuses to pay me, so I'm going to take two thousand dollars worth of stuff out of his home. Now, you're a good kid. You've got spunk, and this isn't your fault. If someone came into my home and did this to my kid, I'd kill them, but where's your dad? Hiding out somewhere over two grand while his kid has to deal with this. This isn't your fault, so I'm going to do you a favour. I'm going to let you choose two things in here that you don't want me to take."

Dave wanted to cry. He could feel his eyes squinting, his lips pouting, but nothing ran wet. He thought of his baseball glove, the T.V., and his hockey equipment. Then he thought of his mom's jewellery box, the ring she'd showed him that her mother had given her and the copper brooch that had been in the family for over a hundred years.

"Anything on the first floor. Just please don't go upstairs, I don't want my mom to see this."

The man looked at him before turning to his partner. "Looks a lot like Terry, doesn't he?"

"Fucker could be his brother," the man with the toque said as a cloud of smoke drifted from his mouth. He walked to the T.V., unplugged it and picked it up with a groan.

Dave didn't look, he just sat at the foot of the stairs.

The man who did the talking pointed to the T.V. "Do you have another T.V. anywhere?"

Dave shook his head. The man gestured to his partner, who struggled with the T.V.'s weight.

"Leave the T.V."

"What?"

"Put the T.V. back."

"Oh, fuck you."

"I'm serious. Put the T.V. back."

"You're telling me because this little shit looks like your son, you're going to leave a T.V. like this?"

The nicer man's eyes burned so intensely that he didn't have to respond, and fifteen minutes later they were gone, just as he'd promised. Dave checked on his mother, and it was clear she had no idea what had happened. He wondered whether or not some of the noises had penetrated her psyche and caused a nightmare, or if she had simply slept the dead sleep of pills.

Dave didn't go back to sleep that night. He just pulled the covers over his head, thankful to lose only the stereo, a crystal lamp, a leather chair and a set of golf clubs. If he'd had red hair instead of brown, or blue eyes instead of hazel, the house would have lost a lot more. If he didn't look so much like the man's son, his mother could have been hurt. But he did, and even though he spent the rest of the night awake from the adrenaline flowing through him, he did so grateful for his brown hair and hazel eyes.

Nine

Dave checked his voicemail for the first time in days to find a reminder about overdue movies he'd rented, two pre-recorded sales pitches for a chance to win a cruise, and a message that actually caught his attention. *Hello, I'm calling for Dave Bolden. My name is Phil Bryer. I'm Mr. Richter's attorney. Please call me at your earliest convenience. My number is…*

Dave didn't listen past "attorney". Attorney meant an insurance claim or a lawsuit, and he didn't want any part of having to rehash the details of that morning. What he wanted was to visit Otto and use his new-found money to put a dent in the money he owed the man for payments on Twenty-Nine Palson. Otto expected an installment at the end of the month, and it felt good to know that now he could pay the debt outright.

Dave had first met Otto Anderson in the second grade. Even at that age, Otto was bigger than everyone else. The two of them had become friends when their mothers started working together. Otto's mother brought him to the Boldens' during her visits, and Dave had introduced him to most of the kids on the street. The better friends their mothers became, the more they saw of each other. Otto's mother talked openly about how she wanted him to be more like Dave. She wanted Otto to be more presentable, more respectful and more responsible. She even signed Otto up for Dave's baseball team, where he was an all-star catcher until the seventh grade, when playing video games and smoking cigarettes took precedence over athletics.

Otto didn't suit being a kid anyway. A part of him had seemed grown-up to Dave since the day they'd met. He was taller than everyone, the first to kiss a girl, the first to smoke; he'd fought a high school kid when he was in Grade Seven. He was out of high school and working full time by sixteen, and he'd slept with a thirty-year-old woman when he was seventeen. Moments blended into each other like that for Otto.

He didn't see another day every morning when his eyes opened, he saw an opportunity, which is why while most of the guys he'd grown up with sat through math lessons dry enough to make their eyes bleed, he cleared three hundred a week bussing tables.

Dave hadn't seen Otto as much as they'd gotten older, but they shared the two most important building blocks of any friendship—mutual respect and a shared history. Both of their mothers had developed cancer around the same time, and they'd spent a period drinking beer together. Long after everyone else at the party or bar went home, they still drank and talked about what the hell their mothers had done to deserve cancer. The more they drank, the more they hated the doctors for not curing their mothers. Otto's had died six weeks after Dave's mom was deemed cancer-free. Dave didn't see Otto for a long time after that. Dave got deeper into his university studies, and Otto got deeper into being Otto, until one night while Dave was cramming for a mid-term, there was a frantic knock at the door.

"I need five hundred dollars," Otto said with bugged eyes. "Don't ask me why, just tell me whether you can do it or not, and I promise I'll pay you back."

Dave gave him the money, fully expecting never to see it again. Two weeks later, Otto returned to give Dave two thousand dollars in hundred dollar bills. Now you don't give someone twenty hundred dollar bills unless you're trying to make a statement, and Otto's was that he wasn't the borrower any more.

The night Dave had found out his dad needed to be in a nursing home, he'd immediately thought of Otto. He needed access to monthly money he didn't have, and there was simply nowhere else to go. Otto gave him the first six thousand interest-free, and the next day Dave put first and last down on 29 Palson Avenue.

Since the day Jack had moved into Palson Avenue, Dave had taken him to a baseball diamond a block over from home at least once a week, and the outings proved even more important to his dad than bringing the sports section.

Dave reared back and fired a fastball at a piece of plywood substituting for a catcher. He was bending down to pick up another ball from a bagful at his feet when his dad extended one from a pile in his lap. Jack sat in his wheelchair a few feet to Dave's right with a baseball gripped tight in his hand and an oxygen mask dangling from his neck.

"You pitch like a poet," he said. He held his hand up limply at the wrist. "All wrist."

Dave smiled. "I could take you back to the home if you'd like that better."

"My son could show you something about pitching. He had the best curveball in the city for a kid so lazy."

"I am your son, Pop."

Dave fired another pitch, and his plant leg exploded so hard that it caused a cloud of dust to rise from the asphalt. His dad looked unimpressed.

"Keep your head up, for chrissake."

Dave grabbed another ball. "Do you ever remember me being particularly lucky?"

His dad stared at the baseball he clutched. "I hear something funny."

"What?"

"I hear something funny."

"It's probably your oxygen tank."

"I hear something."

"I know, but I'm asking you something. Do you ever remember me being lucky?"

"You're a bookie, luck's your pimp."

Dave took the baseball from his dad's hand, which secured

his attention. "I'm your son, Dave. Do you ever remember Dave being lucky?"

"If I was pitching, I'd keep my head up."

"I'm sure you would, Pop, but I'm not asking you that, I'm asking you if you remember your son, Dave, me, as lucky?"

"I'm his father, aren't I?"

Dave nodded and couldn't help but smile at the wit. "Yeah, yeah, you are. And that's definitely lucky, but what about in other ways?"

"I wouldn't know. You've got to take chances to test luck, and I never saw him do that."

Dave stared at him. It was the first honest exchange they'd had in years, and the words made his question seem completely insignificant.

"Pitch another ball, would you? It's not like I can do it for myself."

Dave looked over at his dad for a moment before pivoting to fire another fastball at the plywood. "We've got to get going, Pop. I have a meeting I need to go to."

His dad cocked his head, and his lips formed a mischievous grin. "Why don't you just say it?"

"Say what?"

"You have a meeting with a woman."

Dave began pushing the wheelchair. "It's not like that."

"Sure it is. If it wasn't like that, you would've just said it's time to go like you do every week. You mentioned it for a reason."

"I haven't even met the woman, it's business."

"Liar."

The word choice amused Dave during the cab ride to his destination. For a man who'd spent his life in denial, a life layered with lies, the word came off his father's tongue surprisingly easily. The irony made Dave think of all the times he had heard problem drinkers call people at parties drunks.

He stepped out of the cab and walked up the front steps of a duplex with the address Grayson had given him in hand. He wished it were a date—someone he'd met at a bar, a friend of a friend, or a prostitute. The specifics didn't matter to him. What he needed was someone to invoke a passion that would help him forget. Instead he waited to be presented as a good luck charm, and the absurdity made the truck crashing through his work window more real than the moment it'd happened.

A blond man watched Dave as he approached the address Grayson had given him. The man pretended to stretch, but Dave felt his watching eyes. With a creaseless track suit and shoes that looked brand new, he was the type that spent more time shopping for a gym outfit than actually exercising. Dave guessed they were about the same age.

He turned to the man to catch him staring, before glancing down at a piece of paper with the address to double check that he was at the right door. He rang the bell once with a heavy finger. Grayson opened the door a moment later.

"Good, welcome. Come in," he said, nodding approvingly.

While Grayson talked, Dave noticed Amy sitting on a couch across the room.

She looked to be in her early thirties and was naturally beautiful, except for pained eyes that were red around the rims, and dark bags that weighed on her face. A blue knit sweater hung baggily on her frame, as did a pair of khakis at least a size too big. Press-wood tables, a bland navy blue sofa too skinny to be comfortable, and aqua light stands made her apartment a B-version of generic IKEA.

Grayson handed Dave an envelope, which he slid into the closest jacket pocket. Grayson broke the seal on a bottle of scotch he'd brought over.

"Can I make you a drink?"

"No thanks."

"You're sure?"

"Yeah."

"Okay."

Grayson poured himself a shot and drank it before leading Dave into the living room. Amy stood, and her arms went from her sides to crossed and back to her sides. Grayson rubbed her closest shoulder.

"Dave, this is my sister, Amy."

Dave extended his hand, and Amy moved forward until Grayson stepped between them. He grabbed Dave's arm with a firm grip.

"Forget hand-shaking, hug."

Amy pivoted towards him, with a look that only a sister can give her brother and whispered, "Grayson." She shook Dave's now limp hand to be polite. "I'm sorry my brother made you come."

"He didn't make me come."

"Then I'm sorry he bought you."

Grayson put his coat on by the door. "I'm going to leave now."

Amy turned to him, and her eyes looked defeated, like a kid being left at a new school for the first time. "What?"

Grayson ignored her in favour of addressing Dave. "I'll see you outside when you two are done." He buttoned the top button on his coat and walked out the door.

Amy flushed. She scratched at a red blotch on the side of her neck while pacing a small runway. "I'm sorry, I didn't know he was going to leave."

"Neither did I."

She sat on the couch, and Dave chose a wooden chair to the side. They sat in silence for a moment while Dave tried to think of something to say and Amy struggled to stay still, until the agony of two strangers' silence compelled her to straighten an armchair cover that was already in place.

Dave walked over to a series of bookshelves that had been adjusted to fit records. He guessed that there were a thousand records on the shelves. He removed an album randomly and flipped it over to see that it was The Kensington Market. He had never heard of the band, and the ignorance left him with a curious combination of admiration and jealousy.

"This is a serious collection," he said, holding up the record.

"I have over five thousand. I'd fill a house with them if I could spare the space, but most of them are in storage."

"I've got about three hundred in storage myself." His eyes locked on a Crowbar twelve-inch, 'Too True Mama'. My mother used to play that song all the time. I haven't been able to find this anywhere. Where did you get it?"

"Grayson bought it a few years back. He gets me a lot of my records."

"Play something for me."

"What are you in the mood for?"

"I want it to be your choice."

She walked to the shelf closest to the window, pulled a record from the second shelf and turned to a vintage Garrard RC1 player.

Dave took a seat in the armchair. "If you play the Monkees, we're going to have a problem."

She set the needle on the record, and it popped twice before finding the groove. Raw vocals growled through the speakers, setting off an explosion of pre-punk-fuelled guitar as "Kick Out the Jams" filled the room.

Dave's eyes widened. "The MC5? You could have given me a hundred guesses about what you were going to play, and I wouldn't have been close."

"Best band ever. And underappreciated."

"And crazy. They used to play with rifles onstage, and they were part of that day-long concert at the Democratic convention, the one where all the violence broke out."

"Not part of, they *were* the concert. Most of the other artists didn't even show up because of the chaos. Neil Young was there, but his people wouldn't let him play, so the MC5 played for over eight hours. *That* is backing what you believe in."

Dave smiled. "That's a great story. I take it you know a lot about music."

"My life's goal is to be a walking encyclopaedia of songs."

"That's a big statement."

"It keeps my mind busy." The song ended, and she lifted the needle from the record before turning back to Dave. "Grayson told me what you survived."

"Yeah?"

She nodded.

"Did he tell you why he asked me to meet you?"

She nodded again.

"And how do you feel about that?"

She straightened her back against the couch. "Pretty stupid, but I'm willing to try anything."

"Why?"

"Because I'm unlucky."

"What do you mean unlucky?"

She answered without hesitation. She'd thought about answering the question so often that the words flowed. "I mean, I don't eat peanuts because I'd choke, I don't live in a place with stairs because I'd fall, and if I prepared food with a knife, I'd have no fingers left."

"I don't believe in luck."

She looked at him like she'd expected a more engaged response. "You survived, didn't you?"

The words pricked him. "Survive" rolled too easily off peoples' tongues. Her tone bothered him so much that he had to stand up and move a little to get his response right. "I came to work late because I had a hangover, and I went straight to the bathroom to pull myself together. Do you really believe this luck you and your brother believe in rewards irresponsibility and kills responsible people?"

"It has nothing to do with morals."

"But this idea that there's a force punishing and rewarding, it's ridiculous."

"If you were me, you wouldn't say that."

"Do you really think what's happened in your life is a result of luck?"

She looked at him full on for the first time. He had never seen eyes so tired, yet even in their drained state, their sky blue made him want to keep looking. "I've charted it."

"Charted it?"

"Yeah, I'm negatively synchronized." Dave looked at her like she was crazy, but he didn't want her to stop speaking. "I'm in tune with the wrong rhythms."

"So nothing good ever happens to you?"

"I didn't say that."

"Then maybe it's the way you look at things. You've got to look for opportunities in life. For example, just when I came here, a neighbour of yours was staring at me like he was wondering why I was at your place."

"Which neighbour?"

"Blond hair, about thirty. The point is, maybe he was watching me like that because he wants to ask you out and he's trying to figure out if you're dating anyone. The guy could end up being your husband."

"Or he could be a stalker."

"It's that attitude that has you feeling the way you do. You have a few bad things happen to you and…"

"Four miscarriages are more than a few bad things."

The flow of energy stopped. Dave felt the weight of his words. He liked talking with her, he didn't want her to stop, and realizing the insensitivity of his dogma made him feel bad. Not guilty, but bad like he might have made one of those mistakes that you can never correct.

"I didn't mean to…"

"You *are* special."

"What?"

"I can feel it."

"Feel what?"

"When you've been cursed as long as I have, you get in touch with rhythms, and yours are definitely special."

"You really believe that?"

"Absolutely. Will you spend some time with me again?"

Dave sat back down in the chair. "Sure, give me your number and I'll call…"

"You won't call me."

"I'll call you."

She reached for a napkin on the coffee table, wrote her number in the centre and passed it to him. "We'll see."

Ten

Two weeks after Dave's sixteenth birthday, his mother threatened his dad in a way that he remembered forever. She gathered up sports papers, betting lines, and every note on odds that she could find and threw them in the fireplace. She found the stacks of betting lines in folders in his briefcase, the notes tacked to his corkboard and the schedules he used as bookmarks in black jack and poker books and burned them all in front of him. Embers sparked and bits of burned paper fell between the logs to the ash. Dave expected his dad to freak out, but the man stood expressionless.

"If you ever bet again," she said just an arm's length from the fire, "our marriage is over."

At such an aggressive act, Dave waited for a flow of pent-up words, but that was all she said. When he reflected on the moment, it made sense. There was nothing else to say. The only question was whether or not it would be possible for his dad to stop.

That Sunday Jack suggested they go to a Super Bowl party.

"You've got to be kidding me? After what we spoke about, you want to go to a Super Bowl party?"

"Us. I want us to go to a Super Bowl party."

"Clearly you don't care."

Jack raised a cigarette to his lips as fast as possible, and the other hand lit it in a follow-up motion before he took the type of deep drag he always took when things fell out of rhythm. "Hear me out. Just hear me out, okay? This is always a great party, and the Super Bowl isn't just about betting, it's about pizza, a few drinks, seeing people."

"You should tape yourself."

"Listen, Mr. Smith throws this party every year, and it's not going to do me any favours at the office not to show. I figured we'd all go together, turn it into a family thing, a fun thing, and the boss is all smiles next week."

Ruby looked at her husband like he was a magician. She had never heard anyone speak with as much charisma, and it was that animated charm, so full of promise yet devoid of dogma, that had made him so popular in school, so able to get jobs and opportunities that had nothing to do with merit, and so memorable to everyone who ever met him. She decided to give him a chance. She would go to the party and either enjoy him as the man she loved or catch him in the act of being the man she feared he had become. Besides, after watching him go through seven sales jobs in fifteen years, she was happy to do anything that would keep him employed.

The afternoon of the party, Dave was stressed out, his mother was appropriately suspicious, and his dad pranced around the house as though he were taking them on vacation.

The party was in the back of a pizza shop with open space, the biggest T.V. Dave had ever seen and a herd of men in Buffalo Bills and New York Giants jerseys.

The kickoff sent the room into a frenzy. Whistles, cheers and shouts filled the place, one prompting another until everyone had a turn. Jack tapped Dave on the elbow. He gestured with his cigarette to the pock-faced man standing beside him.

"This is Stan Spiegel. Stan, this is my son."

"Pleasure." Stan raised his beer.

"You're looking at the best poker player I've ever sat with."

But Dave didn't look at Stan. He couldn't take his eyes off the blonde girl standing beside him. There was no way she was Stan's girlfriend; there was no way she was more than sixteen. Her grey slacks and white buttoned down shirt made him think of Catholic or private schools. He wished she were wearing contacts instead of glasses so he could get a better look at her blue eyes.

Stan noticed Dave staring. "This is my daughter, Amanda."

Dave wiped his hand on his pants to remove the sweat before shaking her hand, but hers was just as clammy.

"So who do you have money on?" Stan asked.

Dave looked at Stan's Bill's jersey and considered saying Buffalo before responding, "I'm not a big NFL guy. I'm more of a baseball fan."

"The Blue Jays cost me four grand this year."

Dave looked at his dad for signs that the betting talk might be breaking him down. He watched for an uncomfortable smile, eyes darting to the game, or the way he smoked when he ran odds, but he wasn't doing any of these things. What he was doing was focussing on the conversation while nodding like he was engaged.

The crowd erupted after a Buffalo sack, and Stan ran around the room offering high fives. Jack leaned into Dave. "I got you a present."

He passed Dave a ticket worth two grand if the Giants won with the spread. Dave looked for his mother, who sat wedged between two heavy-set men leaning in too close to her for his liking.

"What about Mom?"

"It's not my ticket. It's yours, a gift."

"Mine?"

"Yours."

Dave looked at the scoreboard to see Buffalo up ten to three. *Now it's mine,* he thought.

"Maybe you should buy Mom a drink."

Jack looked over at his wife sitting between the two men. He popped a cigarette in his mouth before pivoting back to Dave. "Don't lose that ticket."

Jack led Ruby out of her seat by hand and dropped his lips to her closest ear. "Thank you for coming."

"I haven't seen Mr. Smith yet. Have you?"

"Yeah, I saw him. You know what it's like, they treat you like you're just another guest when you show up, and they blast you if you don't."

"Uh-huh."

"I want to show you something."

"What?"

"The kitchen. They've got an old brick pizza oven you have to see."

Ruby smiled. At least he was willing to leave the game. He'd worked for those smiles ever since they met. Sometimes he tried jokes, other times he spoke with passion and sensitivity, and as long as she smiled, he was happy. They inched their way through the crowd to a hallway beside a kitchen that smelled of fried onions and garlic.

"Are you ready?"

Ruby looked at him like the question was weird. Jack pushed open the door to reveal a candlelit room and a table set for two. He kissed her on the cheek.

"Happy Super Bowl."

She couldn't stop smiling as he held out her chair.

"Tony may own a pizza shop, but he's also one of the best Italian chefs in the city, and tonight he's going to make you whatever you want."

He leaned over her to kiss her cheek again, and as he looked at their shadows on the white tablecloth, it felt like they could have been anywhere in the world until a roar from the crowd reminded both of them that they were at a Super Bowl party.

Meanwhile, Dave looked at the ticket as the Giants kicked the extra point to tie the game.

"Is that good?" Amanda asked.

"For New York, yeah. A touchdown is seven points."

"Cool. Do you smoke?"

"No."

"Will you come outside with me while I smoke?"

Dave nodded. They weren't a step out the door before she lit her cigarette. Dave expected her to use it as a prop, to puff and blow to look cool, but she smoked like a true addict. She held deep pulls in her lungs for a while before exhaling a cloud.

"I can't believe my dad dragged me here," she said, flicking her ash. "I have a chemistry test tomorrow, and I have to spend the night around these pigs."

"Chemistry?"

"Yeah, I've got a full semester. Chem, bio, physics and math."

"So you like school?"

"Not really, but if I have to be there, I want to do well."

Dave smiled. He thought of a math test he had the next day, watched her step on what was left of her cigarette, and somehow it made him laugh.

"I should get back to the game." He motioned to the door.

"Do you want to smoke a joint first?"

"What?"

She pulled a tightly rolled joint from her coat pocket. "A joint."

"No thanks."

"You're sure?"

"Positive."

When Scott Norwood's kick sailed wide right on the last play of the game, the Giants won outright, and while half the room deflated, the other half exploded with the euphoria of victory. Stan Spiegel approached Dave with slow steps. Everything about his posture suggested he wanted to disappear. His shoulders slouched, and his neck drooped as if his head weighed a hundred pounds.

"I need to talk to you," he slurred.

Dave thought of the way Amanda smoked, of their going outside together and her joint and waited to be punched.

"How much is that ticket your dad gave you worth?"

Dave heard the question, but the relief of not having to deal with an enraged father slowed his response.

"How much?" Stan asked again.

"What ticket?"

"The ticket your dad gave you when New York was losing ten to three. The ticket that ended up winning outright once he gave it to you. How much is it worth?"

"Two thousand."

"I need you to give me the ticket."

"I can't do that."

Stan let out a sigh that exposed his wheezing lungs. He ran a hand down his face, partly to wipe the sweat, but probably because touch reminded him that this was real, and that this wasn't some alcohol-induced nightmare.

"I just lost five thousand dollars," he said, spit flying from his lips. "Five grand to people I already owe five grand to." He leaned in closer, and his voice was the type of shaky no adult's should be. "They'll take my car. I can't get to work without my car. And I can't pay my bills for a week without my job. Please."

Dave scanned the room for his dad before responding. "Look, my dad gave me the ticket. I think you should talk to him, but you can't do it now, because he's with my mom, and she's not a fan of betting. Maybe tomorrow…"

"I need it *now*. He gave it to you, and I need it. Do you know how many times I've spotted your dad? How many times I've bailed him out of trouble?"

"So tell him."

For a moment Stan looked like he was going to leap forward with a head butt, but fear coaxed him into a few deep breaths before he said, "I'll give you Amanda for the night."

"What?"

"My daughter. I saw the two of you together, I saw you go outside. Give me the ticket, and she's yours for the night."

Dave didn't know what to say. It was as if this were a movie, and someone had hit pause. Stan kept speaking, but Dave didn't hear a word. He never got past the offer of Amanda for money. He turned around and walked to the exit. Stan grabbed at his shoulders and arms, but he shrugged the man off and kept walking past the people in Giants jerseys buying rounds, past the Bills fans sitting dejected and past Amanda, who sat stoned in front of a video game in the far corner. He wasn't fully outside the bar before he started to rip up the ticket.

He never thought about the fact that New York had been down 10-3 until his dad gave him the ticket, he only thought of destroying it, because he would rather have paid two grand not to see the look of stress on his mother's face, not to spend three hours in a room filled with greed and desperation, and not to hear a man try to trade his daughter for his debt than endure all of that, and leave with a ticket proclaiming him a winner, when for the first time in his life, he felt like a loser.

Eleven

Dave wasn't all the way down the front steps from Amy's apartment when Grayson honked to remind him that he was parked across the street. He ducked into the car, wondering whether or not to just tell Grayson what he wanted to hear; to tell him that she looked better simply by being around him, but pride wouldn't allow him to lie.

"How did it go?"

"She's different."

"Certainly is. Did she talk at all or just sit there?"

"She talked a lot."

"Then you're further ahead than me." Grayson started the car, and the Japanese lessons played so loud, he turned down the volume. He mouthed the words for 'Would you like to have dinner?' and glanced over at Dave. "Mr. Thorrin wants to meet with you."

"When?"

"Right now."

Grayson swerved to avoid a delivery truck that made an aggressive lane pass.

"No," Dave said. He shifted his weight to face Grayson's profile. "No way. I picked a stock for him just like he asked. I'm done."

"That's what he wants to talk to you about. You picked a winner."

A primal tingle rippled through Dave, as though he had been injected with the unease he'd felt as a four-year-old on the first day of kindergarten. They didn't speak the rest of the drive.

Grayson made his way through mid-day traffic with efficiency while Dave wondered how they planned to con him, how they'd managed to fix a stock increase, and what they stood to gain from convincing him he was lucky. Grayson turned up his Japanese lessons, and they didn't speak for the rest of the drive.

Thorrin sat in the luxury booth of Mango, a posh uptown lounge with a reputation among the corporate elite for the best steak sandwiches in the city. Grayson and Dave sat in the two chairs across from the padded bench Thorrin sat on. Everything about him was loose. Eyes that sparkled with mischief replaced the look of intensity he'd worn at the office, and a black button-down had replaced his designer suit.

He tongued the last of a French fry from his cheek before reaching beside him to lift two thick envelopes onto the table. He slid them towards Dave. "Start smiling. I bet that's the most money you've seen at one time."

Dave looked at the envelopes while Thorrin poured him a glass of champagne. "How much?" he asked.

"Fifteen grand."

"Bullshit."

"It's time you start believing in your gift. The stock you chose is D & T Amp. They happen to be the direct competition of Core Tech, the owners of the half-ton of memory sticks carried in the truck that crashed into your place of work. As a result of that crash and the subsequent bad press, Core Tech's stock took a free fall, and D & T hit an all-time high."

"Why are you fucking with me?"

Thorrin sipped from a half-full pint and held the mouthful for a moment before swallowing. "I can show you a report to verify the truth, but the reality is the rise was fairly predictable. We weren't the only ones to make money. What's more impressive is your unique connection to the stock. I want you to take a day or two to enjoy the money. Then you'll make another selection."

It occurred to Dave that Thorrin might be high. His eyes darted, passion glazed every word, and his hands moved from one object to the next. Those weren't the words of a calm man, they were the words of dogma.

"Look, I'm grateful for the money, and it's definitely a mind-fuck coincidence that I picked that stock, but I have to say no."

"I don't like that word, Dave."

"The next stock I pick is going to lose money, and I don't want to be responsible for that."

He gave Grayson a deep look in hopes of some assistance, but the man's eyes were locked on a waitress loading up a tray at the bar. Thorrin removed a set of keys from the same pocket as his wallet and extended them to Dave with a closed-lipped smile.

"I have a chalet an hour and a half outside the city; it's yours for the weekend."

"I can't."

"Sure you can. Find a date, put your feet up, stay in bed all day if you want."

"Really, I appreciate the offer, but the last few days have been a lot, and right now I need some time at home to get my head straight."

The keys disappeared into Thorrin's cupped hand. "Fair enough, but the offer stands when you're ready."

Dave looked at his watch. Two thirty on the twenty-fifth of the month meant he had thirty minutes to get Otto his money. He rose from his seat. "I've got to get going."

Thorrin embraced Dave in a parting handshake without getting up. "You enjoy yourself. We'll talk soon."

Dave examined the fifteen thousand during the entire cab ride to Otto's. Thorrin was half right. As an accountant, he had seen more money at one time, but he had never held fifteen grand of his own money at once. He considered the odds of randomly placing his finger on the stock of the company that would profit most from the truck that crashed into his work. It couldn't happen. He had a better chance of being attacked by a shark and struck by lightning in the same week. Thorrin had to be fixing something, but why? He looked at the fifteen thousand again, and suddenly it didn't matter why, because he had enough to pay for seven months of his dad's care.

He stepped out of the cab, over a puddle and into Otto's internet café. The place didn't have a lot of square footage, but it was packed with gamers, computer geeks, MSN junkies, and world travellers sending mass emails about their adventures. It was good business, which made it an even better cover. Dave walked through the café to the back, where he knocked twice on a steel door before entering. Otto wore a black button down shirt and black dress pants. He paced the back of his desk with a phone in hand, but he still welcomed Dave with a handshake before holding up a finger to indicate that he needed a moment. Otto's face always looked angry.

His features were striking, but a protruding brow, large jaw and military box cut left him resembling a rugby player more than a movie star. Dave took a seat in front of the desk.

"Look," Otto said with a scowl, "I've got to go. We're going to have to finish this later. Just make sure you tell them to be polite. You understand me? Be polite. All right."

He put down the phone. "Come here," he said with his arms stretched. He pulled Dave in for a firm hug before sitting in a freshly reupholstered leather chair with large wooden arm rests. He tapped the desk twice with an index finger. "I heard about the accident."

Dave nodded.

"What are the odds of that?" Dave turned his head to look at a fish tank, where a large eel slipped into a mountain of rocks. "Where were you, with a client?"

"No, I was in the washroom."

"The washroom?"

"Yeah."

"That's some timing."

"Yeah."

Otto smiled for the first time. It wasn't a pretty smile, but a "we've known each other since we were kids and you've seen me do some crazy shit" smile. "Well I'm glad you're still with us. You're early though, it's only mid-month."

"I'm giving, not taking."

"Really?"

Dave passed him a thick envelope. "There's fifteen grand in there."

Otto looked at the envelope, clearly surprised, before smiling again. This was what he loved about life. The average person didn't understand that he lived for what ifs, the unexpected, and the absurd.

"What? You got settlement money for this crash already?"

"It just came to me."

Otto nodded in approval of Dave's cryptic answer. "Well, that's good. And I hope it comes to you a lot more too, because I don't like seeing you in this position."

"I appreciate that. And everything else you've arranged, really."

"As far back as we go, I wish I could just give it to you."

"Getting it for me is more than enough; I should be able to get it for myself."

"Well, you just did, right? Maybe surviving the accident is a sign of good things to come."

Dave nodded in agreement, but his face showed that the comment had made him uncomfortable. If five people dying was a sign of good things to come, then he wished he'd died with them.

Twelve

Dave found out about Mr. Richter's funeral by scanning the obituaries. He knew one of Mr. Richter's many long-term clients would put out the notice, and that despite being an only child and having mentioned no living family in the past, and despite not having a wife or kids, this was a man whose death was felt. The crowd of people at the funeral didn't surprise him either. There were at least five hundred chairs and another three rows of people standing. The attendees included clients, friends, golf-club members, people from the numerous charities he had been involved with, local politicians, the parents of the little-league soccer team he'd sponsored, and every store owner in a two-block radius from the office. This was a man who had made a difference. Dave wondered how many people would attend his dad's funeral.

Mr. Richter's funeral made him think of his mother's death. The day his mother had died, his dad had disappeared for four days. He didn't leave a note, he didn't call, and he never mentioned where he had gone or when he would be back. Dave sat in his apartment numb when the phone calls started, inquiries about the arrangements from second cousins, friends he didn't know his mother had, and even her neighbours. He didn't know why he was getting all the calls until he asked his cousin Bonnie, whom he hadn't seen since he was twelve.

"There's a message on your dad's answering machine directing anyone with questions about the funeral to call you," she said.

He paged his dad right away, but he never heard back that

night. The responsibility hit him hard. He had to organize the funeral, and he had to pay for it too.

The thought of paying for his mother's funeral with the three hundred and seventy-five he had in the bank made the muscles in his jaw clench so hard they hurt. He had only been working at Richter's accounting firm a few weeks past six months, and he was still living cheque to cheque.

The task was overwhelming. He wanted to plan it the way his mother would have, only he had no idea what she'd wanted. He didn't know what to put on her gravestone, what type of gravestone to get, what type of flowers to order, or what the priest should read at the ceremony. Without a will, every answer was reduced to his best guess. The thought of disappointing her made him pace until a wave of dizziness forced him to sit back down.

For the first time in his life, he went without sleep that night. He went to work the next day, but he couldn't think about anything except the funeral. Nobody knew his mother had died. He chose to keep her death to himself, because he didn't want to share such a private moment with people he hadn't known very long, and because he didn't think he would be able to keep it together if he was showered with condolences. Just before lunch, Mr. Richter approached his cubicle.

"Are you ready to eat?"

"I don't think I'm going to take lunch today, sir."

"I think you should, it's on me," Mr. Richter said, passing him his jacket from the coat rack.

Dave couldn't say no to Mr. Richter's warm ways. They sat in the front window booth at the local pub and ordered two club sandwiches, then Mr. Richter unfolded his napkin over his lap.

"Is everything okay?"

Dave nodded unconvincingly.

"Are you sure?"

Dave felt his eyes burn. "My mother died a couple of days ago."

"And you've been coming to work?" The silence confirmed Dave's confusion.

"I want you to go home, Dave, take the rest of the week off, be around your family."

The food came, and Mr. Richter thanked the waitress as fast as possible in an effort to preserve the conversation's privacy. When she left, he pushed his food to the side. "When is the funeral?"

Dave winced. Just hearing the word made his head hurt, but something about Mr. Richter's tone compelled him to share his situation.

"I'm not sure. My dad's pretty shaken, and I haven't been able to get in touch with him. He directed all my relatives to call me about the arrangements, so I think I'm going to have to pay for it."

"Can you afford that?"

"I'm going to have to."

Richter looked closely at Dave's eyes and saw that he was unsure, dazed and scared. "I'll give you whatever you need."

"No."

"I understand why that's your response, but I'm going to pay for the funeral. You don't need to be worrying about money right now, and I can afford it, so let's leave it at that. I'm going to give you a blank cheque, and that's the last we'll ever talk about it."

Dave wanted to say no, but the weight he felt leave his body just hearing the offer made him accept the cheque. "I promise I'll pay you back."

"I just said not to talk about it."

Dave's dad resurfaced in time to prepare for the funeral, so Mr. Richter never had to pay for anything. But the fact that he had been willing to stayed with Dave ever after. They never spoke about the funeral or his mother's death again, but every time he looked at Mr. Richter, he remembered the gesture and wished there was a way to return it.

Dave had to admit that Mr. Richter's funeral was impressive.

Listening to so many people speak about the man made him feel better, and the honesty and passion that the stories were told with made him hope he would leave such a strong impression on people. Seeing Mr. Richter appreciated was soothing, but it was still devastating to watch him be buried. Dave left the graveyard with slow steps as though he was unsure about the ground's stability. A woman with shoulder-length brown hair appeared beside him.

"I'm Jody," she said with an extended hand.

Dave shook it to be polite and withdrew his. Instinct told him this was a journalist, so he picked up the pace to make it clear he wasn't interested in a conversation, but she kept up.

"You're Dave Bolden, right?"

He stopped walking. "Are you a journalist?"

"No."

"Then how do you know me?"

"I run a website."

"A website?"

"That's right. It's about miracles." Dave's eyes narrowed again with disgust, but the look didn't deter her. "We share stories about miracles so everyone around the world can be inspired by them. It's important that people know when amazing things happen."

"So you're a cult."

Her faced washed with genuine hurt. She'd approached him the way a football card collector would a Hall of Famer, and he'd dismissed her as a freak. "It's not a cult. I just think you should share your story. You're an inspiration. We had half a million visitors this year. Think about how many people they shared the stories with."

A website. He couldn't get past the imagery. "How did you find out about me?"

"One of our members emailed your story in."

"How did they know?"

"I have no idea, but I want to interview you for the site so that people can read your story from your point of view. You'll get a thousand emails in the first week."

"No thank you."

"Your story can change peoples' lives."

"No thank you."

"I'll pay you five hundred dollars."

A bribe? Five hundred to pimp the story of his dead colleagues? The muscles around his eyes twitched with anger. "Don't try to contact me again."

The idea of a website made his blood boil.

He was at a funeral to commemorate the most gentle man he had ever met, and she wanted him to explain how an eighteen-wheel truck had killed everyone he worked with on a miracle website. He wished he could tell Mr. Richter how twisted she was.

Thirteen

Dave woke after only a few hours sleep. He looked at the clock to see seven ten and decided against trying for more rest. He craved a coffee, so he grabbed his winter jacket to bear the sprinkle of snow blowing outside his window and headed out. Three storefronts before the coffee shop, a series of posters stuck to the plywood surrounding a renovation caught Dave's attention. The MC5 was playing a one-time only concert the following evening. Suddenly coffee felt irrelevant. He pulled out his cell phone and punched in Otto's number. Otto answered on the second ring, and his hello sounded like he had a mouthful of food.

"I need your expertise."

"I like your word choice."

"Can you get me front row tickets to a concert?"

"I can make it snow in summer."

"It's tomorrow night."

"That's fine. Which one?"

"MC5."

"Who?"

"The MC5. You know, 'Kick out the jams, motherfuckers.'"

"Whatever. I'll make a call and have the tickets dropped off at your place tonight."

"Thank you."

"For you? It's my pleasure. I've got to go. I've got another call."

Dave closed his phone and motioned to stop an empty cab, but the first one coasted past him, so he stepped off the curb and pointed at one a few cars behind. The driver was so tall, he had to hunch to keep his head from touching the ceiling. His neck was skinny, and a scar in the shape of a bow-tie peeked out from the collar of a black T-shirt.

"That guy drove past like I wasn't there," Dave said, pointing at the cab disappearing in the distance.

"Sometimes these drivers, their minds wander." The man spoke with a rich East African accent.

"Coxwell and Gerrard, please."

"No problem." The traffic light turned red, and the man seized the opportunity to turn and face Dave. The whites of his eyes were glazed yellow, but they burned with intensity. "You were born here, yeah?"

"I was."

The light turned green, and he accelerated into the next lane.

"You have no idea how fortunate you are. I'm from Rwanda, and I can tell you that people here, they wouldn't believe how some of the world lives."

"Tough living, I imagine." Dave wanted to be polite, but his mind was still on the concert.

"I tell everyone that will listen, your nightmares can't compare to my reality there. I had to leave my family at fourteen to avoid being forced into the rebel army, and I walked across the desert to reach free soil. I started the journey with my best friend, but on the ninth morning, he never woke up, so I had to leave him. Can you picture such a moment? Tongue swollen with dehydration, mind hazy from a lack of food, your heart heavy because you know you will never see your family again, and your best friend lying dead before you."

Dave stared at the rear-view mirror to meet the man's eyes and did his best with the look to show that he'd taken the story in.

"Embrace your life," the driver said. "You live a life my people only dream of."

Dave nodded. The cab's radio crackled and the dispatcher's tired voice filled the vehicle. "Car number three-twenty-two just had a code purple. Driver fine, passenger injured, police on site."

The driver turned to Dave. "Good thing that driver ignored you. He just got carjacked."

"What?"

"They say the driver is fine, but the passenger is injured, and that would have been you."

Dave nodded. A carjacked cab in daylight. One could live a long time and not hear a story like that, let alone be present for the madness. He considered the probability. The cab wouldn't have taken the same route if he was in it, so therefore the driver's belief that he had narrowly escaped tragedy was a false connection.

He tipped the driver ten dollars and approached Amy's place determined to forget that he'd heard the cab was robbed. Sadness had shadowed him since his own accident, and he craved fantasy, not more reality.

He pressed Amy's buzzer, but after a few minutes, she still hadn't answered, so he considered leaving for a moment before pressing the buzzer once more.

Hurried steps approached the door from the other side before it opened, and Amy took a step back with surprise.

"Hey."

Her brow furrowed into a look of confusion.

"I thought I'd do better than call," he said. "I hope that's okay."

"Of course."

"Can I come in?"

She nodded and stepped to the side so he could enter. "Did my brother pay you to come back?"

"No. I know I should have called, but I've got a surprise that demands face-to-face contact."

She held up a phone that she gripped so tight, her knuckles were white. "Sorry, I'm dazed. My phone number is cursed, and I just got another weird call."

"And how would you define a phone number as being cursed?"

"It's been mistaken for a non-residential number."

"That happens."

"Three times a day for the last two months."

"Are you sure they're not prank calls?"

"I thought they were at first, but the people on the other end were as disappointed with me answering as I was with them calling. Do you still think I'm not unlucky?"

"Having your phone number mixed up doesn't make you unlucky."

"The first set of calls were from people trying to order double-headed dildos."

"That's weird, but not unlucky," he said with a laugh he couldn't contain.

"Then for a week I got calls from a lab trying to give me a patient's biopsy results."

"Look, that's definitely strange, but…"

"Think about the odds of having your phone number posted on a website that specializes in dildos and mistakenly entered into a lab by an overworked receptionist in the same month. Things like this don't happen to normal people."

"True, it's rare and darkly funny, if you ask me, but those calls don't affect you, so you can't say they make you unlucky."

"I just got a call before you buzzed that mistook me for a teen suicide hotline."

Dave took a moment to take in her expression. Both the strain in her eyes and worry on her face suggested she expected to get such bizarre calls.

"What did you do?" he asked.

"I told her she had the wrong number and that I'd look up the right number for her, but she hung up."

"That's disturbing, and I'm sorry you had to take that call, but I have a surprise for you that might help take your mind off it."

She set the phone down. "I didn't think you'd call, let alone come over again."

"Well, I did. Do you know the MC5 is coming to town?"

"Of course."

"Are you going?"

"I can't go to concerts. I'd get trampled."

"This is your favourite band, right?"

"It's too dangerous."

Dave stepped closer to her and smiled. "I have VIP tickets, and I want to watch it with you."

"I can't."

"You have to. Who else can give me the details you can?"

"I would love to go with you, and I can't believe you're asking me, but…"

The phone's electronic buzz cut her off before she finished. Instinct told her to step back from the phone. "You have to get it," she said, gesturing to Dave.

"Let it go to voicemail."

"Your energy can save her."

"Save who?"

"Please answer the phone."

The buzz seemed louder to both of them now.

"You should answer your phone."

"I'll go to the concert if you get it."

He looked at the panic in her eyes and felt compelled to do anything he could to change the expression. With a quick pivot, he answered the phone just after the fifth buzz. "Hello?"

"Aren't you supposed to answer faster?"

The voice on the other end was smooth and the accent clearly Newfoundland. Dave placed the tone as late teens. "What number are you looking for?"

"The teen suicide hotline."

"I'm sorry, but this isn't…"

"What's your name?" the voice asked.

Dave looked at Amy, who appeared reassured just by having him on the phone. "Dave."

"Will you talk to me, Dave?"

"I'm not a counsellor. This is a private number."

"You're going to be the last person I talk to."

Dave took a breath, put the phone in his other hand and wiped the sweat from the hand that just held the phone on his pants. He looked again at Amy and she mouthed, "Please."

"Who am I talking with?" he asked the voice on the other end.

"Cole."

"Okay, Cole. How old are you?"

"How old are *you*?"

"I'm thirty-five."

"Seventeen."

"And why did you call this number, Cole?"

"Because I'm tired of hating myself."

"Can you guess what I'm going to ask next?"

"I'm gay."

"And?"

"What do you mean 'and'? I'm living a curse."

For the first time, Cole was aggressive, so Dave matched the tone. "I mean it's not a big deal to be gay, and it's certainly not a curse."

"Tell that to my parents."

Reflex told him to tell the teen to tell his parents to go fuck themselves, but reason warned that the situation demanded a more measured response. "Your parents are hard on you?"

"My dad wants to take me to a strip club in Montreal for my birthday next week."

"Tell him you're not interested."

"He wants to pay one of the strippers to have sex with me."

"I'm sorry he told you that. But you'll be eighteen then, right? Tell him that you're an adult, it's your choice now, and you're not interested."

"They love me, and they tell me it's not my fault I've been cursed, but that I'm destined to go to hell, so I should do everything I can to make amends for who I am."

"How can you possibly believe that your sexuality is a curse? Is it a curse that I have brown eyes?"

"They say ten per cent of the population is homosexual. The odds were overwhelmingly in favour of me being straight, yet here I am. My destiny is to disgrace my parents."

"Your destiny? Is it the blind's destiny not to see?"

"Of course."

"You need to shift the lens. You get to choose what you believe in, and right now you believe in things that punish you for who you are. You can just as easily choose to believe in things that love you for who you are."

Dave hoped for a positive response or a change in tone, but instead there was a silence that reinforced the conversation's stakes. "Are you with me?"

"Yeah, but you don't understand what it feels like."

"Of course I don't. But I know what it feels like to wonder if I believe." He looked at Amy a moment before continuing. "Last week a truck crashed into the place where I work and killed everyone except me. I ask myself all the time why I lived, and what it boils down to is what I want to believe. Did I live for a reason, or did they die because it's possible?"

"And?" Cole asked, now fully engaged.

"And I believe it happened because it's theoretically possible for a truck to drive off the road and through a business's front windows."

"I'm sorry that happened to you."

"I'm sorry you hate yourself. You seem like a cool guy."

A beat of silence felt like minutes, until Cole said, "I'm going to hang up, Dave."

"Are you sure that's a good idea?"

"I've got a lot of thinking to do, but thank you for sharing that story."

"Take care, Cole."

The teen hung up, and Dave put the phone on the table. Amy looked at him like he glowed.

"Do you believe you're special now?"

"I almost threw up."

"If I'd answered the phone, he would have hung himself."

"You need to change your number."

They shared a tension-releasing laugh. It felt good to exhale and even better to drop his shoulders.

"You owe me a concert."

"I'll be there."

She smiled at the thought of spending more time with him, but just the word "concert" made her stomach swirl.

Fourteen

When Dave picked Amy up in a cab, her eyes had the liquid, thousand-yard stare of fear, so he squeezed her closest hand and put the concert tickets in her lap.

"Front row," he said with pride.

"Amazing." Her lips were so tight that the word fell more than flowed from her mouth. "Will you hold my wallet for me? I don't want to lose it."

Dave nodded, slipped the wallet into a pocket and pulled a flask from his breast pocket. He sipped until his gums burned and extended it to Amy, who to his surprise, filled her mouth.

"Easy," he said. "We've got a long night."

She let out a cough, nodded and returned the flask. "I get panic attacks."

"Okay." He rolled down the window. "Just breathe."

"Ask me a question about music, it'll relax me."

"Alright. When did the MC5 last play in Toronto?"

"March 25, 1970. Varsity Arena."

"How can you possibly know that?"

"More questions," she said with a heavy swallow. Precedent told her the tightness in her throat meant she was losing control. She fought back a gag and motioned him to continue with a finger. "Harder questions."

"Okay. Who opened for them that night?"

"Small Faces and Canned Heat."

Another gag. "Harder."

"Who was in Canned Heat?"

"Alan Wilson and Bob Hite." She took a deep breath and

inhaled as if smoking. "Harder."

"Why were they called Canned Heat?"

"After the 1928 Tommy Johnson song 'Canned Heat Blues' about an alcoholic addicted to Steno, more commonly known as canned heat."

Dave smiled. "You're too cool to be panicked."

"What?"

"With as much as you know about music, you could sit down with the Stones, and they'd pour you a drink."

She smiled and looked out the window, surprised to see they had reached the venue. They stepped out of the cab and were walking toward the building when a homeless man shook a tin cup that jingled with coins.

"When you're happy and you know it…spare some change."

He shook the cup twice to punctuate the rhythm, and Dave handed him five dollars.

The club smelled of draft beer, and the floors were already sticky with spillage. The place was packed, but the space was tight, so it was difficult to guess how many people were there.

Dave led the way through the crowd with the swagger of a man with front-row tickets. He took a swig from the flask and passed it to Amy.

"Thank you for coming. I know this isn't easy for you."

She took a sip and winced. "This is a great flask."

"My dad used it for years."

"Did he give it to you?"

"Not exactly."

He thought of the week after his mother's funeral. To be supportive, he had picked up some Chinese food after work and brought it to his dad's place. As soon as he'd opened the front door, he'd heard his dad's drunken moan. The moan was not panicked, but slow and deliberate like a child with a toothache.

"Oh my god it burns."

Dave moved toward the sound as fast as possible. "Dad?"

"Oh my god it burns."

Dave entered the living room to find his dad's pleather easy-chair tipped over, and Jack's legs dangling over the leg rest.

"Oh my god it burns."

A nineteen-thirties movie played on the television. Dave turned it off and hovered over his dad, whose eyes swirled as he looked up at the ceiling with his arms splayed over his head. A flask lay beside him.

"What's going on, Pop?"

"Oh my god it burns."

Dave leaned down to take the flask away from him and noticed white foam spilling from his dad's mouth. Thoughts of alcohol poisoning or a drug overdose flashed through his head until he saw a toothbrush a foot away.

After Dave's mother had died, his dad had started brushing his teeth at the kitchen sink. He was drinking so much, it was simply easier to stumble to the kitchen then negotiate the stairs. That night he'd picked up his muscle relaxing cream instead of his toothpaste, and minutes later, he was lying on his back with a burning mouth.

Dave knew taking his dad's flask wouldn't stop the man from drinking, but making him think he'd lost his favourite flask was a punishment, and after finding him in such a pathetic state, he'd wanted to do something to ensure Jack would remember the night.

Amy returned the flask, and Dave snapped back into the moment. "Have you always been lucky?"

The question annoyed him, but a closer examination of her eyes revealed a belief he couldn't say he had in anything, and it felt good to be the object of such hope.

"If you knew how average my life has been, you'd know why I'm smiling at that statement."

She looked at him like there was a better chance of her believing he could fly and reached into her oversized bag. "I got you a present."

"Yeah?"

She nodded, pulled out what was clearly a wrapped record and passed it to him. Dave looked at his reflection in the silver wrapping and wished he didn't look so tired. He tore open the top right corner and pulled out the record to reveal a twelve-inch of Crowbar's "Too True Mama". Excitement ran through him, and despite the crowd of people around them, he looked at her like she was the only person on the planet.

"Thank you."

"That's the song your mother used to play, right? I was sure it was, then I panicked and thought it might be 'Oh What a Feeling'."

"This is the one," he said, holding the record high.

"I'll hold it in my bag for you, so you don't have to carry it."

He passed her the record and gestured to the bar. "Are you up for a shot?"

She nodded, and he started through the crowd.

As soon as he turned, the comfort Amy enjoyed began to dissipate. She took a deep breath in an effort to stave off a gag and pivoted to open up the room, when she felt the hard stare of a man with close-cut brown hair. *He's not looking at you,* she told herself. *It's in your head.* She turned away and looked back to see him moving through the crowd in her direction. A thick moustache robbed his mouth of expression, and his eyes were solemn and over-intense in their focus. A quick glance at the bar for Dave could have relaxed her, but all she saw was a sea of bodies.

She moved along the front row, and the man moved with her. A gag forced her jaw to clench, and the man stepped in front of her. She started to scream when the man held up a police badge at eye level.

"Please come with me to the back room."

He gestured to a red exit sign to the left of the stage, where a woman with dark hair and glasses stood looking stern.

"I don't understand."

She looked for Dave again but couldn't see him.

"I'll explain when we get to the back. Let's not draw attention."
He put a hand on her elbow and steered her toward the exit sign.
"I really don't understand. I'm just here for a concert."
"I'm sure you are."

Dave gave a bartender with heavy blue eye make-up and a face like wax a five dollar tip and was heading back to the front row with two shots of tequila when he saw Amy being escorted out of the room. He handed the shots to the closest guy and bee-lined for Amy.

In the back, the detective with the moustache spoke first. "May I check your bag?"

"For what?"

"May I, or are we going to the station?"

"I don't know what you're talking about."

"We've been watching you three months, Crystal. We know everything."

"Crystal? I'm not Crystal."

"Of course you're not."

"I'm not Crystal. My name is Amy Leonard."

"Then show me a license and your health card, and you can enjoy the concert."

Panic sent a wave of tension through her head that made her eyes hurt. "I don't have my wallet. I'm afraid of losing it, so I gave it to my date."

"Show me your bag."

Amy passed her bag to the detective just as Dave entered the room.

"What's going on?"

"You can't be back here, sir," the female detective said.

Dave gestured to Amy. "We're on a date. I came here with her."

The male detective looked at his partner, who dropped her head to a photo stuck to a clipboard. The woman's eyes narrowed for a moment before she nodded.

"What's her name?"

"Amy Leonard."

"Do you have ID?"

"I have her ID." Dave removed Amy's wallet from his jacket and passed the male detective her license and health card. The detective showed his partner, whose eyes bugged.

"Incredible." He passed Amy back her identification. "Please accept our apologies, but the resemblance is uncanny. We've been watching this woman for months. She's one of the city's biggest ecstasy dealers."

He held up a photo of the woman they'd mistaken Amy for, and Dave stared at it in shock. The features were not just similar, the two women could have been twins. Both had slightly swollen upper lips, brows that gave them a perpetual look of worry and the purest blue eyes he had ever seen.

The crowd erupted, and within seconds, the guitar riff of "Kick Out the Jams" vibrated through the room.

"Once again, we apologize. I hope you understand. Please enjoy the show," the detective said and extended an arm to the door.

They left the room, and Amy turned to Dave. "You see?"

"I'm sorry that happened. That was crazy."

"If you weren't here, I'd be on my way to the station."

"I got mistaken for a guy who was breaking into cars when I was at university."

"Did you look like him?"

"Enough to get stopped on the street."

"Did you see how much I look like that woman?"

"They say everyone has a doppelganger."

"And mine's a drug dealer."

The crowd erupted at the end of the first song, and Dave smiled. "We're still at an MC5 concert. Let's have a drink and enjoy the moment."

"I want to go home."

"Are you sure?"

"Positive. I'm never going to a concert again."

Fifteen

The phone woke Dave on the third ring.

"Hello?" he said, doing his best to hide that he'd been sleeping. He looked at the clock and saw eight forty-five. He'd slept four hours. Regular patterns had eluded him since the accident, so he'd decided to simply sleep whenever exhaustion allowed him.

"May I speak with Dave Bolden, please?"

Dave looked at the rain splashing against his window pane. The voice was too alert for such a dull day. He sat upright.

"This is Dave Bolden."

"Oh hi, Dave, I didn't recognize your voice. It's Cheryl Reid from Vatic Media."

Dave didn't respond. Vatic Media had been a client before his place of work was destroyed. The name conjured thoughts of his colleagues' shattered bodies.

"Dave?"

"Yeah, I'm here."

"We're sorry about your tragedy."

"Thank you."

"I'm calling because we want to offer you a job."

"A job?"

"You've always done great work for us. I'm hoping you can come in today to discuss things."

"What time?"

"As soon as you can."

"How about lunch?"

"Lunch works for me. Do you know where we're located?"

"I do."

"Okay, I look forward to seeing you."

He hung up, surprised by the call. A job. He considered the details: Vatic Media, mid-sized company, growing, and comparable pay to what he'd earned with Richter Accounting. The opportunity should have excited him, but he couldn't stop thinking about the fifteen thousand he'd paid Otto. It would take him three and a half months just to clear fifteen thousand at Vatic Media, let alone have fifteen thousand left over for his dad's care. Thoughts of sixty-hour work weeks, performance reviews, managers, the hustle for clients, and the wrath of clients left him anxious. In truth, he didn't want to work any more, not yet anyway. A new feeling washed over him. Part of him wished that Thorrin was right, and he did have the power of luck on his side.

Dave put a tie around his neck for the first time since the accident. He flipped to channel twenty-six, where two stock ticker tapes ran across the bottom of the screen in opposite directions. Maybe if he hit the library, took out every book on the stock market and obsessed over the business channel, he could get competent enough to have a good run with Thorrin. The thought lasted as long as it took the screen to change to a commercial. Numbers always came easy, but the market's science eluded him. He looked at the screen as though what he saw was in a different language, and the host spoke in a code that made him feel inferior—up, down, street names, warrants, EBITPA, ask and bid, short selling, book value, resistance levels and poison pills.

Partnering up with a broker that would give him recommendations in return for fifty per cent of Thorrin's kickbacks was another option.

But the gains weren't worth a broker's risks. Between insider trading and the risk of losing a guy like Thorrin's money, there was no incentive for a real broker to enter such absurdity.

The first thing Dave noticed at the interview was that Cheryl Reid looked older than he remembered. Her hair was tucked behind her ears, and her lips were locked in a smile so toothy, it looked cartoonish. She hugged him for a three count. "We're so sorry."

Dave wanted to say "Be sorry for my colleagues, they died," but he managed to squint with his lips raised in a weak smile.

"Let's start with a tour." She led him through a hallway with dull lighting to a cluster of cubicles. "This is the main space." She knocked on the side of a cubicle, where a woman with short hair faced a computer screen. The name tag read: Ann Hemple. Ann turned her chair to face the knock. "Hi there," Cheryl waved. "This is Dave Bolden."

The two exchanged a quick handshake before respectively wiping their hands. Dave wiped his hands because they were sweaty, and Ann probably wiped hers because she wondered where his hands had been.

"Ann is doing all the accounts by herself right now, so you'd be working closely with her if you come aboard."

Strike one, Dave thought.

A phone buzzed, and Ann spun towards it as if it couldn't have rung soon enough. She wore an oversized hunter green suit jacket and slacks, and her eyes looked medicated. Cheryl waved goodbye before continuing the tour.

The next stop was a kitchenette with a fridge, a microwave and a plate of morning glory muffins. Ann pointed to a calendar marked with yellow happy faces.

"We have group softball on Tuesdays in the spring and summer, yoga in the fall and winter. And Fridays after work we usually get together at the pub to start the weekend."

Dave caught himself staring at a sticky note reminding everyone to ante up for the weekly office lotto tickets. This wasn't a place he wanted to work. He didn't want to work anywhere yet, and maybe never in an office again.

"I've got to be honest," he said, slowing her momentum. "This is all a little much right now. I mean it's wonderful for you to make this easy for me, and it looks like a great place to work, but

I need some time away from the workplace right now."

"How much time?"

"I don't know."

"Okay. Well, we respect that, of course, but we need assistance as soon as possible, so I can't promise you the job will be available at a later date."

"I understand."

He couldn't get out of the building fast enough. The overhead lighting, the smells of photocopier fluid and cheap coffee, the constant clicking of keyboards and hustling on phones filled him with the need to see what remained of his former workplace. He'd spent more time at Richter accounting than anywhere, and that reality hit him hard as the cab stopped in front of what was left of the office.

"They should put a pizza place here," the driver said with a gesture at the hollowed-out front. "The neighbourhood needs a pizza place."

Time seemed to slow as Dave stepped out of the cab. People passed him in both directions, but none of them did more than glance at the broken storefront. He inspected the orange plastic fence someone had unravelled over the perimeter. The sagging in the middle proved the fence hadn't done its job. He imagined squatters smoking around the rubble that had once been his office or teenagers smashing whatever they could find that wasn't already destroyed. Other than dust and dirt, the front door looked like it had the last time he'd walked through, which surprised him considering the devastation just a foot away.

A car honking pulled his attention to the road, where a minivan almost pulled into a Lexus SUV. For the first time, he noticed a man watching him from three storefronts down the street. The man didn't smoke or take it all in while he waited for someone, he just stared at Dave.

Dave looked at the man long enough to notice his black bubble vest, jeans and Maple Leafs hat. The stare made him uncomfortable, but the office's shell drew his eyes back to its frame. What if it became a pizza shop like the cabbie wanted? The thought frustrated him. People would remember the space for pizza, and his place of work, the place where four of his friends had been killed, would disappear except from his memory. No one else had survived. No one else knew the place for what it was, so while the family members of his dead colleagues might remember their loved ones' stories of the office, he was the only one left who'd known the place intimately.

He glanced down the street again to see that the staring man was now closer.

With his feet planted, legs stiff and a newspaper rolled up in one hand, he didn't hide his gaze either. Dave sighed. He wasn't in the mood for the city's unpredictable; he was in the mood for a beer.

The Saunders pub had hosted many a Friday liquid lunch for Dave, so when he entered, Frank Saunders limped his way out from behind the bar and hugged him tightly.

"What took you so long? We were on pins and needles here, you bastard."

Frank smelled like he'd had a few beers himself, but it was his style to talk to the customers, drink with the customers, and listen to the customers. He ran his hands through the sides of his thick, white hair while exhaling. "Damn, it's good to see you."

"Thank you."

"Okay, no talking today then. But know this, you don't pay for another drink here as long as you live."

"Frank…"

"You hear me? Not as long as you live. Now go take a seat, and I'll get you a pint."

Dave avoided the front booths where he'd often taken clients for lunch, walked past the two-seaters where he'd had after-work drinks with Shannon and slipped into a back booth. Frank couldn't have served the pint fast enough.

"Bless you," Dave said as he lifted the pint to his lips.

"My pleasure. When it settles down, I'll join you for a drink."
Dave raised his pint.

A part of him wanted to spend every night in a bar, where
music underscored every moment, until the beers slowed time,
and he entered a world that just happened. A world where
conversations started with ease, witty replies flowed off his
tongue, and all he had to do was sip at a beer.

Another mouthful was slipping down his throat when he
looked up to see the man who'd stared at him outside walking
towards his booth. His stomach tingled in anticipation of the
worst. Perhaps he was somebody Thorrin had sent, or maybe
this guy had mistaken him for the man cheating with his wife
or a guy who owed him money. He didn't get to the next set of
possibilities before the man sat down.

"Do I know you?" Dave said.

"No." Weary eyes dominated the man's face. He spread large
hands on the table and leaned on his forearms. "But I've been
waiting for you to come back to the crash site."

"For me?"

"Every day."

The man wasn't polished enough to be associated with Thorrin.
"Why's that?"

"Because you survived."

Dave sat back in his seat. The words made him uncomfortable
and unsure of what might happen next, so he locked eyes with
the man and searched for any clues about who he was sitting
with. The man's face was drained, and his eyelids were a sore pink.

"Are you a journalist?"

"No." The man slid both his lips into his mouth and bit
down on them for a moment before continuing. "I'm the driver
of the truck."

Dave saw a flash of steam rising from the truck's grill and
replayed the broken bodies of his colleagues. He didn't know
what to say.

"I saw you when they were putting me into the ambulance," the man said. The words raced from his mouth as if he couldn't say them fast enough. "But they were asking me so many questions, there was no time."

"You don't need to do this."

"I disagree. I *have* to do this. Don't you want to know how it happened?"

"It doesn't matter."

"It's the only thing that matters. I've barely slept since the crash. I get these pains in my head like it's going to implode. I need to tell you. You survived, you deserve to know."

Another flash of the truck filling the office space forced Dave to close his eyes for a second before he reopened them. "It won't change anything."

"I need to tell you."

Dave shifted his weight. The muscles in his forearms flexed, and his eyes narrowed. "Do you really think that if I know you swerved to avoid a kid or blew a tire that it'll make this any better? It doesn't matter to me how it happened."

"I'm not doing this for you."

They stared at each without saying anything. Dave had lied to the man. Seeing the driver changed everything. The truck had a face in the flashes now. Dave envisioned the man slumped over the wheel as he stepped over broken glass and debris.

"The crash was my fault," the man said.

Dave didn't respond. He was doing his best to ignore the flashes and stay focussed on the driver. "I've been double shifting the past two months. I hadn't slept in three days. I didn't eat that morning, and the next thing I know, I'm in an ambulance. The doctor said it was a seizure. Said it was brought on by exhaustion, but she's not sure."

"That's not your fault."

"People died because I passed out."

"You could have just as easily passed out at home."

"I shouldn't have been driving."

"I don't know what you want me to say."

"Neither do I."

Dave thought of the man having a seizure. It could have happened anywhere, but it hadn't. He could have died, but he hadn't. He finished the last of his pint before setting it back on the table and spinning the glass with his closest hand. "Do you think maybe we lived for a reason?"

"How so?"

"You could have easily died in the crash, and if you'd crashed just a couple of minutes later, maybe hit a few more red lights before you reached my office, I'd be dead too."

The man adjusted his hat. "Are you asking if I believe in a higher power?"

"I'm asking if you believe in luck."

"Luck?"

"That's right."

"Luck had nothing to do with this. The truck crashed because I had a seizure."

The tone shook Dave enough that he shifted his weight again. "It's hard to make sense of this."

"I'd settle for making peace with it." The man stood up. His body moved slow, as though it hurt his back and legs to straighten. "You take care."

They shook hands, and Dave was surprised to find the man's hand so cold. He watched the driver leave the pub and wondered what would become of him. Would he live the rest of his life plagued by the belief he that he'd been responsible for ending four lives? Knowing how it happened didn't make Dave feel better about surviving. All the knowledge did was emphasize the variables that had worked in tandem to allow him to stay alive.

Sixteen

Dave entered his dad's room with a bouquet of daisies. "Afternoon, sir, I brought you something to help with that smell that's been bothering you."

"The cleaning products?"

"Yeah, I thought some flowers might freshen things up."

"Good for you."

His dad lay stiff in bed with a newspaper folded by his side. He had yet to turn his head towards his son.

"Okay," Dave said as he set the flowers down on a dresser. "You want to be like that, then we'll just get to the problem. Where is it?"

Jack didn't respond.

"Do you understand they're going kick you out of here if this continues?"

"They stole from me."

"They didn't steal from you. They warned you that gambling wasn't allowed here. Now where's the money?"

Jack pushed himself to a sitting position, and his feet swung to the ground with a loud thump.

"Where are you going to live if they kick you out?"

"I'll be at the cottage."

"The cottage? I'm sure you'd love that, and I'd love a million dollars right now, but neither of those things are going to happen. Do you know what I have to do every month to keep you here?"

Jack turned his head to the window, and Dave couldn't help but notice how awkward his dad's profile looked. With a curved back, matted hair and heavy eyelids, there was no denying he was a shell of the man Dave remembered. Dave grounded himself in a chair and pulled it nearer his dad.

"Look, I didn't mean to put that on you, but I need you to tell me where the money is. If we give it back to everyone that placed a bet, I can probably straighten this out."

As if someone had plugged him in, Jack snapped forward. "You'd have to be a bloody fool to take the Jets by two touchdowns. They got what they deserved."

"That's not the point. The point is you promised not to bet in here, yet you encouraged and organized people to bet then took their money."

A rattle in Jack's breathing warned that the conversation was too intense, so he waved a hand across the room. "It's under the dresser."

Dave thought of the summer before his first year at university. His dad had made him promise not to tell anyone, including his mother, what he was about to show him. What Dave perceived as melodrama made him laugh until Jack flashed him a look that made him feel uncomfortable, even at eighteen.

"You think money's funny?" Dave didn't respond. "Is it funny to you that you don't have money for tuition? Is it funny that you're planning on taking a loan that'll eat into your paycheques long after you've graduated?"

Dave wiped at an eyebrow. The high stress of gambling had hardened his dad over the years, and he'd become prone to these types of dogmatic rants. It saddened Dave to see him that way, but it made him angry that his father was right.

"Now, do you promise?" Jack asked, lighting a cigarette.

Dave managed a weak nod.

"Say it."

"I promise."

"Good man," Jack said, pointing at Dave with his smoking hand. He hunched at the base of the dresser like a baseball catcher with his fingers clasped. His eyes burned with intensity. "I keep a stash of money here, taped underneath my sock drawer. Now, I'm telling you this for two reasons." A sigh of frustration escaped his lips as he reached beneath the dresser. The strain on his face demonstrated that removing the money was more effort than he had expected, before he revealed the thickest roll of money Dave had ever seen. "The first reason I'm telling you this is because I'm paying for your tuition."

The words filled Dave with a sense of relief he had never before experienced and a sense of appreciation he would never forget. His facial muscles locked in a youthful smile. "How?"

"You mean thank you," Jack said, blowing out some smoke.

"Of course. I'm blown away, thank you." Dave paused for a moment. "You know, I'll pay you back."

"You pay back debt. You're my son, you don't owe me anything. I made some good plays, and there's a little more to go around this time." Another deep drag filled his lungs before he stubbed out what was left of the cigarette into an ashtray painted like a roulette wheel.

He rubbed his knees and shifted his weight to the ground, where he could lean his back against the dresser. "Now, the second reason I'm telling you this is because I want you to know it's here in case anything happens to me."

"Don't say that."

"Don't be naïve. People die all the time. Heart attacks, car accidents, aneurysms, strokes. Now I don't see that being a reality any time soon, but if I'm not around, I want you to come and get this money for your mother."

Dave recognized the sincerity in his dad's eyes, a look that suggested he was entrusting his son to care for the love of his life. "I understand."

"Only if I'm not around."

"I know," he smiled.

"I'm not joking."

"I know that too."

He never told Dave what would happen to the money if his mother died first.

"Under the sock drawer?" Dave asked as he pulled himself back to the present.

Jack pushed the oxygen mask to the side of his face. "Where else would it be?"

Dave hunched down to pull the money off the bottom drawer, where he found two fifties, ten twenties and twenty fives. The bills made the crisp sound that only money can as he counted it a second time.

"Why would you take their money? You know some of these guys don't have much left over."

"It's not like we've got a lot to do here."

"You've got a gym, a games room, a library."

"We have distractions."

For the first time that day, Dave took a close look at his dad. White flakes caked the corners of his mouth, and a crease in the pillow case left a red line stretching from an ear to his chin. This wasn't a man who put a priority on appearance any more.

"How are you feeling today?"

Jack looked at him like the question was as stupid as it sounded.

"Are you thirsty? It feels pretty dry in here."

Jack stared at his bare feet and the network of veins spreading towards toes with yellowing nails.

"How about a game of cards?" Dave asked as he removed one of a stack of packs from the shelf.

The heavy steps Jack took reminded Dave just how difficult life had become for the man. Movement from the bed to the table by the window was strenuous now, so the destination needed to justify the effort.

"Are you still doing your stretches? You don't want to spend too much time in bed, it's not good for you."

"Deal the cards."

Dave took a bag of coloured poker chips from the shelf and counted out twenty blues, ten reds and five whites each while Jack looked at the far wall as though a movie was projected there. He'd started locking into the thousand-yard stares five years before. No one had caught on then that it was the start of his ending.

Dave tapped the cards on the table to get his dad's attention. "Stud?"

"Hold 'em."

Dave dealt the cards, and Jack suddenly focussed. After a quick glance at his two of diamonds face down, he was running the probabilities. He'd played enough hands in his life that this was second nature, but it never lost its excitement. He wasn't just playing the man or the cards, he was playing himself, and even in this watered-down, one-on-one game, it was likely the most alive he'd felt that week.

Jack waved at Dave in disgust. "Keep your hand up, will you?"

"Sorry."

Jack put two blues in as a bet.

"I can do that," Dave said looking at a pair of nines—one heart and one diamond.

Dave flopped the queen of hearts and the two and three of spades. Jack dropped in two more blue chips.

"Still stone-faced, huh? Well, you're not fooling me." Dave matched his bet.

The next card revealed a six of diamonds. Jack didn't bet.

"Okay, now we're getting somewhere," Dave said as he tapped the tips of his index fingers together. "I'll go two more reds."

Jack flipped the chips in like it was a burden. Dave turned over a ten of spades with the last card. Jack took another look at his cards before karate chopping the air.

"No bet, huh? You sure you're paying attention?" Dave loved these situations, because he could provoke glimpses of the man he remembered.

He loved those flashes of the man who enjoyed the little things, had a knack for making the most of every moment and a passion for interaction. Jack's eyes flared. The barbs pricked him, but he had done this long enough to control his game and to bide his time.

No doubt a part of him wanted to toss his cards in Dave's face, and swear at him until he had no breath left, but the gambler in him knew better. Dave upped the bet another red chip. Jack pushed his bet along the table to the pot.

"It's all you," Dave said as he tapped the table.

Jack laid down the ace and king of spades to display a flush.

Dave revealed his pair of nines. "You won't be able to keep that up all day. I knew you wouldn't stray from your best ten hands, and your eyes told me you didn't have the real deal, I just didn't know you were suited."

Jack pulled the pot towards him as if it were a thousand dollars. "It's the first of the month. Where's my treat?"

Dave pointed to the vase with the flowers. "I brought you flowers."

The table shook as Jack threw the cards. "It's the first of the month. We had a deal."

"All right."

Dave got up to close the door. With privacy ensured, he removed a mickey from the breast pocket of his jacket and poured a stiff drink of whiskey into his dad's coffee mug.

"A little more." Jack gestured with an index finger.

"That's good for now."

"You would think you were turning a profit, you're so stingy with your pours."

"Would you rather I didn't bring it at all?"

Jack ran his tongue over the roof of his mouth after the first sip. "Aren't you going to have some?"

"Naw."

"Why not?"

"I'm not in the mood."

"Come on."

"Not today."

Jack began muttering under his breath, but audible enough to hear. "Not today? Turning a drink down to a man's face."

"How do you feel about easy money?"

"Easy money?"

"Yeah."

"There's no such thing."

"Not even when things are just happening for you, like you couldn't get it wrong if you wanted to?"

Jack took another mouthful, and his eyes got a little brighter with every drink. Suddenly he stood up and raised his mug. "Luck is believing you're lucky."

"Point taken. To whom do we owe that gem?"

"Tennessee Williams," Jack said as he pushed his mug across the table. "Now did I earn another drink?"

"You certainly did." Dave poured him another two ounces while he sat back in the chair.

"Have a drink with me."

A part of Dave wanted to drink the whole bottle. One drink after another, reliving all the best stories he could get his dad to tell, but circumstance ate at him. Chance, fate and luck swirled through his mind. Somehow he was still alive, and somehow he had more money than ever. His dad knew odds as well as anyone. He'd studied probability, analyzed point spreads and card scenarios every day, and he swore by information over instinct. Precedent told him who to pick in sports, and with poker he only played the best ten hands. The best nine playing hands and what he called the random keeper—a seven and a jack. Math ruled his betting, and while he'd never walked away with the pot of gold, he'd stayed afloat for decades.

"Dad, in all your years of gambling, what's the most you ever won?"

Jack stared at the wall again. This time a drop of drool from the liquor worked its way down to his chin.

"Dad?" Dave tapped the mickey on the table to get him back to the moment.

"Huh?"

"Gambling. What's the most money you won at one time?"

"In one play or at one time?"

"Either or."

Jack's mind drifted to memories of twelve years earlier. Memories of a black tie event in a mansion and the Yankees battling back from two games down. He knew Atlanta fans were on a wave of hysteria with just two games between them and their second championship in a row, and he knew that would blind them from the start of the game's most storied franchise regaining its glory.

"Twenty-two thousand," he said. "Fifteen on a baseball series, seven playing poker, all in the same night."

"Twenty-two grand in one night, and you don't think something was working in your favour?"

"Intelligence was working in my favour. The Yankees had the best mix of young players and veterans a team had ever assembled. And with the Olympics in Atlanta that year and having won the year before, the pressure was too much."

Dave looked at this dad. He hadn't been that articulate in weeks. He missed those stories. He spoke with ease, honesty and the type of detail Dave never seemed to find in his own life. "What about the seven grand?"

Jack smiled before finishing his drink. "I caught a pro losing his composure. A lot of them are like that when they start losing, you just have to be there enough that you're at the table when it happens. He started making irrational moves, bad bluffs, over-aggressive bets. I was just one of the ones who took him—the room carved him up for thirty thousand before he left."

"He must have wanted to die."

"No, no, he wanted to play. A friend of his had to drag him out of the place."

"So the money just came to you that night?"

"I jumped on the opportunities."

Dave looked at his dad and decided to take Thorrin's money as long as could.

Forget worrying about his misconceptions, seize the opportunity, and take the money while you can. He didn't need to hear his dad say the words; he knew that would be his answer.

"The other day you said I don't take enough risks. If you're on a hot streak, at what point do you stop risking profits?"

Something out the window captured Jack's attention.

"They're stealing from me," he muttered.

"I'm asking you a question, Pop. At what point do you stop risking profits on a hot streak?"

"You don't," Jack said without turning from the window.

Seventeen

Despite Thorrin's assurance that the driver would buzz him when he arrived, Dave waited outside. Adhering to time made him feel in control, so when Thorrin said the car would arrive at two, he made sure to be outside at one forty-five.

A short man with slicked-back grey hair and a disarming smile that exposed crooked teeth opened the back door for him. "How are you, Mr. Bolden?"

"Fine, thanks."

It felt wrong for a man some thirty years his senior to call him "Mr". Plexiglas divided the front seats from the back, except for the centre, where a communication slot was open, so he sat in the middle of the horseshoe seating.

The driver looked at him through the rear view mirror. "Mr. Thorrin was worried about heavy traffic, so he left you a few beers in the fridge there. If you feel like a snack, there's most everything you can think of in the two doors beneath the bar, and the T.V. converter's on the table."

"Thank you."

"Buzz me here if you need anything," the man said, pointing to an intercom.

Dave nodded with an awkward smile. It was weird to think that the man's job was to make him comfortable and drive him across the city. He opened a beer before turning on the T.V. It took effort to remember being in a living room as nice as this limo.

With a cold drink in hand and five movie channels at his disposal, he imagined Thorrin in the limo as he talked on speakerphone watching stock prices every morning, held meetings on the way to more meetings every afternoon, and had sex that most people only fantasize about every evening. Or maybe the limo was just a vessel. Maybe he used the Mercedes as a sign of success as he moved from one transaction to another, and it was more of a mobile office than the clichéd dream of conquering the corporate jungle.

Either way, he wished the limo were less impressive. He wished the seats weren't so comfortable, that the ride wasn't so smooth, that the flat-screen didn't make whatever channel he turned to so captivating, and that the whole experience didn't make him happier simply by being there. But it did. The longer they drove, the more he wished he were lucky enough to randomly pick stocks. Fuck the stress of keeping his dad in a home, fuck borrowing money every month and instead, spend away every memory of that freak occurrence until the details that haunted him were buried beneath opulence. If only he knew what the brokers were saying.

A doorman with a receding brush cut greeted Dave as he entered Thorrin's building. With marble tiles, wall-length mirrors, and high-back wooden chairs in each corner of the room, everything about the aesthetics demonstrated wealth. The building was a hundred-and-two years old, and despite numerous renovations and additions over the years, the original brick and wood remained preserved.

"Afternoon," the man said with a heavy Quebecois accent.

"Good afternoon, I'm here to see Mr. Thorrin."

"Of course." The doorman pointed to a corridor with an elevator on either side. "You want the top floor. I'll let him know you're coming up."

Dave pressed the day-glow orange P and braced his stomach as the elevator rose thirty-two floors. He had never been to a penthouse. A bell prefaced the doors opening before he stepped into a foyer with two giant ferns in black pots the size of toilets. The foyer was the size of his apartment.

"Good to see you," Thorrin said, stepping out from a front door that stretched from floor to ceiling. "Come on in."

In was an open-space concept with windows on every wall. Dave took a seat on one of two couches separated by a glass coffee table. Thorrin stepped behind a wooden bar, complete with two draft taps and three glass shelves of liquor with lights illuminating the bottom of each bottle.

"Do you want a drink?"

Dave looked at the three taps. "I'll take a pint."

"Light or dark?"

"Dark, please."

It was hard to take his eyes off the wall-sized aquarium across from the couch. More than twenty jellyfish bobbed around the tank, and all of them glowed a vibrant orange.

"That's not their natural colour; it's a filter in the lighting. I can make it orange, yellow, purple or red." Thorrin passed Dave his pint, set a stack of silver coasters on the coffee table and sat on the couch beneath the aquarium.

Dave took a quick sip of his beer then another mouthful. "Why am I here?"

"You're here because you ask questions like that." Thorrin smiled. "Most people who get inside my place are just happy to be here. You are highly intelligent, Dave. I've met maybe five people in my life like you, and I've done business with all of them."

"You're assuming a lot about me."

"Observing, never assuming. I picked it up hanging around my father's restaurant as a kid. I was adopted, and my adoptive mother, God bless her, died when I was seven, so I spent a lot of time at my father's work." He twisted his beer on the coaster, and his thumb wiped a streak up the glass's side. "I used to watch people all day. People on first dates, people having affairs, business lunches, job interviews, lawyers talking to their clients, addicts talking to their dealers. You learn a lot watching body language."

"What kind of restaurant did he have?"

"Neighbourhood. Basic, dependable. He did well for a few decades, but that last ten years drained the life out of him. He could see it happening, but he refused to evolve. Wouldn't change the menu, wouldn't renovate, wanted to keep up all the old photos of people that none of the customers knew any more. Ultimately, he was a terrible businessman."

Dave watched two jellyfish bump into each other. Orange looking jellyfish in a living room were just too cool to ignore. It occurred to Dave after Thorrin stopped speaking that the home was so large that it was silent. The lights didn't buzz, the air vents didn't blow, and there was no racket from the street below. The place was completely self-contained.

"Do you live alone?"

"I do now. My wife, Katherine, died nine years ago. She battled cancer for four years before that, so it was an awful stretch. She was raised Catholic, and I always supported her belief and escorted her to church, but I believed more in her than her faith. Naturally, when she got sick, I thought about life and death in ways I never had before. There's no way around it when a loved one gets sick. But about a week into her treatment, I realized I was more scared than her. I was consumed by fear, by all the what-ifs, but she accepted her situation and embraced every moment. And I mean every moment, not just the easy ones. She still enjoyed putting me in my place, and it's not like she started suffering fools. When she died, I adopted her philosophy. Life is about moments, and I decided I'd spend my life searching for the most intense ones."

"She sounds like an amazing person."

Thorrin nodded, and a glow in his eyes confirmed that he appreciated Dave's sentiment. "Do you plan on having kids?"

Dave filled his mouth with beer before shifting his weight in the seat. "One day."

"Well, if you're thinking about kids, make sure you have the financial backing to support them. You don't want to be like my father."

Dave thought of his own dad. Part of him hated the man for making his mother stress about money and for making her scared that they might have to sell the house or car every month. He agreed with Thorrin; he didn't want his kids to worry about money.

Thorrin ran an index finger over an eyebrow. "I owe everything I have to my college roommate. We met our first year at university playing football. You ever play football?"

Dave shook his head. "Baseball."

"Right. Anyway, my roommate and I met that year. We never left the practice squad, and we never played football again, but we lived together for the rest of university. The guy was a millionaire by twenty-five, and I'm going back more than a few decades, so you can appreciate how rare that kind of money was then. His whole business philosophy was to focus on scarce resources. Staying ahead of the demand, the anticipation of evolution. He got me my first break in oil, and I never looked back. Software in the seventies, video in the eighties, bottled water, cosmetic surgery, the internet. He taught me to find things people don't even look for."

"Smart man."

"Brilliant man. Do you want to be rich, Dave?"

Dave raised his pint glass. "It would help."

"Help what?"

"Help with my financial responsibilities. I could get a home, travel, the usual things."

"When you say financial responsibilities, you mean your father?"

"Yeah."

"And is being an accountant going to provide you with these financial freedoms, the freedom to provide for the next generation?"

"Not the way I'm doing it."

They looked at each other for a moment without saying anything. Thorrin deliberately backed off, and Dave hoped he wouldn't ask another question.

Thorrin drained his pint and rose from his seat with the empty glass held only by his fingertips. "The thing about us is, we need each other."

"Really?"

"Oh yeah. You've got the gift of luck, but you act like an unlucky person. Without me, you'd never realize your gift."

"What do you mean 'act like an unlucky person'?"

"I read a study on luck. The researchers gathered up fifty people that claimed to be lucky and fifty people that claimed to be unlucky. Now you couldn't just sign up for this. Each person had to have some proof behind their claim. A lottery winner, gambling addict, those types of things. They took these hundred people, gave them each a copy of the same magazine and told them their task was to count how many photos there were. Now, the unlucky people immediately started with questions. 'What if it's just a headshot?' 'What if it's in black and white?' 'Does a full spread photo count as two pictures?' All fifty of the unlucky people, every last one of them counted forty-seven photos, which was correct. Every one of the lucky people, bless their souls, stopped at page two, where a sticky note said, 'Stop counting, return this magazine to the instructor and collect your two hundred dollar prize.' Unlucky people are so focussed on meeting tasks, pleasing people, taking the straightforward path, that they miss the opportunities right in front of them. And that's you. You never saw what you were capable of until I came along."

Dave was wondering how many sticky notes he'd missed over the years when Thorrin lightened the mood with a smile. "Do you like movies?"

"I do."

"I have over a hundred thirty-five millimetre prints. How do you feel about *On the Waterfront*?"

"I've never seen it."

"Well you're going to."

And they did. They watched *On the Waterfront, Strangers on a Train* and *The 400 Blows*. They watched almost six hours of movies in a screening room with high-back seats, surround sound and pint after pint. Thorrin worked his way through three buckets of popcorn while Dave wondered if he was ever going to forget this visit.

Eighteen

Watching T.V. wasn't an option any more. Dave had tried it as a late-night tool to distract his mind, but now he couldn't tolerate the fantasy. The predictable storylines, repetitious character traits and exaggerated moments used to entertain him, occasionally even thrill him, but now they were just offensive. Cop shows with their glamorized violence, sitcoms with their cookie-cutter characters making the same mistakes week after week in the name of allegory, and "Reality T.V." dripping with melodrama that tapped into the most basic instincts. Television provided packaged living organized into any genre he felt like watching, but watching wasn't living, and after living the destruction of his workplace and the death of his colleagues, no matter how much he wanted to lose himself in T.V., it had lost its magic.

With the T.V. off, he could hear his neighbours arguing about spending too much and staying out too late until the voices rose to inaudible roars. Dave hated yelling, so he walked to the window for some deep breaths to remind him of sleep. He wanted it more than anything, and not just for rest. He wanted to sleep so he could forget, just for a night, the tragedy that had befallen him and his coworkers. He wanted to wake up without images of their broken bodies and without the guilt that circumstances had allowed him to survive. But he couldn't sleep. Every time he shut his eyes, he saw flashes of the truck and horrible details, like the way Shannon's broken jaw drooped to the floor and the way Mr. Richter's hands looked like they were reaching for something. He knew the truck had crashed into his work simply because it could, but it didn't stop it from being awful.

The door buzzer startled him. He looked through the peep-hole, surprised to see Amy, and opened the door. She wore a black bubble jacket with a faux-fur collar and flashed a mischievous smile that he didn't know was in her repertoire.

"I want to take you somewhere," she said.

"Now?"

"Yeah."

"Okay, where?"

"It's a surprise."

They hustled from the apartment through a steady rain and stepped into a four-door white Honda from the late eighties. The exterior was covered in spots of rust, but the inside held up surprisingly well. Dave guessed one hundred thousand kilometres.

"You know I don't normally drive? Especially not in this weather."

"I'm honoured."

"You think I'm weird, don't you?"

"No."

"Yeah, you do. I can tell by the way you're looking at me."

"I don't think you're weird; I think you overanalyze things."

She looked at him like he'd spat in her face. "I've been in five car accidents. I broke my collarbone once, and I've had whiplash twice."

"Then maybe I should drive."

Her eyes warned that jokes like that weren't welcome. "The insurance company labelled every accident the fault of the other drivers."

"Well, driving is dangerous."

"Yeah? Have you ever been in a car accident?"

The car pulled into a large parking lot. There were so many cars that it took a lap to find a spot. Amy parked beside a black van emblazoned with a mural of a motorcycle riding over the clouds.

"Are you excited?"

"I'm curious."

They stepped out of their respective doors to see a sign for "Bingo" in gaudy fluorescent lights. Dave waited a moment to make sure that she wasn't walking across the lot to what looked like a diner before following.

"Your surprise is a bingo hall?"

"That's right."

"*Now* I think you're weird."

"Yeah? Remember you said that in an hour, because I'm going to prove to you that you're lucky."

"At bingo?"

"Follow me."

She led the way up a makeshift red carpet, past a man holding a fully dressed hot dog in each hand and into the hall. The place reeked of desperation. Men and women with cigarettes dangling from their mouths and plastic cups of beer in their hands traded barbs as they hit their bingo cards with their dabbers as if they could win a million dollars. The smell of deep fried food and the veil of cigarette smoke made Dave wince in disgust as he sat beside Amy at a table. She already had four bingo cards for each of them.

The bingo reader yelled, "B Eight."

Dave shifted his weight to avoid Amy's frantic dabs. "B what?" he asked.

"Eight," she said and passed him a dabber.

A forty-something woman beside Dave with a face like a prune flashed him a stern look for infringing on her cards with his elbow.

"Sorry," he said. He leaned back from the smell of her perfume.

Amy spread his cards out in front of him for faster dabbing. "Haven't you ever played bingo before?"

"When I was a kid."

The bingo reader yelled again, "G Forty-seven."

Amy moved from one card to the next in rhythm. Her eyes were focussed and unfazed by the chaos around her. Dave gave up.

"So what's your game then?"

He looked at her with care. Her eyes looked bluer, more expressive and more alive than they had at her place. She dabbed the top of his hand.

"What's *your* game?"

"I don't have one." He wiped at the ink the dabber had left.

"Sure you do. What do you bet on?"

"I don't bet."

"I Fourteen," the bingo reader announced to a series of grumbles.

Amy dabbed her cards then Dave's. "You don't gamble at all?"

"Never."

"Never? Not cards, horses, football?"

"I've never been interested."

"O Sixty-eight."

The woman beside Dave jumped out of her seat, and her eyes bulged as her chair tipped to the floor. "Bingo! Bingo!" The peak of her teased hair seemed to reach for the ceiling as she pumped her fists in the air. She might as well have won the lottery.

Dave turned to Amy. "Looks like *she's* the lucky one."

"You just weren't paying attention."

"I think I'm done."

"No."

"I'll watch."

"No, you have to play."

A deep male voice that Dave associated with strip clubs came over the loudspeaker. "Ladies and gentlemen, today's door prize winning number is three, eight, one…"

Amy's eyes widened. "Let me see your ticket," she said, tapping his arm.

"What?"

"Your door ticket, the stub."

"What about yours?"

"I want yours."

The announcer continued to milk the crowd's greed. "Once again people, that's three, eight, one…"

Dave searched through his pockets, past his keys, wallet, a gum wrapper and bank machine slip before pulling out the stub. "Here you go."

Amy scanned the ticket. "Three, eight, one…"

"Four," the announcer continued. "Seven, five. Three, eighty-one, four, seventy-five."

Amy mouthed the numbers as he spoke.

"Those are your winning numbers, people."

"Three, eighty-one, four, seventy-five." Amy jumped from her seat and waved the stub as high as she could. "He won, he won." She turned to Dave and pointed a finger at him as if he were a celebrity. "Right here, he's the winner."

Embarrassment made him want to hide from the pointing fingers, the sneers of jealousy, and the announcer waving him up on stage. He would have left if Amy hadn't grabbed him by the hand and led him to his prize.

Dave didn't say another word until they were back in the car. He couldn't stand the bingo hall's incessant buzz of chatter and stink of sweat, but watching Amy made him happy. The way she interacted with people showed a different side of her. Her face was flushed, her hair was a little messy, and it looked good on her. She started the car.

"Are you excited?"

"I'm not big on attention."

The car pulled out of the lot, and she honked twice in excitement. "I told you I'd prove it to you."

Dave squeezed the sides of the box sitting in his lap. "Winning a high-speed blender does not make me lucky."

"Do you know how many people were in there?"

"You're reading too much into it." He put the box into the back seat.

"You still don't believe, do you?"

"Not at all." He wanted to tell her to keep her eyes on the road, but that felt rude.

"Well, you should."

"Look, I don't know whether to be flattered or creeped out by this belief that you and your brother have, but you've got to listen to me. I'm not lucky."

"No?"

"That's right."

The car began to accelerate. The engine was not used to working hard, so it growled as they picked up speed.

"I'll prove it to you."

The speedometer read ninety-five kilometres per hour. A tingling in Dave's stomach warned him that this wasn't fun.

"Slow down."

"We'll be fine."

Her fingers tightened around the steering wheel as the car picked up speed towards an intersection with a red light.

"We'll be dead." Dave raised his voice. "Now slow down."

"No."

He looked at the red light, then for cars coming from the west or east. Then Amy shut her eyes.

"Are you crazy? Open your eyes."

"No."

"Open your fucking eyes."

He leaned towards her like he might grab the steering wheel, but they were too close to the intersection, so he raised his forearms in front of his face and braced himself for contact. But the contact never happened. They blew through the intersection unscathed except for the fear that left his stomach nauseous. Amy slowed down before pulling the car over to the side of the road. Her face glowed.

"Tell me you're not lucky now."

"You're crazy."

"No, I just believe."

The words slowed the moment. Things began to come back into focus, and his heart steadied. Her belief in him felt good.

"Kiss me," she said.

"Kiss you? You almost killed me."

She leaned into him and kissed him until he kissed back. They were gentle kisses, and they followed each other's lead until she pulled away. They looked at each other for a moment. Dave appeared surprised but stricken, and Amy flashed a closed-lipped smile before she leaned towards him again.

The drive back to his apartment felt like a natural progression for both of them. Amy put on a CD of ambient music, and they drove without saying a word. They hoped the momentum would carry them back to the apartment with the same feelings.

Once inside the apartment, Dave began to tighten up. It had been awhile since he'd had sex with anyone when he was sober, and even longer since he'd had sex with someone he'd liked before he'd lusted. A part of him wanted to sit down and listen to Amy tell stories about her childhood and high school years for the rest of the night.

She kissed him before he took off his jacket. Unlike the gentle kisses in the car, her lips moved with passion. There was no talking at that point, and for the first time since the accident, Dave enjoyed being alive.

Nineteen

The doorbell woke Dave from a deep sleep. It buzzed again, and he sat up to look at Amy's naked back before heading to the door. He didn't bother putting a shirt on. He expected a salesman, maybe a charity asking for donations or at worst a neighbour, but instead, he opened the door to see Grayson. Exaggerated blinks, as if he were dreaming, failed to make the image go away.

"Good morning, Dave," Grayson said, raising a styrofoam cup of coffee to eye level.

"Grayson." He thought of being beaten to death, stabbed in the stomach, or shot in the back of the head. "Ah, just give me a minute, I want to throw on a shirt. Come on in."

Grayson stepped inside with a nod while Dave did his best not to look guilty, but the more he thought about Amy lying in his bed, the more unnatural the faces he made became. He hustled to the bedroom, where Amy was now awake but still lying down under the covers.

"What's up?"

Dave's eyes bulged as he snapped an index finger to his lips. "Shh." He mouthed, "Be quiet."

"Why?"

His shoulders now hunched as the index finger returned to his lips. "Shh."

"What? Don't be weird."

Bending down, he pulled her head close to his lips. "Your brother's at the door."

"Why?"

"I have no idea. Is there any chance he knows you're here?"

"No, no chance."

"Okay, just wait a minute. And stay quiet."

He slipped a T-shirt over his head and returned to the living room, where Grayson now sat in an armchair with a newspaper spread over his legs.

"So what's going on?" Dave asked.

"Thorrin wants to have breakfast with you."

"Now?"

"Is that a problem?"

"No, just unexpected. I'm going to need a few minutes."

"Of course."

Grayson's eyes dropped back to the newspaper, and Dave headed back to the bedroom, where Amy was now sitting up and doing her best to listen. Dave sat beside her on the bed to whisper. "I've got to go."

"Where?"

"To breakfast."

"Why?"

"Because I don't want your brother finding out that you're here, so if I have to go out to breakfast to avoid that, I'll go out to breakfast."

They stared at each other for a moment. Dave expected her to be stressed, but her face was playful. His stomach didn't allow him the same levity.

"I'm going to make this breakfast as quick as possible. Will you stay here until I get back?"

"Yeah."

"Okay, I'll see you in a bit."

They kissed awkwardly. Dave was far too worried about their lips making noise, so Amy shooed him away with one hand over her mouth to cover up a laugh.

Dave stepped into the car surprised to hear something different from the Japanese lessons coming from the stereo. He guessed it was Mandarin.

"Korean," Grayson said. "I'm thinking of investing there."

Knowing that Grayson had come to his place on Thorrin's behalf and not to murder him for having sex with his sister was a relief.

"What does he want to see me about?" Dave asked.

"Do you like football?"

"No."

"Ever bet on football?"

He thought of his dad's charts, formulas and all the hours the man had spent reading magazines. "I don't bet."

"Thorrin wants you to pick the point total for the New York Dallas game."

"What do you mean point total?"

"The combined score."

He shifted his weight in the leather seat. "I have no idea. I don't follow football."

"Just pick a realistic number."

"A realistic number."

"That's right, something you feel good about."

"Sixty-nine."

A red light stopped the car's progress, and Grayson turned to Dave for the first time. "Sixty-nine, huh? Alright, you want to be a smartass? You still just made a bet."

Grayson parked the car in front of a posh restaurant with tinted windows. Dave followed him inside to Thorrin's booth, where he sat with a dark-skinned East Indian man to his right and an attractive white woman a decade younger to his left. Both of Thorrin's guests were enjoying fruity drinks with wedges of orange while he picked at a plate of fruit with all the kiwi slices forked into a pile on the side.

"Welcome, Dave." They shook hands, and Dave sat across from him. "You picked the points, I hope."

Dave nodded.

"Good man." He put a hand on the Indian's closest shoulder. "Dave, this is a friend of mine, Senthur Farook."

They shook hands, but when Dave pulled away, Senthur held him in place. "It's an honour."

The compliment was ignored until Senthur released his grip. His features were delicate. With smooth skin and carefully styled hair, he could've been a model, but his eyes were veiled as if he had seen things that stopped them from shining.

Thorrin locked his focus on Dave. He had that look people get when they know something you don't. "Senthur is close to doing business with us, but he'd feel better if he saw how fortunate you are firsthand."

Discomfort flowed through Dave's body. *Fortunate.* A business deal based on how fortunate he was? He had just sat down. He needed to stop the absurdity, but before he could think of the right words, Thorrin had a firm grip on his closest forearm.

"This is Mr. Senthur's associate," he said with a gesture to the woman on his left. The word "associate" tends to be reserved for old white men in suits, but she was beautiful. She had shoulder-length brown hair, large eyes, and a nose that turned up at the tip enough to create a bulb but not enough to be piggish. Her smile made everyone at the table wish it was directed at them. "So, what we want you to do, Dave, is tell us her name."

"What?"

"Tell us her name."

"I have no idea who she is."

"I know."

"I'm not a mind reader."

Senthur rose, his hands to the table, and spread five one thousand dollar bills in front of him. Dave had never seen a thousand dollar bill before. He scanned the restaurant to see if anyone had noticed, but Thorrin's voice demanded his attention.

"We have guests, Dave, don't be rude."

"You're betting on this?"

"Tell us her name."

Senthur raised his glass, saying, "Take your time."

"This is stupid."

The response prompted Senthur to push the money into a pile. "You're not in the mood?"

Thorrin put a hand on Senthur's wrist to stop him from taking the money off the table. "Oh, he's in the mood. He just prefers to make me sweat a little, and as much as I enjoy the drama, I have to insist that you choose a name, Dave."

Dave looked around the table for signs that this was a joke, or that Senthur and the woman were merely plants to further disorient him. But the expressions were too real for a set-up. Senthur's eyes were too intense and filled with too much anticipation to know what was going to happen next.

"You're serious?"

"Very."

He turned for a last appraisal of her features. Her eyes, nose and teeth all seemed exaggerated until a name flowed from his lips. "Karen."

Senthur began to slide the money from the table while gesturing at the woman with his glass. "I'm sorry, my friend, this is Cassie."

Thorrin sat stunned that Dave had chosen the wrong name until the woman stirred.

"He's right."

Senthur's head snapped towards her. "What?"

"He's right about my name."

"How so?"

"I go by Cassie, but my legal name is Karen."

Thorrin clapped aggressively, nodded at Senthur and took the money from the table.

"How did you know that?" Senthur looked at Dave as if he weren't human.

"I didn't."

"Very impressive."

Dave's attention shifted from Thorrin to Grayson and back again. "What are you trying to accomplish with these set-ups?"

"This wasn't a set-up."

"It had to be."

Senthur tapped Karen on the arm. "Show him your license."

She finished her drink before grabbing her purse. This wasn't a person who went unnoticed. Everyone at the table watched her shake the last of her drink's crushed ice into her mouth, the way her long fingers slid into her purse, and the way her smile took up half of her face as she absorbed the stares. She removed her license from a green suede purse and passed it to Dave. He looked at the license to see: Karen Nina Marshall.

Thorrin stirred his drink with the oversized straw. "Why did you choose Karen?" he said to Dave.

"I don't know."

"Sure you do. You could have said any name, but you said Karen."

"She looks like somebody I knew named Karen."

He'd met Karen Nichols his sophomore year of university. Karen was an aspiring actress that looked far too cool for someone majoring in accounting. The closest he'd come to asking her out was at a pub. They were waiting in line for drinks together when he took the opportunity to compliment her on her performance as Lady Macbeth in the department's fall play. He'd never seen the show, but he'd seen her name on the promotional flyers for weeks.

What he hadn't known was that the play had received vicious reviews citing her overacting as the central flaw. She took his comment as sarcasm, and they never made eye contact again, yet she remained in his fantasies well into senior year. He hadn't thought about her in over a decade.

Senthur turned to Thorrin and gestured to Dave with his drink. "I like him."

Thorrin met his glass to make a clink. "Who wouldn't?"

Dave sat at the table for an hour, until only Thorrin and Grayson remained. They celebrated with drinks, but his mind was still on the money. So what if they were cooking the books on these bets, and he was their front? Watching some eccentric gambling junkies with money to burn get hustled was an easy price to pay to even his debt with Otto and put enough money away for his dad to live at Palson Avenue for the rest of his life.

"Do you want a ride home?" Grayson asked.

Dave nodded then leaned into Thorrin. "When do we do this again?"

Thorrin's eyebrows rose. "You're initiating this now?"

Dave nodded.

"Let's do something with numbers, something to do with accounting."

Thorrin and Grayson shared a smile. They looked at him like a young fighter who had finally found his confidence in the ring. Thorrin extended Dave's cut from the bet with Senthur.

"Something with numbers it is."

Twenty

Dave's finances were the most organized part of his life. This didn't mean he'd saved money or managed his bi-weekly cheques well, but it did mean he was well aware of exactly how he'd wasted it all. He tallied up the money Thorrin had given him since they'd met, and a smile filled his face. This was the type of money that bought more than things; this was the type of money that made problems go away.

The phone buzzed, and he answered it, hoping to hear Amy's voice. Grayson greeted him instead. "Are you still feeling confident?"

"I feel like making money."

"Then you'll be happy to hear Thorrin set up a challenge for six this evening. I'll text you the address this afternoon."

"I'll be there."

He hung up wondering what awaited him. Maybe he would have to predict someone's tax return, or whether or not a specific business turned a profit that day, or maybe he would have to state how many people in a room owed on their taxes. Whatever the case, with Thorrin pulling the strings, he felt confident more money was coming.

It wasn't that he didn't want to believe that luck worked in his favour, but the same way he didn't believe in religion, the Prime Minister's addresses or alien sightings, he didn't believe in luck. He had to admit, however, that the string of unlikely coincidences was rare, so he figured it was time to get another perspective.

After looking up books online, he settled on a bestseller titled *Lucky You* and contacted the author and professor of math from the local university, Dr. Nora Burns, via email. He detailed his story of survival at Richter's accounting firm, and two hours later he had a reply and meeting for coffee with a woman who had sold more than a million copies of books analyzing patterns of luck in peoples' lives.

The first thing he noticed about Dr. Nora Burns was her youthful face. She was younger than he'd expected, no more than forty, and while she wore the spectacles of an academic caricature, a beaded bracelet around her neck and tattoo band around her wrist made him think of a world traveller.

"Thank you for meeting with me," he said while watching her pour the most cream he had ever seen anyone add to their coffee.

"After reading your story, I had to."

"Do you think luck was involved?"

"It's impossible to say without knowing more about you, but with a situation like yours, it's worth an investigation."

"The last thing I want to be is investigated."

"I understand. Just hearing stories like yours helps my research."

"Like mine?"

"Like three generations of males in Montreal who were hit and killed by taxis exactly twenty years apart, on the same block. Like the seventeen members of a Saskatoon church choir that had seventeen different reasons for showing up late on the morning of May 1, 1950, when the church blew up from a gas explosion."

"So?"

"Do you mean do I believe in luck?"

Dave nodded. She set down her coffee and leaned back to get a good look at him, as if she was deciding whether or not he was worthy of the information.

"I'll tell you what I know for certain after years of research," she said as she broke a blueberry muffin in half. "People that are considered lucky have common traits. First, they are people who put themselves into chance situations more often than the average person, and second, they share a resilience that allows them to persevere in all aspects of life. Which means that luck isn't a blessing as much as it is a learned skill. And being unlucky is the reflex of living a stunted life with an increasingly pessimistic attitude."

Dave thought about her words for the rest of the afternoon, and the deeper he dug, the more he had to admit that her theory was not that different from his dad's view on luck. "You can't win if you don't play," the elder Bolden would say. And as trite and clichéd as his dad's words sounded, Dr. Burns would agree. Boil the two ideologies down, and they were the same. Academic or street-wise, they both argued that luck and risk need each other.

Meeting Thorrin at a penthouse condo to participate in a high-stakes challenge against chance definitely qualified as risky, so as he sat down at a table across from Thorrin, a Chinese man with frosted tints and an older blonde woman with hair like a helmet, he did so confident that he moved with life's flow. The condo was so stunning, it was difficult to concentrate on the moment. Everything looked like it had been bought that morning, and as he looked over the railing at the indoor lap-pool below them, he wondered if his dad had ever seen such extravagance.

Dave did a quick sweep of the room. The blonde wore a bright red suit and smelled of rich tobacco that made him think of cigarillos. The Chinese man was no more than thirty, and his positioning under a halogen light that hung from a long cord revealed thinning hair.

"This is him?" the woman asked Thorrin with a dismissive gesture at Dave.

Thorrin nodded.

"Hmm." Her sigh emphasized just how unimpressive she found him.

The slight seemed to stoke Thorrin's competitive nature and prompted him to rub his hands together. "Shall we?"

The blonde raised her glass of wine, and Thorrin locked eyes with Dave. "This is Kevin," he said, nodding at the Chinese man. "Tell us how much money is in Kevin's chequing account."

"Chequing account? I thought we agreed on taxes."

Thorrin stood from the table and walked to a window overlooking the downtown core. Dave knew to follow. He leaned into Thorrin and spoke in a whisper. "We agreed on taxes. I can't guess how much money is in his bank account."

"You can and you will, or you will owe me every dollar I put on this wager."

"What?"

"You heard me. Tell me how much money is in that man's account, or you owe me my bet."

The mirth was gone from Thorrin's face and replaced by a stern focus. He walked back to the table and smiled at the blonde. "He's worse than a kid before a school concert."

She sighed and motioned to get on with things. Dave's brow contorted into worry. He appraised the Chinese man, but he couldn't visualize a number, let alone predict the truth. The situation's magnitude became clear. He could lose thousands of dollars he had no way of paying back. He lifted his hands from the table and wiped the sweat prints with his forearm so the blonde wouldn't see. Instinct told him to apologize, to barter some type of payback plan, but he knew it was too late to stop. He closed his eyes and took a deep breath. Then his thoughts wandered to the only time he'd ever seen his father cry.

It was the night before he'd started university, so he'd gone to bed early, but just after two in the morning, the sound of breaking glass had jolted him from bed. He could hear his dad swearing, and it was easy to tell the man was drunk. He stepped into the kitchen ready to tell his dad to call it a night when he saw him struggling with a lighter that he held to a line of loose-leafed paper.

"What's going on, Dad?"

"They're supposed to be automatic."

"What do you have there?"

Dave reached for the paper, and as his dad lowered the lighter, his liquid eyes became clear. He'd seen his father frustrated many times, deflated even more, but something about the look in his eyes pooling with tears shook him to the core.

"Automatic," his dad said again.

Dave looked at the paper to see the number 152,360 written so many times, there was more ink on the page than white space. Dave held the paper to eye level.

"What does this number mean?"

"It's how much I would have made tonight if a holder hadn't fumbled the snap on a convert. They drive eighty yards in a minute twenty to take the lead, and a fumbled convert stops me from covering the spread. There hasn't been a fumbled convert attempt in three years." He pointed to the paper as if he were pointing at a rare diamond. "That number would have changed my life, *our* lives."

Dave handed him back the paper and struck the lighter for him. His dad held the paper over the fire until the edge turned orange with flame, and the two of them watched as every number on the page burned to ash.

"Do you have an answer, Dave?" Thorrin's voice snapped Dave back into the present. He turned to the Chinese man, and for a moment the man looked like his father.

"One-hundred and fifty-two thousand, three-hundred and sixty."

The Chinese man pushed his chair back from the table. "Did you see me downstairs?"

"I've never seen you before today."

The man passed Thorrin his bank slip to prove that Dave was dead on.

"A little more impressive than he looks, isn't he?" Thorrin smiled at the blonde, who gawked at Dave in disbelief.

The Chinese man looked at Dave like he might pounce across

the table. "How could you possibly know the number? I just took out eighty dollars five minutes before I came here."

"I guessed."

"Then I have some lotto numbers I'd love you to take a guess on."

Thorrin laughed and tapped the man on the hand. "Those guesses belong to me."

The words forced Dave's focus back to Thorrin, and it was clear from the look in his eyes that he might have been smiling, but he wasn't joking.

Twenty-One

Dave returned from another breakfast with Grayson to find Amy on his couch reading a detective novel belonging to him that he'd never read. She lowered the book from eye level. "How was breakfast?"

"Weird."

"Why weird?"

"It doesn't matter. Right now, it's your turn."

"What do you mean?"

"I'm going to prove to you that you're not unlucky."

"Really?"

"Oh yeah."

"You sound determined."

"You sound skeptical."

"I am."

"Well, not for long."

He took a blindfold from his pocket and passed it to her. "What's this for?"

"I don't want you to see where we're going."

"It's a bit much, isn't it?"

"You don't have to put it on until we're in the car."

They drove for ten minutes before she wrapped the fabric around her eyes. "Are you sure I can't just close my eyes?"

"You could, but I don't trust you."

"Don't be cheeky."

With the blindfold on, she heard the sound of the brakes, the rattling of parts, and the grinding of gears. She took a CD from her pocket and held it out to him. He took the CD and looked at it to see "Groovy Tunes" written in black marker across the disk. He put it in the player.

"You ever heard this song?" she asked.

Dave gave the wailing gospel singers another second. "No."

"I'll burn you a copy. This is the Swoops. You've probably heard their tracks on at least a dozen samples that are on the radio today. Only this is the real moment in time."

She reached for the blindfold, but Dave tapped her arm. "Don't ruin the surprise. This is part of the fun."

"I just don't want you to be disappointed."

"Don't worry about that."

"I am, you sound confident."

"Work with me here, will you?'

"This isn't an argument, it's not like I want to be right, it's just the way we are. The way we were born."

"The way we were born?"

"That's right, you were born in May, weren't you?"

"Where'd you see that?"

"I didn't, May's the luckiest month."

"You know I should tape you when you start with this, because if you heard yourself I think you'd be surprised."

"Sigmund Freud, May. Pope John Paul II, May. John Wayne, May. Walt Whitman, Browning, Emerson, May, May, May. Do you want me to continue?"

"So everyone born in May has a blessed life?"

"I was born in January. Do you want to know who was born in January?"

"A lot of failures and a lot of successes, just like the other eleven months."

"Wrong. Do you think it's a coincidence that Elvis Presley, Richard Nixon, Grigori Rasputin, Benedict Arnold, Martin Luther King, and Virginia Woolf were all born in the same month?"

"Yes. And I think a lot of people would argue that those people were anything but unlucky."

"And I believe you believe what you say, which is why I know you'll be disappointed with this surprise."

Neither of them said a word for a while after that. As the car drove, Amy imagined a life where they were married, where she looked out the window as they drove to the cottage every weekend with two children, maybe three. In this fantasy, they had a house and a family. That's what she wanted out of life. Every bit as intensely as some people desire wealth and others power, she wanted a family to share life with.

Those thoughts repeated themselves until the car stopped.

"We're here," Dave said. He pulled down her blindfold to reveal that they were in a parking lot. After adjusting to the light, Amy's eyes focussed on a small plane at the end of a field covered in a layer of snow.

"Where are we?"

"Parachute school."

She looked again at the field, where someone now folded a parachute, and thoughts of falling, broken bones and blood dominated.

"What do you mean?"

"I mean you're jumping out of a plane. You're going to jump, and you're going to be fine."

"There's snow on the ground."

"They won't let us jump if the weather's not right."

"I can't jump."

"Yeah, you can."

"No, I can't."

"Look, you keep saying you believe in me, right?"

Her eyes narrowed like she hated him for using her words against her. Then a man floating to the ground fifty yards away let out a guttural scream that drew attention to how small he looked. Dave grabbed her closest hand.

"Let's go."

Instinct told her legs not to move, but she accepted his lead.

The warmth of his hand made her want her entire body to
be as warm. She concentrated on relaxation techniques while
Dave signed them up for their instruction. *Two times sixteen is
thirty-two, thirty-two times three is ninety-six.* But the numbers
didn't steady her breathing. The battle wasn't against nerves
or imagination; she was about to challenge a force she was
convinced swayed with the gods of life and death.

The trainer looked more like a schoolteacher than someone
that jumped out of planes, and as he spoke her mind waded
through every negative adjective she knew.

"I am your instructor, although I prefer jump master,"
he said in an accent she placed as Slavic. "You're both doing
tandem jumps, so the training isn't long. We're doing most
of the work." He gestured to another man with muscles that
bulged from his orange diving gear. "Thirty minutes of your
time is all we need, and another fifteen minutes to get you to
the jump altitude of ten thousand feet. If the weather holds up,
you'll have finished your jump an hour from now."

Amy didn't speak for the next thirty minutes. She nodded
when she had to and heard what she had to hear, but her mind
could not move past ten thousand feet. Dave led her to the plane,
and she struggled to control a tick in her jaw that made her head
jerk. *Nothing is going to happen as long as I'm with Dave,* she
told herself. *His luck will save me, his luck will save me.* She didn't
process any of the questions the instructor asked as the plane
took off; she just answered on reflex. She told him her height and
weight, shook her head when he asked if she had a heart condition,
nodded when he told her to make sure she breathed, and panicked
when he pointed to a waiver and said, "Sign here, please."

The higher the plane rose, the harder she squeezed Dave's
hand, until they reached jump altitude. The sky looked endless,
blue and dreamy that high up, as if it were its own playing field.
If only fear hadn't been numbing her body, she might have been
able to enjoy the view.

Dave kissed her hand, and she held tight as she inched her way behind the jump master. A shared harness connected them, but she wished she was connected to Dave. He flashed her a wink and leapt with his jump master out of the plane, which ignited a dizziness that burned through her.

She heard the instructor say, "Don't look down" and immediately looked out the plane door. It occurred to her that maybe it was her fate to jump to her death and end this streak of bad luck forever. She wished she wanted to fall so she could end the anxiety, but every cell in her body fought to keep her inside, where her feet could feel something beneath them.

She imagined a crowd below, taunting her. She knew a certain number of people in the world wanted something to go wrong, for her to jump too straight and piledrive her body weight; for her chute to bunch up, or for the cord to snap. Those are the stories that live on for decades.

She looked at the twelve inches or so of blue grating in the shape of diamonds that stood between her and the door, then a chip in her jump master's harness caught her attention. This wasn't the harness's first job. She slid her toes forward.

"Three breaths and go," the jump master said.

The alternating yellow and red stripes on his back made Amy think of stunt men, the collapse of lungs and suffocation.

It was impossible to see any details on the ground from that height. For all she knew, they were above water, mountains or a forest. She looked straight out into a blue sky so vibrant, it made her realize she had never really seen blue until then.

This isn't a bad way to die, she thought. The jump master raised a thumb, and she tipped her body weight forward until gravity took over. With her arms splayed and her face rubbery, she felt anything but graceful.

The red and yellow stripes on the jump master's back blurred into a unified streak, until the parachute opened and tugged on her hard enough that she thought her spine was going to rip from her back. She reacted more than thought with primal screams, her fingers balled into fists, and eyes too afraid to be shut yet too disoriented to stay open. Her body dropped again. This time she saw a flash of blue sky that she was convinced was water. Up looked down and down looked up. Only the tugging helped her distinguish between falling and recoiling, then she felt a beautiful weightlessness.

"Great jump," the instructor yelled.

She closed her eyes until they landed and wondered for a moment if she was going to throw up before her lungs filled with air.

Dave ran over and kissed her forehead. "Congratulations."

The instructor grabbed her shoulders. "Don't you feel alive?"

She wanted to vomit, but yes, she was very alive.

Thirty minutes later, her heart still hadn't returned to normal as they sat across from each other in the closest diner. The place hadn't been renovated in thirty years, but it was clean. Dave raised his pint.

"You did it."

"I did." Her mouth didn't feel ready for a sip of beer.

"Don't you feel relieved?"

"I feel shaken."

"What about the rush? Doesn't it feel better knowing it's okay to take a chance?"

"I didn't get hurt because I was with you."

He put down his glass without taking the next sip. "I didn't jump with you. You could have died, but you didn't. You could have been injured in any number of ways, but you weren't. And you weren't because you're just another person."

"Another person who was with you."

"You can't really believe that."

"I live it. If anyone other than you took me skydiving today, I'd be a tragedy on the evening news."

He dragged his pint across the table so that the glass

screeched before leaning in enough that other people couldn't hear him. "I'm grateful to make some money from whatever hustle Thorrin's running with your brother, but you're too smart to believe in this hocus-pocus. There is no such thing as lucky or unlucky, things happen because they can."

"That's what you believe."

"That's how it is. Babies die because they can, people get heart diseases because it's possible, and cars crash because drivers make mistakes."

"Why are you in denial?"

"I can ask the same of you."

The waiter asked if everything was okay, and they both nodded politely. Amy waited for the waiter to head to another table before shifting her weight. "Does the thought of believing that you're special scare you that much?"

"No, I'd love to believe I'm special, but I'm not. What scares me is the fact that *you* believe I am."

Twenty-Two

As soon as Dave stepped into 29 Palson, an orderly escorted him to his dad's room. With his hair pulled into tight cornrows and a clean-shaven face, the orderly appeared to be in his late teens, but he had to be at least twenty-five.

"I appreciate you coming. He almost did quite a number on himself."

"Thank you for calling," Dave said, rolling his folded newspaper into a baton.

As soon as they entered Jack's room, the orderly nodded to Dave and left. Despite an open window, the room smelled like a combination of rank body odour and sweat that had dried into unwashed clothes for a number of days. Dave walked up to his dad, who lay in bed with his back raised by three pillows.

"What are you doing taking your mask off?"

Jack didn't answer. Listening to him breathe was difficult. If Dave closed his eyes, it would have sounded like he was listening to a science fiction movie, where people in protective suits take filtered, pressurized breaths.

"Don't pull that zoned-out crap today. I know you heard every word I said."

They locked eyes for a moment before his dad spoke. "Did you bring today's line?"

The liquid in his eyes was thick, his face drained of colour, yet he still savoured being a smartass.

"They told me you took your mask off. You're playing with your life doing that."

"I want to see the line."

"I'll give you the line when you listen to me. Why'd you take the mask off?"

Again, no answer, so Dave kept the newspaper gripped tightly in hand while they sat in a stalemate. He inspected his dad. The man couldn't have been comfortable. His back arched in the wrong places, and his neck twisted so that it must have been kinked. A tug on the closest corner of his pillow grabbed his attention.

"Sit up. I'm going to give you a massage."

"I don't need you touching me."

In his singlet, his body looked its age. Sun spots covered his arms, and the once-taut skin now hung loose on his biceps. Dave pressed his thumbs into the slouched shoulders.

"Jesus," Jack shrugged, "I'm not cookie dough."

Dave dropped the newspaper into his dad's lap. "Here's your line."

"Who are the Raptors playing?"

"The Knicks."

"Spread?"

"I don't know."

"Put me down for the Knicks if it's less than five."

It had been a year since his dad had started confusing him with his bookie. Dave had never met this Alex, but he guessed they didn't look alike. He attributed the references to Alex to his dad's yearning for gambling, but a part of him also believed it was a deliberate slight to reinforce a disappointment he had felt in his son for years.

"I met a woman," he said while his thumbs worked both sides of the spine.

Jack was too focussed on the newspaper to hear anything. Number of games, multiplied by the total odds, multiplied by the total wager. The massage stopped.

"Her name's Amy."

Jack smacked the paper. "Bloody hell, you smudged the Chicago game with your sweaty palms."

"Will you listen to me for a second, Pop?"

"What?"

"I said I met a woman named Amy."

He held the newspaper close to his face to inspect the smudge before saying, "Get out while you can."

"Out of what?"

"The relationship."

"We're not in a relationship."

"Your line of work and love don't go together."

"I'm not your bookie, Pop."

"My wife was the only thing I cared about more than gambling."

"I know." He started working on the shoulders again. He rolled soft circles with his index fingers until his dad began to relax. "When did you know Mom was the woman you'd still be talking about fifty years later?"

"Immediately. The first time we spoke, I knew I was experiencing something different, something I would remember for the rest of my life. In 1958, the city was as tight as a drum. Not one of my friends had a car, none of them had career jobs, and the chances of starting a relationship were limited to weekly dances or the bowling alley.

"I'd earned a reputation over the years as a sweet talker, so when I pointed at a beautiful brunette with a fresh bob and said 'That's going to be my new girlfriend, boys,' no one flinched. I wanted to make it interesting, so I said, 'I've got a ten that says I have her phone number in the next five minutes.' I knew Charlie Waters since we were six, and I knew he couldn't resist a bet, so he says to me, 'You're on, Jackie. You got five minutes starting ten seconds ago.' Your mom was in a conversation with a redhead that looked five years older, but I didn't wait for a lull. I said, 'You know, I come here every Friday, and I have never seen anyone stand out the way you do. I just wanted to come over here and tell you that you look beautiful.'"

Dave laughed. "And what did she say?"

"She said, 'Is that the best you can do?' So I look at her, confused, and she says, 'I got promoted today, and the best you can come up with is you're beautiful?' So I probed, and she told me she got promoted to mailroom supervisor. I invited her out to dinner the next night to celebrate, and I never looked at another woman with lust again. She gave me her number, and I folded it up and slipped it into my pocket. When I went back over to the boys, they started clapping, but I told them I didn't get the number and paid Charlie his ten bucks. Your mom was too special to be playing games with."

Jack raised his hand so that Dave had a good view of his wedding band. The look of sadness in his eyes made Dave feel bad for reminding him of his wife. Dave missed his mother too. He missed her strength, her unwavering care, and the peace she gave any situation simply by being there. But he didn't miss her the way his dad did. He hadn't started and ended each day beside her, he hadn't created life with her, and he hadn't felt like one half of the same soul.

Jack pointed to a photo of a cottage on an island he taped to the wall above his bed. "I want to be at the cottage."

The photo drew Dave in for a closer look. It had been years since he'd seen a picture of the cottage, so flashes of catching garter snakes, diving off the floating dock, listening to his dad tell stories by the fire long after his mother had gone to sleep, driving the boat, the smell of boat fuel, and fishing hit him as he absorbed the details. He hadn't fished since his last trip to the cottage.

Jack's eyes dropped back to the bed. All the regret in the world couldn't bring the cottage back. Jack had inherited the place from his mother, and over the years he'd used it as collateral for loans and lines of credit when gambling had left him short.

Dave tried to forget the day the bank had seized the property, but the details were too poignant to erase. He'd been sure his mother was going to divorce his dad, that the irresponsibility had proven to be a disease beyond her cure, but she hadn't even yelled at him. Instead she lay in bed with him for the better part of two days. She didn't touch him or talk with him, she just lay with him and shared the silence.

"I'd like to be there too, Dad."

"Yeah."

They didn't say anything after that. Dave didn't care why his dad took his mask off any more. He just wanted to rub the man's shoulders until the knots came out.

Twenty-Three

"This is my first time in a restaurant in six months," Amy said as she squirted a drop of sanitizer into her palm.

Dave knew what to expect. "Food poisoning?"

She nodded.

"Not this time."

Dave had brought Amy to his favourite restaurant. Despite it being expensive, he loved the fusion menu, the low lighting and the lounge décor. Amy did her best not to think of vomit or diarrhea, but as she scanned the menu with feigned enthusiasm, her imagination turned chicken into choking and sweet sauce into sweating.

"You have to try the chicken satay," Dave said. "It comes with a peanut sauce that will blow your mind."

"I don't eat chicken," she said without taking her eyes from the menu.

"Why not?"

"Because they have bones."

"So you're afraid of choking."

"I don't eat anything with bones."

"Because you're unlucky?"

Dave's tone sent a ripple of anger through her body. "Don't be a dick."

He looked around to see if any of the other patrons had heard her before leaning into the table. "What?"

"Don't treat me like I think I'm a victim. I don't feel sorry for myself, and I'm not looking for reasons to feel bad."

The tone made Dave smile. This was another side of her, and

he wanted to see more of the complexity. "I was joking, but I can see it upset you, and I didn't mean to do that, so I'm going to go to the washroom, and when I come back, we can enjoy our meal."

The washroom smelled of vanilla. As he washed his hands, he thought of how he'd like his washroom to smell the same, until something on the floor captured his attention. Money has a way of cutting through life's muck, and the only thing left to be determined was the denomination. He bent down to find that it was a twenty, picked it up and stuffed it in a pants pocket.

When he returned to the table, Amy passed him a glass of wine. "I thought it would be nice to have a drink. I hope you like red."

"I love it." He preferred white but had no interest in fuelling her paranoia, so he sat down and raised his glass. "I just found twenty dollars on the floor of the washroom."

"Of course you did."

"Don't say that. This is the first time I've ever found money in my life."

"Maybe you haven't been looking."

"Looking where? On the floor? I was just washing my hands, I glanced down, and there was a twenty."

"And you never wonder why it's that easy for you?"

"I just said I've never found money. And besides, it's only twenty dollars." A waiter with thick wrinkles in his forehead approached the table with a platter of cold spring rolls. "Compliments of the restaurant," he said in an Eastern European accent.

"Thank you." Dave picked up the platter to offer Amy a spring roll.

"What's in them?"

"I'm not sure." He picked up the largest one and took a big bite before inspecting the rest. "Vegetables. And coriander. Are you a fan of coriander?"

Amy nodded as she reached for the closest spring roll and

took a small bite. Not five chews later, her eyes bugged. She pushed the seat away from the table and shoved a finger in her mouth.

"What's wrong?" Dave asked.

What was wrong proved more unexpected than choking. She probed for the pain's source until she hit something pointy like wire, only thicker and sharper. Pain raced along her jaw line.

Dave now stood beside her, but she ignored everything he said. The tip of the metal slipped through her fingers twice before she got a good enough grip to pull. The more she pulled, the more the pressure on her gums was relieved, until she felt the object dislodge itself. For a moment she considered not looking at whatever had just stabbed her, but she needed to know what had almost lodged in her throat.

This time Dave's eyes popped when her fingers left her mouth to reveal a black staple. Not a nine-to-five office staple, but an industrial strength, staple-gun staple.

"Is that a staple?"

She placed the staple on her bread plate. Sharp and wet with blood, the metal couldn't have looked more out of place.

"Did it cut you?"

"I bit into it."

"I'll get the manager."

"I just want to go."

"Are you sure?"

The look in her eyes as she nodded made him want to go to the kitchen and beat every staff member that had anything to do with the staple in her food until their apologies brought happiness back into her eyes. He passed her the car keys.

"I'll meet you in a minute. I'm just going to settle up here."

The waiter approached, but Dave knew Amy didn't want to draw any more attention to herself, so he stepped in front of the man. "Is everything okay, sir?"

"Not even close." He held the bread plate with the staple in the centre only inches from the waiter's face. "She bit into her spring roll, and this stuck in her gums."

They hadn't taught the waiter about this in staff meetings. He had a response for hairs, dish cleaning bristles and bugs, but an industrial staple forced honesty.

"That's disgusting, sir. Of course the wine will be on us, and I'm sure the manager will write you up so that your next dinner is free of charge."

Dave looked at him like there wasn't going to be another dinner.

"Is there anything we can do for your lady friend?"

Dave pointed to the kitchen.

Inside the car, Amy inspected her mouth in the pull-down mirror. Her gums hadn't bled much, but a puncture mark as if she'd stabbed herself with a toothpick stood out below a molar. She couldn't stop thinking about what would have happened if the staple had made it to her stomach, or even worse, lodged in her throat. As her hands shook and her gums throbbed, she couldn't imagine this happening to anyone else.

Dave hunched into the car holding a paper bag. He put his closest hand over hers, which was surprisingly cool. "I'm sorry that happened to you. Does it hurt?"

"A little."

"Can you eat ice cream?" he asked, pulling a covered plastic dish with two scoops of chocolate from the bag.

"How'd you get that?"

"It was the least they could do."

"It wasn't their fault I walked into their restaurant."

"Don't say that. What happened to you sucks, but it happened to you because some sous chef rushed his job or the chef smoked a joint. The reason it happened had nothing to do with you."

She tossed the ice cream container on the dash unopened.

"That's easy for someone who just found twenty dollars to say."

"Twenty, not twenty thousand. You're too smart to think like this."

"And you're too arrogant to see what's in front of your face. You found twenty dollars, and I had a staple in my spring roll. Even you should see the pattern."

Amy opened her mouth again to inspect her gums. She thought of tetanus, blood poisoning, and the flesh eating disease. "I need to rinse my mouth out."

"I want to take you to a friend's place," Dave said.

"I just want to go home."

"You need to see this. You'll be doing me a favour."

"I almost ate a staple, Dave. I want to go home and rinse my mouth out."

"I really need to share this with you. We'll be a half-hour, tops."

"Okay."

She grabbed the ice cream from the dash and ate it without saying a word while they drove. It was some of the best chocolate ice cream she'd ever had, but she couldn't stop herself from probing every spoonful with her tongue in search of a staple, glass or fingernails. It wasn't until the car pulled into a hospital parking lot that she paid attention to the surroundings.

"I don't need medical attention."

"We're not here for you; my friend's a doctor."

"I don't like doctors."

"Then just think of him as my friend."

Every step toward the hospital's front doors made her more uncomfortable. The sight of a nurse on a smoke break made her think of judgment, pain and death. Dave pointed to a row of plastic chairs.

"I'm going to go find him. Why don't you grab a seat?"

She stepped closer to him so that no one else could hear. "Promise me you're not getting him to look at my mouth or to ask me questions about why I think it happened."

"I promise."

The only seat available was beside an extra large man with sweat stains under each arm and a small bag of sour cream and onion chips in his lap that accentuated the size of his hands, so she chose to stand. A young girl with headphones caught her attention next. The girl hammered a pop machine with a fist until it dropped her desired can.

She couldn't have been more than sixteen, yet heavy bags under her eyes in the shape of upside down triangles made Amy wonder what was going on in such a short life to leave her so drained.

Dave returned with a big smile. "Good news. Now I didn't tell you this before because I didn't want to build it up then have it not happen, but we're all set. A friend of mine from university, Rick, is a doctor here, and about a year ago he asked me to come in and read to a group of kids. Now I haven't done this for awhile, but it's a pretty special experience, and he was able to fit me in. I thought you'd want to check it out."

"Tonight?"

"After our dinner, it had to be today."

They stepped onto the elevator beside a nurse scribbling on a clipboard.

"I can't picture you reading to kids," Amy said.

"I never would have thought of it on my own, but Rick is a persuasive guy, and after my first visit I got hooked on how excited the kids get."

"Then how come you haven't been for awhile?"

"That's a fair question. I could say work or too many late nights, but I don't have a good reason. But I do know you made me want to come back, so let's have look."

They stepped off the elevator to a series of unused stretchers. Amy followed him down the hall until he met a man coming out of a side room.

"There you are."

The man raised a mug of coffee. Dave gestured to Amy. "Rick, this is Amy."

"Pleasure to meet you."

She wiped the sweat from his hand on the thigh of her pants, surprised to find his so clammy. Purple bags under his eyes made him appear older than he was. Puffy and sensitive, they were part of the price for regular nights with little sleep.

"They're ready when you are." The doctor pointed into the side room.

Amy followed Dave inside the room to see about a dozen kids, none of them more than six or seven, playing with action figures and toy cars in small groups. All of them were bald or close to it, their skin drained, whether they were light or dark-toned, and their eyes rimmed with the distinct yellowing of sickness. A nurse with a smile that filled her face stood from a chair.

"Welcome," she said in a thick Caribbean lilt. She turned to the kids, and they all looked at her as though they were used to her leadership. "Our reader's here, people. Gather around the chair, please."

Dave grabbed the book set out for him on the desk before sitting down: *The Little Bear Cub*.

"Good evening. My name's Dave, do you remember me?" Some of them did, lots of them didn't, but only a girl whose attention was focused on a plastic flower answered.

"No," she said. "I don't."

"That's okay, I haven't been here in a while."

The girl held the flower up to the ceiling before breaking into laughter.

"I'm going to read *The Little Bear Cub*. Whose selection was that?"

A Chinese girl with a fake tattoo of Superman's S on one of her forearms stretched her hand high.

"Great pick."

Dave read, and the more he read, the more it surprised Amy. He hadn't struck her as the type to make funny voices for kids. Stoic, intense, thoughtful—absolutely, but she had never seen him so vulnerable, and for the first time, she thought of him as a father.

Dave waited until the drive home to connect his plan for taking her to the hospital. "So what did you think?" he said, waiting for a stoplight so he could turn to face her.

"You were amazing. I mean, you were amazing with the kids."

"Thank you." The light turned green before he wanted it to, so he had to continue with glances away from the road. "Every one of those kids is terminal. No one our age is unlucky when kids as wonderful as them are dying."

Her eyes narrowed as if he'd just spat in her face. "That's why you brought me there?"

"There's no way you can believe you're unlucky after seeing those kids."

"I thought you brought me there to share an experience with me."

"I did. An experience that's related to how you view life."

"You are the most dogmatic person I've ever met."

"I'm trying to make you feel better."

Spasms in her hands turned to full shaking as frustration surged through her body. "I don't know what you want me to say."

"I'm not looking for you to say anything specific. I'm just saying, next time you feel unlucky, think of those kids."

As angry as he'd made her, she wanted to believe in his passion. No child should die, and maybe that was enough to cling to. The day had solidified a few things in her mind.

Seeing Dave read to kids made her the type of happy that sparked her to imagine reading a book with him to kids of their own.

Twenty-Four

The nightmare always started with Dave in the toilet stall and his head hurting so much, it was difficult to think. He winced at the Tylenol's bitter taste, then the realization shot through his body. In one minute, the truck will crash through the front windows, and in one minute they'll all be dead. The obligation to save his colleagues overwhelmed him so much that he never moved. Sometimes he thought of running into the room and pulling the closest person as far back from the windows as possible, other nights he thought of ways to lure people to the back of the office or washroom, but every night he stayed in the toilet stall. He didn't want to see the truck, he didn't want to die, so he tried to call out instead. "Come here. Get away from the windows, get to the back wall." But nothing ever came out. He couldn't will a word, syllable or yelp. Then the sound of the crash came. The volume was so loud that he ducked his head and used his forearms to cover his ears. It's at this point that he wished he were dead, and that he could trade places with his colleagues' shattered bodies for being such a coward. But he never died, and it was always at that exact point that he woke up.

It took a moment of steadying his breathing before he noticed the door buzzer. He sat up and listened for a second to make sure this wasn't another dream. One glance at the clock reinforced that anyone knocking at the door that early was not someone he wanted to see. Grabbing a T-shirt from the back of a chair, he moved towards the door with heavy legs to find Grayson's smug smile filled the peep-hole as though he were working a Hollywood camera.

"You're kidding me?" Dave said loud enough that he hoped Grayson could hear before pulling the door open.

"Morning," Grayson said, raising what was left of a banana.

"You can't keep coming here whenever you like."

"We brought the office to you," he said, stepping aside so Dave had a clear view through the window of the stretched Mercedes idling in front of the complex.

"Give me a minute."

The clock clicked to eight fifty. As much as Grayson's intruding presence unnerved him, there were worse ways to start a day than with a limo ride. His mind raced in anticipation of what they wanted as he stepped outside. Were they blaming him for lost money? Or had Grayson found out how often he was seeing Amy?

The same stout driver he'd met before opened the limo's side door. This time he was chewing gum like his heart would cease beating if he stopped.

Dave ducked his head on the way into a seat beside Grayson and across from Thorrin. The flat-screen flashed stock prices and codes. "Good morning," Thorrin said. He passed Dave a mug of black coffee followed by a tray of cream and sugar, which Dave waved off.

This was the first time Dave had seen Thorrin in leisure wear. Dressed in a beige short-sleeve shirt and slacks, he looked more relaxed, like he was heading for the golf course. "Grayson told me you don't like to bet," he said, placing his own mug of coffee in a holder on the glass table between them.

"That's right."

"Well, you should." He tossed a folded newspaper from the seat beside him into Dave's lap. "New York beat Dallas thirty-five, thirty-four. You picked the game dead on."

Dave thought of the day he'd told Grayson to pick sixty-nine as a point total. He opened the paper to find the game score and accompanying article circled in red. He considered the odds of getting the score right. Number of games, multiplied by the spread, multiplied by the wager. He'd watched his dad obsess over probabilities enough to know that even fanatics find it difficult to predict a score.

Grayson sifted through a bowl of mixed nuts in search of a cashew before turning to Dave. "How much do you know about football?"

"Almost nothing."

"And the beauty is you don't need to," Thorrin added. Grayson and Thorrin often finished each others' sentences. Having a conversation with them was more of a teamed verbal assault than a rank and order relationship, and their words flowed as cohesively as rhythmically.

Thorrin shook a manila envelope until two stacks of money fell onto the table. "Here's your share of the football game."

"I don't believe you came to my place this early to pay me, so what's up?"

"I want you to pick another stock for me."

"That's not a good idea. Even with you guys making this work, I feel better about sticking with something I know."

"Grayson's made it incredibly easy for you."

Grayson tapped a printout to draw attention to the paper in front of him. "We've noticed that you're most effective when pressure is intensified, so I made a list of the year's most precarious stocks for you to choose from. Some have gone from duds to through the roof and others quite the opposite, but all of them have proven entirely unpredictable, even for the country's most renowned experts."

"I don't feel good about it."

"You're doing an excellent job of proving that luck has nothing to do with intelligence, Dave. You need to stop blaming us for scamming people and start embracing what you can do. I want to do business with you, and it isn't negotiable. I like you, so I'd prefer to do this as partners." Thorrin pulled a red Sharpie from his breast pocket, spun the printout towards

Dave and passed him the marker. "Now let's be civil and make some money. You're an accountant, you know how this works. Anyone who makes large sums of money takes risks. Risks that could ruin them at any moment. Stockbrokers, land developers, professional athletes, film and television producers, plastic surgeons. They all take risks that could ruin them financially at any moment. But if they're good, then they're rare, they're doing something few are capable of, and as a result, they are paid extraordinary amounts of money. Risk is a part of success."

Dave nodded as the limo turned onto the highway.

"I told you before that my associate Senthur is on the verge of doing very large business with us, but what I didn't tell you is what his business is. Senthur is a gambling addict, so much so that traditional outlets don't satisfy him. Cards, sports, horses all bore him now. What he looks for is people who are rare. People like yourself. In about five minutes, we'll be meeting Senthur, and you can see how this works first hand."

Thorrin's phone buzzed. He slipped in an earpiece, put up an index finger to indicate that he needed a moment, and launched into full business mode. Dave had already stopped listening. His head swirled with thoughts. Being in the limo was like being high. He felt a ripple of insight flow through him. He felt like he was in an alternative reality, equal parts dream and nightmare, where different rules applied and anything could happen.

Dave picked up both stacks of money and rocked them gently like a balancing scale while examining the printout. His eyes focussed first on a tech stock before drifting to a company called Metal Co.

"Eighty," he said, raising his eyes from the sheet.

Thorrin lowered his coffee. "What?"

"Eighty per cent."

"I see." Grayson looked at Dave as if watching a poodle that had just bared its fangs. "There you go, I knew you weren't that boring."

Thorrin wasn't as amused. "That's a sixty-five per cent increase. Sixty-five per cent for someone who's been nothing but difficult."

"If I'm the one picking the stock, then I'm the one doing the work, and that's eighty per cent."

Thorrin and Grayson shared a look. These were the moments Thorrin waited for. With all the adrenaline, passion and desperation, it was difficult for him to contain his excitement.

"Twenty. I'll give you twenty, but with the increase comes increased responsibility. As of now, you are responsible for the money I'm willing to spend on a potential stock. If you win, you get your cut. If you lose or if you choose to be stubborn and walk out of here without selecting a stock, then you owe me the money I spent or planned on spending."

"Let him know how much money you're talking about," Grayson said, opening a package of almonds with his teeth.

"Two hundred thousand dollars."

"And we will collect every penny," Grayson added.

"I don't have that kind of money."

"Then it's in your best interest not to owe it."

"What would I have to do to convince you that I'm not lucky?"

"Just pick the stock, Dave."

"Listen to me. I don't want to owe you money I can't pay you."

"This isn't negotiable. You know the situation, and you know what you need to do."

"You're not listening to me."

"Stop talking."

"But…"

"Stop talking."

The limo turned into the driveway of a mansion and idled for a moment in front of ten-foot tall iron gates as they opened.

The drive to the house was at least twenty yards long and lined by lush trees with branches that cast a shadow over the road. Dave considered the possibility that they were going to murder him before reassuring himself that they wanted too much from him to kill him. The sight of a blue SUV and a maroon Acura in front of the mansion eased his mind a little.

"You're going to love this," Thorrin said, exiting the limo.

As Thorrin lead the way up a flagstone path, the mansion's front doors opened, and Senthur stepped out. In an orange collared shirt and beige slacks, he looked ready for a resort.

"Welcome. Good to see you again," he said, choosing to shake Dave's hand before Thorrin's. Dave nodded and followed the man through a gaudy living room the size of a baseball diamond where maroon and gold dominated, past a kitchen that looked like it could service a high-end restaurant and out sliding doors to a huge backyard. Twelve-foot-high bushes formed the property's circumference, which was at least two hundred yards long and another fifty or so wide. Senthur took a seat at a round table overlooking a long stretch of grass. A comparatively small swimming pool was covered with its winter tarp behind them. Senthur looked older than the first time Dave had met him at the restaurant but just as serious.

Senthur gestured around the table, first at a lean, stoic East Indian man to his left. "This is Elango." Moving clockwise, he gestured to a thick Slav in his forties. "Vlad." Vlad nodded. His wrinkled brow looked like it had butted a few people in his time. "And Artem," he said without looking at the man, who looked to be in his early twenties. Artem's neck was the width of his head.

The more Dave saw Senthur, the more it became clear that he was extremely introverted. Unlike Thorrin, he didn't need the spotlight or control. This was a different type of rush for him.

Senthur looked around the table and over at Thorrin, who couldn't contain a grin. "Are we ready?"

The table nodded in unison, got up and made their way to the grass. Dave followed until Grayson put a hand on his forearm.

"Not us. We'll be watching from here."

The young Russian glared at Elango while he stretched his calves and waited for the Tamil to break the stare, but he never did.

Thorrin leaned into Dave and pointed to the two young men as if they were cars or motorcycles. "They're going to have a race. Only they're not running to beat each other, they're running in hope that the dog won't choose them."

"A dog?" The word conjured up horrible images in Dave's imagination.

Almost on cue, a man with a beer belly and a mane of greying hair came around the corner doing his best to restrain a thick, snarling pit bull. The handler's pocked face gave him a hardened look that contrasted with his soft hazel eyes. Unlike his handler, the dog was pure muscle, compact, and from Dave's perspective, all teeth.

Dave turned to Thorrin. "They're going to run from that thing?"

Thorrin nodded. "You want to pick who's going to win?" The man was high on adrenaline. His eyes bugged, his words followed each other so closely they almost formed a new language, and both index fingers tapped the table with an anxious rhythm. This is what he lived for.

Senthur clasped his hands together as if praying. "Let us begin."

Dave looked back at the dog straining on the thick, leather leash. Its short marble fur appeared more like painted skin, and with eyes set far apart and ears like a pig's, it looked more demonic than dog. The dog personified evil, and the "e" in evil made Dave see the name Elango. "Elango." Dave said the name without looking at Thorrin, who smiled, walked over to Senthur and whispered in his ear.

Elango walked to Grayson and the makeshift starting line.

"You'll get a ten-second head start before the dog is released," Senthur said. He did his best to address each man evenly.

Artem didn't move until Vlad whispered into his ear. Artem joined Elango and assumed a sprinter's position.

"Speed isn't an issue," Senthur said in his quiet way. "One of you will be down in twenty seconds, regardless of how fast you are."

Dave looked at the dog and turned to Thorrin. "What do they have to pull the dog off?" Thorrin gestured to a sack and a pole with a noose in the handler's hand.

"The key is not to look back," Grayson said, looking at nobody in particular.

Senthur now stood parallel to Elango and Artem. Vlad lit a cigarette off to the side.

"We'll start the clock on my whistle, and ten seconds later we'll release the dog."

Senthur's eyes locked on Elango. "Ready?"

The man nodded.

Senthur pointed at Artem next. "Ready?"

Artem nodded. The pit bull strained on its leash.

The dog didn't weigh more than fifty pounds, but the combination of its teeth, black eyes and guttural snarls made it seem monstrous.

Senthur raised a whistle to his lips, counted backward from five, and both men raced forward. Elango appeared focussed on anticipating when the dog would be released, but Artem raced ahead, hoping not to be the easiest target. The dog handler released the pit bull, and it charged right for Elango. He could sense it coming, so he glanced over his shoulder in time to see it bearing down on him, but instead of accelerating or zigzagging, he dropped to the ground hard enough that his chin snapped off the dirt.

The dog leapt over him and up to Artem. In a smooth motion, it tackled him to the ground and began thrashing until blood spittle flew through the air. Dave looked away, but he could not escape Thorrin's screams of elation. He did not see a man being mangled by a dog; Thorrin saw the thousands of dollars he'd won.

Twenty-Five

"This can't happen again," the supervisor at 29 Palson Avenue told Dave from his seat behind a desk overcrowded with piles of paper. "Part of our function is to run a stable environment, and your father seems to be doing his best to make it just the opposite. I've put the details in writing to make this official. This is his last warning."

Dave shook the man's hand before heading to his dad's room. Jack was watching celebrity poker on television. A housecoat covered most of his chest, and his bare feet rested on a hassock.

"I'd give anything to sit at a table with these pretty boys," he said, turning to Dave. "Three hours, and I'd clear the table."

"What were you thinking?"

"What?"

"A game of cards is one thing, but you had to know that was going to get you in trouble. I thought we had a deal."

Jack's arms flailed forward in a panic. "Is there a spider on me?"

"Where are you going to go if they kick you out?"

Heavy swipes at Jack's housecoat caused his chair to jump. "Look at my chest. Is there a spider on my chest?"

"No, there's no spider on your chest."

"It sure as hell felt like there was."

"Focus for a minute here," Dave said, turning off the television. "Why would you get yourself in this kind of trouble?"

Company, Jack thought. *And at my age, money is a faster way to company than charm.*

Luckily for Jack, there were more escorts listed in the free weekly newspapers than plumbers, electricians and mechanics combined, so access wasn't a problem. The challenge was raising the three hundred he needed to pay for the visit and the extra one fifty to get her to pretend to be a family member when signing into the senior's home. Considering he was already on warning for sports betting, he decided on a game of poker. Assuring they wouldn't be caught was as easy as inviting Chris, the day-time attendant, to play. Chris saw the invitation as an opportunity to win money from a group of fading minds, and in return, Jack could operate without fear of being reprimanded.

The rest of the table was a mixed bunch. Gerry Nunes wanted in because cards reminded him of the kitchen game he used to play every Wednesday with his brothers and cousins. With everyone else dead, he saw the two hundred dollar buy-in as a small price to rekindle old feelings. Don Dickerson played for the company. Nobody had visited him in over two years, and other than reading the newspaper, no one saw him do much of anything. Tracy T figured it was worth playing for the chance at a drink. Her daughter wanted her dry, so sneaking a drink had become more difficult over the years, but Jack promised he would bring a flask. They called her Tracy T because her last name was difficult to pronounce, and she hated hearing it butchered. "Better T than the mess spilling out of your mouth," she would say. "My father is rolling in his grave because of you."

As far as Jack could tell, Byron Jennings posed the only threat. Byron had dealt cards for fifteen years at charity casinos, and while he swore he'd never gambled himself, Jack didn't believe him. He was too smart not to be an opportunist.

Whether Byron talked about jazz or politics, he was equally charming, and Jack couldn't remember anyone being angry with him.

Three hours into the game, the table was clear except for Jack and Byron. Jack had won more pots, but Byron struck when the pots were larger. Chris was bounced in the first hour, so Jack had to pay him fifty dollars to stick around. Jack took three deep breaths from his oxygen mask before looking at his cards to see a king and a queen. Byron led with an aggressive bet that Jack matched without hesitation before erupting into a deep cough. The flop revealed a two of diamonds and a four of clubs, but neither card upped the betting until the dealer laid down the king of hearts. Byron twisted his thick wedding band four times before raising two hundred dollars. Jack's right eye began to twitch. He'd tried for years to control the tell, but adrenaline betrayed him. He took another pull from the oxygen mask before pushing in all of his money.

The room burst into a series of catcalls. Byron dropped his eyes to the table.

"You're first," Jack tapped the table.

Byron laid down a full house before allowing himself a smile that revealed both of his missing teeth. The table clapped and hissed. The twitch in Jack's eye turned into incessant blinking, but no matter how many times he closed his eyes, the cards stayed the same.

"All right," the attendant said. "Everybody out. We've had our entertainment for the day." He folded three chairs he'd brought and ushered everyone out, until only Jack and Byron remained. "Can I trust you guys alone?" he asked.

Jack stuck up a middle finger, but Byron nodded. Byron waited for the door to close before removing his ante from the stack of money and pushing it towards Jack.

"If you agree not to tell anyone, then it's yours. I'm assuming you organized today's game for a reason, and I don't want to get in the way of that. Money's no good to me in here anyway. But you know what is?"

"What's that?"

"Favours. And I'd say you owe me a few after this."

Jack nodded.

"Good enough then. You enjoy whatever it is you need that for."

The escort arrived just after five, which gave them an hour before dinner. She didn't look like a typical escort. With short brown hair, a full face and an oversized green sweater with matching khakis, she would have blended into any university library. She accepted the envelope of money and sat beside him. The agency had told her she was going to a senior's home, but she wasn't ready for Jack's appearance. His warm eyes relaxed her, but his sagging skin and numerous sun spots made her think of her grandfather.

"Should I close the door?"

"Please," Jack wheezed.

She closed the door before returning with her hand out. "I'm Amanda."

"Welcome, Amanda, I'm Jack."

"So uh, how would you like to start?"

"With the radio."

"I'm sorry?"

"I'd like you to dance with me."

"Dance?"

"That's right."

"Just dance?"

"There's no 'just' with dancing. Now press play on that machine. I've already set up the music."

Amanda walked across the room to the tape player, which gave him time to shift his weight out of the chair.

"Do you know how to waltz?"

"I don't. Sorry."

"I'm joking. Regular slow dancing is just fine."

Sinatra filled the room when she pressed play. From her point of view, it looked like Jack might fall at any moment, but he leaned his weight on the oxygen machine to steady himself. She grabbed his closest hand, wrapped her other arm around his waist, and as they swayed to the music, Jack closed his eyes. His movement was limited, but there was no question he knew how to dance. In contrast, Amanda hadn't slow danced since high school.

"Do you have a cottage?"

"No."

"I had a cottage for years. Beautiful place."

"Are you sure all you want to do is dance? Three hundred is a lot of money to dance."

"Worth every penny."

"Don't they ever have dances here?"

"It's not the same."

She couldn't remember the last time a man had held her so gently. Most nights she was the object of sexual frustration or pent-up aggression, so when he led her in a spin, she had to giggle. "You're a very nice man, Jack."

"Thank you, my dear."

At that moment the door opened. Jack was too lost in the moment to notice, but Amanda knew it wasn't good.

"What the hell is going on here?" An attendant with a handlebar moustache held up the clipboard where Amanda had signed in. "You don't have a niece, Mr. Bolden. You thought that'd just slip by us?"

Amanda turned off the music.

"And you," the attendant pointed at her. "You've got a minute to get out of here before I call the cops on your skanky ass."

"Hey," Jack said, taking a step closer to him.

"Be quiet, Mr. Bolden. You're going to be lucky to be here after I write this up, so I suggest you stop the bleeding while you can."

Amanda grabbed her purse and brushed by the attendant. Jack was too busy replaying the music in his head for the threats to affect him.

"Okay," Dave said after listening to the story, "why don't we get you out of here for a bit, get some fresh air."

Neither of them said a word on the way to the beach. Dave worried about what he would do if his dad got kicked out of 29 Palson while Jack still replayed the music and the few minutes of dancing. Dave wheeled his dad to a spot by a bench on the boardwalk. The breeze coming off the water was colder than Dave had expected, so he pulled out two blankets from beneath the wheelchair and laid one over his dad's legs, wrapping another around his shoulders. A series of waves formed small whitecaps at their tips as the water rushed into the beach.

"This isn't the cottage, but it's a nice view," Dave said, picking up a rock from the wet sand.

"It smells like bird shit." Jack erupted into the type of painful cough that only emphysema can bring on before raising his oxygen mask to his mouth with a palsied hand. Dave watched to make sure his breathing steadied before pitching the rock over the sand and into the water. Jack lowered the mask from his face.

"How much did you lose?"

"What?"

"You've got a look on your face that only losing money can cause. How much?"

"I didn't lose money."

"Don't lie to me."

"I'm not, I actually made a lot of money."

"Then you're a bloody fool for walking around with such a long face."

Dave picked up another rock the size of a baseball. "Have you ever owed a lot of money? So much that you're like an indentured servant?"

Jack looked around his wheelchair at the boardwalk. "There's bird shit everywhere."

"Yeah, yeah, there is, Pop. But I'm asking you a question. Have you ever borrowed so much money that the people who lent it to you might as well own you?"

"I've borrowed a lot of money in my time."

"Okay, well, I'm in a similar situation. How do I get back to even, how do I get out?"

"You outplay them."

"What do you mean outplay them?"

"Anyone who has leverage on you in life is playing you. Your greed, your needs, your love, your desperation. Play them instead."

Jack burst into another round of horrible coughs until Dave steadied the oxygen mask. Jack took a few deep breaths before lowering the mask sooner than his lungs wished.

"The cottage never smelled like bird shit."

"I know."

Twenty-Six

At home, alone with his thoughts, Dave had to admit that things were changing. He'd felt life's rhythms altering for weeks, but instinct had told him to deny that a pattern was forming and to deny that Thorrin's money was dangerous. But the silence wouldn't allow him to deny it any longer. Without routine, Dave's touchstones had disappeared. It wasn't that he identified himself as an accountant, but somewhere in the routine of nine-to-five, the familiarity of voices and the cause and effect of daily work, he'd defined a comfortable reality. He couldn't make sense of his new circumstances, and with the fall of his daily routine fell the workdays, bi-weekly paycheques, vacations, weekends, and the anticipation accompanying a Friday afternoon that used to make sense to him. Sometimes the routine frustrated him, but it always made him comfortable.

The shower's cold water jolted him as he stepped underneath the spray. He adjusted the hot water tap first, then the cold tap, but he couldn't get the balance he wanted, so he settled for cool. All he wanted was to clean up, then go to sleep, but his mind wouldn't relax. Thoughts scrambled frantically in an effort to make sense of the past few weeks. The truck crashing through the office storefront, Grayson's smug smile, the limp bodies of his colleagues, a series of bizarre guesses, money and more money. His head ached. A squeezing sensation on both temples prompted a harsh gag. He bent his head down to begin a series of deep breaths through his nose to steady the heart, relax the nerves, and relieve the stress reactions.

Part of him wanted to call Amy and ask her if she would leave the city with him.

They could move to a small town, out west, or to any country she wanted as long as they disappeared. But he couldn't abandon his dad. The man didn't have anyone else left who cared about him, so escaping wasn't an option.

Hunger made Dave weak, but his stomach warned him not to eat. Things were escalating fast, and it was only a matter of time before he would be the one running from the dog. The thought of owing Thorrin the money for any stock he couldn't predict also stopped him from sitting down. He paced the apartment while considering how to get out of the situation. Going to the police and claiming extortion was an option, but between the danger that he would be putting himself in with Thorrin and having to get a cop to believe the whole story, he knew it wasn't a realistic option.

He hunched down under his bed, removed the box where he kept his money and brought it into the living room. As he spread the stacks over the table, it surprised him to see just how many there were. Thinking about how he'd guessed a stranger's name or picked the winning score of a football game left him numb. He remembered feeling like that when he'd thought about death as a kid. However, these choices he made were coming true. He knew it was beyond his control, and the reality of that helplessness left him uncomfortable.

He wanted to believe that he'd survived the truck crashing into the office simply because it was possible, but every passing day made it more difficult to be sure. Since he'd met Thorrin, the questions had mounted in his head, and as he looked at the money in front of him, denying them was no longer an option. Nothing looked the same any more. His apartment looked dirty, the T.V. shows he used to love felt dated, and his reflection in the mirror appeared drained.

Things had changed, and it was hard to live without wondering why everyone he worked with had died. He gathered up the money before returning it to the box. The compulsion to admit how he felt led him to the phone. He didn't want to be alone with his thoughts for another second. The double beat of his dial tone reminded him he had messages. The first message was a hang-up. Two weeks before, he would have pressed star-sixty-nine immediately, but he erased the message without hesitation. The voice of message number two was vaguely familiar if not exciting.

"Mr. Bolden, this is Phil Bryer again, please call me."

Again, he erased the message. *Fucking vultures.* Whether it was an insurance rep or a journalist, he hated them the same for calling him, only because he was the sole survivor or seeing him as some sort of gatekeeper to knowledge that might save money or make money. He was sure of their motives, and somehow they knew how to contact him. His thumb pressed the "erase" button just to be sure before keying in Amy's number. After the first two rings, he considered hanging up for fear of waking her, and after the third and fourth, he feared she wasn't home, until she answered on the fifth ring.

"I'm sorry to wake you up, but I really need to speak with you."

"It's okay, I wasn't asleep, I was listening to music."

"Can I come over?"

"Of course. What's wrong?"

"I've just been up thinking, and I'd feel better if I saw you."

"Then come over. I'll leave the door unlocked."

He couldn't get there fast enough. Every moment felt out of sync.

Visions of his colleagues' broken bodies intensified, and the more he thought about that morning, the less he was sure about what he remembered. *Was I in the bathroom for one minute or five before I heard the crash? Did I really have to go the bathroom, or did I just want to delay the start of work?* These were the details that had saved his life, yet he wasn't sure about any of them.

He stepped into Amy's place to find her sipping tea on the couch. In a tight-fitting T-shirt and track pants, she looked more like somebody going to the gym than somebody who was tucked away reading in bed. She got up from the couch and passed him a cup of mint tea before wrapping her arms around his chest.

"Come here." She pulled him close.

"I'm sorry for doing this, but…"

"Don't be. Come sit down."

His eyes were sore. He took a sip of tea as a show of thanks before rubbing at both sockets.

"I want to tell you," he started before pausing. His voice was unsteady. "I want to tell you that I miss the people I worked with. I've been trying to deal with it as part of life, and that worked at first, it was just how I felt, but in the last few weeks everything's changed. I don't know why I survived, and I can't stop thinking about how great it would be to just go to bed one night, get up in the morning, go to work and have them all be there."

"Of course you do." She reached for his hand, but he pulled away. The thoughts compelled him to be on his feet.

"If there is something working in my favour, why did I survive? What's the purpose of someone like me living and them dying? And why are all these fortunate things happening to me right after something so terrible?" He stopped pacing to drop his weight back onto the couch. "I don't know what to think."

Amy eased his head and shoulders down into her lap. "Maybe you're not supposed to think. Maybe you're supposed to just let it happen."

"I thought I knew how to deal with this."

Her closest hand ran down his arm before stopping to massage his wrist. "Have you thought about what you want to do next?"

"You mean with a job?"

"Yeah. Do you still want to be an accountant?"

"I don't know. But I don't think I'm up for working in an office any more."

"Can't say I blame you. I couldn't stand being in an office."

She bent down and kissed him before he could get out his next word. The kiss surprised him. He wasn't ready for the tingle that the warmth of her lips brought, but she kept kissing him, so he kissed back. Kissing her was easy. Their lips worked with each other until they lost time in the rhythm. Amy sat up to reposition herself so that she could lie beside him. With her hands stroking his hair and neck, it wasn't long before his eyes shut, and he slipped into a deep sleep where the darkness shut out everything that stressed him.

In the morning, Dave woke to the sound of whispering in his ear. It took a moment to make out the details, but he recognized the voice as Amy's right away.

"I have to go to work," she said. "I'll leave my keys on the front table."

"Work?"

"Yeah, it's Monday morning."

He cleared the sleep crust from his eyes. "I didn't know you worked."

"How do you think I survive?"

"I thought Grayson said he took care of you."

Raised eyebrows displayed her disappointment that Grayson had spoken of her like she was below him. "Well, he owns the place, so he I guess he is taking care of me."

"Where do you work?"

"I manage a laundromat. And I've got to get going."

"Can I come?"

"You want to come to a laundromat?"

"I'd like to see where you work."

"Okay. Can you be ready in five minutes?"

A clear sky greeted them as they stepped out of the apartment. The air was fresh more than cool, so Amy unzipped her jacket. "I can't believe you didn't get a ticket," she said, pointing to his car. "People always get tickets here."

"Maybe they saw how pathetic I looked and took pity on me."

The self-deprecation received a glowing smile.

"Or maybe I should bring you everywhere with me."

"I could handle that."

They turned the corner, and Dave noticed a large LAUNDROMAT sign hanging from two poles about fifteen feet above the sidewalk.

With black type on white, despite its age, the sign really popped. Dave was wondering how much longer the rusty hinges connecting the signs would stop it from crashing down to the sidewalk when Amy spread her arms.

"We're here."

"Very cool."

They stepped inside to see that the place was empty. Other than some scattered newspapers on the folding table and a couple of Bounce sheets on the floor, the space was clean. The machines looked like they had been around since he was a kid, and the beige walls and brown-tiled floors gave it a timeless feel.

"There's not much to it," she said, gathering the newspapers. "But it gives me a lot of time to listen to music, and most of the people are really nice." She took a key from her pocket, unlocked a cabinet and removed a stereo. She patted the top of it like it was a cat. "This is my best friend when I'm working."

"This would be a great place to work."

"You think so?"

"Sure. You're your own boss, you get a lot of time for music, you're providing an essential service, and you get to talk to people."

She smiled. "People don't normally get excited when I tell them I work at a laundromat."

"Then you're telling the wrong people. Is there a variety store around here?"

"Yeah, just down the street."

"Good, I want to buy a lotto ticket."

She turned, and her eyes sparkled as if he had just invited her to a Caribbean island. "Really?"

"Really."

"Oh my god, you're serious." She hopped three times in place.

"Why not? There's definitely been some good things happening to me. What do we have to lose?"

"You have everything to gain, but don't involve me in this, or it won't work."

The variety store smelled stale, as if nothing had been moved for years. The counter was relatively clean, but even the chocolate bar rack had a layer of dust. Dave looked at all the types of tickets laid out beneath the counter's glass.

"What should I get?"

"Not the scratch ticket. Ask how much the weekly pot is."

He looked at her for a second like she should ask herself before turning to the owner, who was in his fifties, with a blotch on his bald head that looked burned or diseased. "Hi, what is the pot for the weekly lotto?"

"Eight million," he said in an Eastern European accent Dave placed as Ukrainian.

"Get a weekly ticket," Amy said so fast it came out as one word. "But wait until I leave, I don't want to be around when you get it."

She left the store as fast as possible, and the clerk made eyes at Dave to indicate he thought she was crazy.

"She's just excited. And very superstitious."

The Ukrainian man laughed deeply and fully at her expense. Dave scribbled down a series of numbers before passing them to him.

"Good luck," the man said as he passed him the ticket.

Dave held the ticket high. "Thank you."

"I mean with your lady friend." The clerk burst into another full laugh that Dave knew was at his expense.

He looked at the ticket and thought about how weird it was that a small square piece of paper could be worth eight million dollars. He waved it from shoulder to shoulder as he stepped out of the store so that Amy could see it was official.

"I can't believe you did it."

"Do you want to hold it?"

"Are you crazy?"

Dave smiled at the purity of her reaction. He folded the ticket once before placing it in his wallet. "How close are you with your brother?"

"Grayson?"

"Is there another one?"

"No, it's just the question came out of nowhere."

"He keeps showing up in my life, so I'd like to know how close you are."

"I'd say we're close. At least as close as he is to anyone. He's twelve years older, so it's not like we grew up sharing secrets, and we don't see each other a whole lot, but he's a good big brother. Why?"

"Because Grayson and this man he works for are taking this belief in me too far."

"How so?"

"They won't let me stop working with them."

"Why do you want to? You're making money, aren't you?"

"You're not listening. They won't let me stop. I refused to pick a stock, and they told me I'd owe them what they would have invested if I don't. That's two hundred thousand dollars, and they said they'd make sure they'd get their money."

"Grayson wouldn't do that."

"Well, he did."

"Are you sure you're not reading into what they said?"

Dave stopped in front of the laundromat. "Look, I don't want to be in this situation, especially not with your brother. Not when we're starting what we're starting here. They took me to see some form of extreme betting the other day. These guys were racing, and they let loose a dog to see which guy it would attack; I don't want to be involved in this stuff. I need your help. I need you to go to Grayson, tell him that we've started a relationship, tell him he should let me out."

"Dogs?"

Dave nodded. Amy didn't respond as fast as he'd anticipated. He was hoping for an "Anything for you", but her eyes warned that the request wasn't that simple.

"There's got to be more to this. I know Grayson is a cutthroat businessman, but he wouldn't be part of something like that. Someone must be making him do it."

"Will you talk to him?"

"Yeah, I'll talk to him."

"Do you think you can convince him to let me out of this?"

"I'll try."

Twenty-Seven

Dave was sifting through Amy's record collection when she returned from her bedroom.

"Grayson agreed to talk about your relationship, but he wants you to be there. He said he doesn't want to get caught in a triangle of misinformation."

"All I care about is that he agreed to meet."

Grayson met them at a dessert café. He already had a slice of cheesecake and a piece of maple fudge in front of him when they entered. He greeted Amy with a long hug and Dave with a quick handshake.

"So…what did you want to see me about?"

Amy wiped her hands across her thighs. "I want you to know…I want you to know that I'm seeing Dave."

"I know."

"Really?"

"Yeah. I knew something was up; you're happy."

"You're okay with it?"

"I'm okay with anything that makes you happy."

"Thank you."

Grayson took a bite of the fudge and gestured to Dave. "I knew it would be good for you to spend some time with him."

Amy's eyes dropped to the floor. Being reminded that she'd met Dave through Grayson made her uncomfortable.

"You two are obviously more than friends, which is fine by me as long as it benefits you. But remember, I have a business relationship with him that precedes your relationship, and if that business doesn't work out, it's going to be awkward."

Dave dropped his hands below the table so Grayson couldn't see that they were unsteady. "Actually, I want to talk about that."

"That sounds dramatic."

"Dave says you're forcing him to work with you," Amy interjected.

"And what else has Dave said?"

Grayson locked eyes with Dave, so Dave answered. "I told her you said that I'd owe the money you planned on investing if I didn't pick a stock, and I said you threatened that you'd make me pay what I owed."

Grayson leaned back in his seat, and a wry smile filled his face. "He's not lying to you."

Amy looked like she might cry.

"He's just being melodramatic. We said all of that. We just don't mean any of it."

"I don't understand."

"His luck only becomes a factor when he has something at stake, so the more risky a venture we bring him in on, the more important it is that he believes the stakes are high, even grave."

"So he wouldn't really owe you the money?"

"No."

"Really?" Dave asked.

"That's right, it's all motivation."

"And you would never hurt him?" Amy asked.

Grayson released an amused scoff. "I'm an executive, Amy, not a thug."

Dave felt confident enough to press the moment. "So I'm free to stop working with you whenever I want?"

"Of course you are, but being that everyone is profiting from this partnership, including the two of you, I see it as my duty to make sure you participate." His eyes locked on Amy. "If you don't like the idea of him being coerced, talk to him, get him motivated to make a profit, and we can avoid these dramatic charades all together."

"What about the extreme betting?"

"We took you to see how much money people are willing to invest in a man with your gift. I promise you that you won't ever be running from a dog."

Grayson forked the last of his cake until his phone buzzed. "I've got to get going." He kissed Amy on the cheek one more time. "Stay this happy."

They watched him leave, and Amy ripped open two more packs of sugar and added them to her coffee before stirring the liquid counter-clockwise. "What if you're lucky?"

"Amy…"

"What if you're lucky, and you have this incredible life waiting for you, if you just accept it?"

"That would be very sad."

"Exactly."

"But if there is something to this string of events that has been working in my favour, there's nothing I can pursue as long as Thorrin feels I'm his employee."

"Maybe the incentive they are giving you is what you need to bring out your luck."

"Incentive? They intimidate me, manipulate me and hustle me. None of that is incentive."

"Yet you're making more money than you've ever made in your life."

"It's bound to stop, and I have no interest in owing them money."

"What if it doesn't stop, and you're walking away from a fortune?"

"Everything stops eventually. And if there is something working in my favour, I have no control over it."

"Because you haven't embraced it."

"What exactly do you want from me?"

"I want you to embrace your potential."

"I can't embrace anything as long as Thorrin's in my face. So let me deal with that, then we can talk about potential."

Two hours later, Dave walked through the internet café towards Otto's office.

Seeing a bunch of teenagers and tourists at Otto's place of work always surprised him, but they made for effective camouflage, and the business actually turned a profit.

He knocked twice on the back door before entering to see Otto hunched over a birdcage, where a lime-green parrot sat on a perch.

"Good morning, Otto. Good morning, Otto," Otto repeated in his best parrot-talking-human voice.

Dave smiled. "It's almost noon."

Most people would have been embarrassed, anyone else at least startled, but Otto didn't even turn. That was his gift. He had the ability to become totally lost in himself at any moment.

"Fucking bird. I paid two grand for this thing. The guy assures me it'll be talking in four weeks. I've had this thing three months now, and not a fucking peep."

Dave removed three stacks of money from his jacket and put them on Otto's desk. "That's the rest of what I owe."

After a quick inspection, Otto tapped each stack. "Should I be expecting the cops to follow you through the door? How'd you get all this?"

"The stock market."

"Well, you're on quite a run. Got any leads for me?"

"No, this just came together."

"Things seem to be coming together for you a lot lately."

"That depends on how you look at it."

Otto ran an index finger and a thumb over his chin. "Well, you don't owe money any more, and any day you don't owe money is a good day. Now get out of here before you pass this streak on to my clients and put me out of business."

Twenty-Eight

As he sprinkled some pepper over a bowl of tuna, Dave decided it was time to move. The apartment didn't feel like home any more. Every morning he woke up alone there, he felt like he was in a stranger's place, and every night he lay in bed, he felt the vacancy. The colour of the walls seemed different than what he remembered, the scatter rug a shade or two darker than when he'd bought it, and the brown couches he'd loved so much before now felt like somebody else's decision.

He forked two stabs of tuna into his mouth before deciding to call his landlord. He sifted through the top drawer of a cabinet in search of his personal phone book, past the yellow pages, several take-out menus and a pad of paper before realizing he'd left it at work. A wave of dizziness warned him not to sit down. A flash of his desk at work crumpling like a pop can replayed itself in his mind. He thought of his phone book in the top drawer of the desk, yet another thing gone forever, and reduced to a memory no more reliable than dreams. He considered how long people would have thought of him if he had died and everyone else had lived. Most acquaintances would have mourned him for a week or two, but before long, he would fade into the recess of their memories, reserved for things they didn't want to think about. And his dad, well his dad already claimed he didn't know who he was some of the time, so he figured it wouldn't take him long to choose to forget that Dave ever existed.

The thought of telling Thorrin he wasn't going to participate in his tasks any more made him a type of nervous that caused him to lose control of his body. His stomach churned with unease, his palms and upper lip sweated, and the speed of his heartbeat left him too worked up to do anything routine.

This wasn't the first time he'd felt this way around an older man. Small talk was never a problem, and dealing with new people proved easy enough, but asking permission or confessing anything left him as insecure as a ninth grade student with a speech impediment the day of an oral presentation. And it never got easier with age. Whether he was ten, twenty or thirty, he always avoided being vulnerable around older men.

The day he'd quit his triple A baseball team in Grade Twelve, he'd planned on telling his dad as soon as he got home. He decided against excuses or avoiding the issue and focused on admitting that he would rather work part time and spend his money taking any girl that would go with him on dates instead of enduring another practice for a game he'd lost interest in. But the plan changed when he walked through the front door. When his dad asked how practice went, instinct told him to feign a story about working on his curveball. It wasn't just the fear of his dad's anger that stopped him from telling the truth, the biggest motivator was avoiding the disappointment. He tried to tell himself that he didn't care about making his dad proud, but when he stood there with a chance to be an adult and an opportunity to show he was his own person, he clung to the comfort of lies. It took two days before the coach called home to tell his dad that he'd quit the team. He could tell right away from his dad's tone what the conversation was about, so he tried to psyche himself up for a battle to defend his decision. But his dad never asked him about his decision. He just gave Dave the penetrating look of disappointment that his son feared so much. Dave felt that look every time he was with him for the next seventeen years.

The same feelings had haunted him when he'd decided to quit his job as an accountant. The need to take some time off had underscored his thoughts for months.

He had no plan or alternative career in mind; he just needed a change of pace for awhile. One morning after a meeting with a particularly dull client, it struck him that there was no better time to take action. He drafted a resignation letter as fast as possible, but he knew he would have to wait a day to give it to Mr. Richer, because he was out of the office. The rush of freedom, possibility and change flowed through him after he left work. It was all about to happen, but when he returned to work the next morning, he felt so anxious that he had to skip breakfast. In an attempt to shun the jitters, he walked straight into Mr. Richter's office, repeating "I quit" in his head, but there was no quitting with Mr. Richter. He was the type of nice you're lucky to meet five times over the course of your life. The word "quit" burned in his mind, but he couldn't will it to leave his lips. He couldn't disappoint Mr. Richter.

Amy had created an opportunity to get out of his bizarre situation with Thorrin, and he hoped he could look the man in the eyes and not have his tongue betray him. He didn't sleep a minute that night. After four hours of lying in his bed running scenarios through his imagination, he decided to wait out the rest of the night on the couch in front of the T.V. Reruns of Seventies sitcoms followed one after another, but they did little to distract him. Losing Amy worried him. He figured it was possible Grayson would retaliate by ending their relationship, so he asked himself if it came down to it, would he suck it up with Thorrin to preserve what he had with Amy, or lose Amy to free himself from Thorrin?

In the muck of his sleep-deprived mind, the question had merit, but the more he thought about it, the more he realized that even if he kept working with Thorrin, eventually he would lose his money, which would put his relationship with Amy in just as much jeopardy.

Just before seven, he fell asleep. Exhaustion shut him down, and when he awoke four hours later, the fear in him made a plea that it would be better to tell Thorrin the next day, but he knew where that feeling had led him in the past, so he sprang up and headed for the shower. Thirty minutes later, he stood in front of Thorrin's receptionist, who recognized him and escorted him to Thorrin's office. Dave wondered how many business people in the city would sacrifice their morals for such access. With dark hair and a deep tan, the receptionist looked younger than she was. Her face was full, but an easy smile drew emphasis to her beauty. She walked Dave through the open space to Thorrin's office.

"Here you are, Mr. Bolden." Nobody had called him Mr. Bolden before he'd met Thorrin.

Thorrin was looking out his floor-to-ceiling windows when Dave entered the office. His suit jacket hung on his chair, and when he turned to Dave, his face wore the weight of a stressful start to the day.

"Dave." He spread his arms. "I've been having a bitch of a morning, but I'm feeling better already with you here. What brings you by?"

Dave took a breath. He could feel a shift in his body, and suddenly his legs were limp and his words eager to please.

There was no time to waste, no way to set it up to make things easier, so he stepped forward and spoke. "I want to tell you to your face that I don't want to work with you any more."

Thorrin looked at him for a moment before sitting down in the chair behind his desk. "That's aggressive."

"I appreciate that you believe in me and I'm thankful for the money, but at the end of the day, I'm just not what you want me to be. Eventually I'm going to lose you money."

"So you're playing hardball with me?"

"I'm just trying to be honest."

"No, no, no. That's fine. You're like any good businessman, you want what you're worth." Thorrin opened a side drawer of his desk.

"I just want out."

Thorrin removed a stack of money from the drawer and placed it on the desk. The stack was too thick for Dave to guess its worth.

"Maybe I have been remiss. You deserve a bonus—it's good for motivation."

"I'm not trying to extort you."

He pushed the stack across the desk. "Pick up the money."

"This isn't about money."

"Everything's about money."

"Not this."

"Pick up the money. Go on a shopping spree, get drunk, get a blowjob and stop pretending this is so strenuous."

"I want out."

"Let's not forget you asked me to set up more challenges at one point."

"I want out."

"Yeah?"

"Yeah."

Thorrin rubbed at the nape of his neck, and his face contorted in disgust before he stood up. Again, it surprised Dave how tall he was. "At this point I'm starting to *want* you out. You're ungrateful, you're rude and you're a whiner. But you're a resource, and if you think I'm going to dump someone as profitable as you, you're out of your mind. You want out, buy your way out."

"How do I do that?

"You pay me what you're worth."

"And what am I worth?"

Thorrin leaned on the window ledge. From Dave's perspective, his body was outlined by the seemingly endless overcast sky. Dave knew there were people who never saw a view like that in their entire lives.

"Why don't you take risks?" Thorrin asked.

"What makes you think I don't?"

"I wouldn't be in your life if you were a risk-taker. You would have never been an accountant, and you wouldn't have needed me to show you your gift. I'm offering you a chance to be rich, and you're doing everything possible to pull away."

"I take risks."

"When?"

"When I'm in control."

A smirk filled Thorrin's face. "Then you don't take risks at all. When I started in this business, I was making a hundred thousand a year at the top investment company in this country, and I risked the immediacy of that money in pursuit of one hundred million. And do you know what I found out? I discovered that the money's great, but in the end, the rush of the risk is even better."

"Not for me."

"Not for you? Okay, you want out? Pay me a million dollars and leave the city. I don't want anyone else around here benefiting from you."

Dave felt his throat tighten. "I'll leave the country, but I can't pay you a million. I have six thousand dollars in the bank."

"Then you keep working with us."

Dave thought of owing Thorrin money, losing Amy, and stress eating at him every day. The combination gave him the strength to hold his ground. "I didn't come here to ask you. I came here to tell you I'm out."

Thorrin's head snapped straight, and his eyes opened larger than Dave had ever seen them. "Don't be brash. It's not good for your father's health."

"Are you threatening my dad?"

Thorrin stood again, removed his suit jacket from the chair and put it on. "Directly. I'll have him dragged into an alley and shot in the back of the head like a junkie, if it comes to that. And don't even think of looking at me like a desperado because you'd be dead before you gathered up the nerve. But it doesn't have to be that way." He sat back down in the chair. "I'm going to write down an address. Do you remember Senthur?"

With his mind still stuck on the talk of his dad, Dave offered Thorrin a blank stare. Thorrin snapped his fingers twice to get his attention. "You remember Senthur?"

Dave thought of guessing the woman's name, the men racing from the pit bull, and the sound the man had made when the pit bull tore into his back. He nodded.

"Good." Thorrin passed him a piece of paper. "Now you have two choices. You can be civil, meet us and make more money than you will in the next year, or…" He couldn't help but smile, for these were the type of moments that charged him. "Or you can buy your way out. Either way, I expect to see you tomorrow at noon."

Twenty-Nine

After Thorrin's threat, Dave needed to see his dad, even if his dad didn't particularly want to see him. With his shoulders slouched, Jack wiped at a glob of oatmeal that had dried to his shirt while he stared at a soccer game on the T.V. as if Dave weren't in the room. Dave didn't mind, though, because if anyone could set him straight about luck, it was his dad. The man had floated on the highs and sunk in the lows, and if there are forces that control outcomes, Dave was confident his dad knew about them. He sat in a chair adjacent to Jack's bed. A bag of baseballs leaned against the dresser, and he traced the seams of one while he spoke.

"In all your years of gambling, did you ever meet anyone who was really lucky?"

Jack didn't answer, so Dave tickled his feet until he pulled away.

"What the hell's wrong with you?"

"Have you ever met anyone who was really lucky?"

A question about gambling surprised Jack enough that he turned from the T.V. before answering, "I saw a few guys go on some runs."

"But were they lucky? Was there anyone winning every time?"

"The casino's the only one that wins every time."

Jack erupted into a coughing fit that forced Dave to rub his back. Coughing as violent as that would unsettle most people, but Dave had watched it so often that the back rubbing response had become routine. Once the coughing stopped, Dave removed a coin from his pocket and put it in his dad's hand. "Flip this for me?"

"Why?"

"I want to see if I can guess what'll turn up."

"Don't be a jackass."

"Humour me."

Jack sat up. "You're being weird."

"I'll bet you a dollar I pick it right."

"Make it five."

Jack's fingers struggled to manipulate the coin, but this was competition, so he focussed. Dave watched every detail as the coin flipped through the air. "Heads." He rushed over to the far corner, picked up the coin and smiled. "It's heads."

"Monkeys can do that, boy." Jack had already turned his attention back to the T.V.

A rush surged through Dave that led him to a shelf, where he removed a pack of cards. "Do me another favour?" he said, taking the cards from the pack.

"No."

He put the deck of cards in his dad's hands. "Pick a card for me."

"No."

"Just pick a card for me, see if I can guess it."

Jack tossed the deck across the room sidearm, and the cards scattered over the ground. "Luck's for losers. You hear me? A winner makes their luck. Study the odds, learn the best plays, work your craft. That's how you profit. There isn't a man alive that got rich by crossing his fingers. I made every bet with that mentality. And if you embraced that more, if you weren't so afraid of what could happen, maybe you'd be pitching curveballs for a living instead of counting other peoples' money."

Dave looked at him, and his eyes screamed, *And look where it got you*, before he bent down to pick up the cards. Two weeks before, he would have nodded while his dad ranted against luck, but something had changed. He would never admit it, but it felt good to believe he had a gift. He turned to his dad with the cards extended.

"I believe that worked for you, but there might be another way."

"And there might be a golden egg in my shit, but I wouldn't want to be the one checking my drawers." Jack watched his son for a moment. He had always loved the way Dave's brow furrowed when he had to control his temper and wished he was capable of the same look. "You're a good boy," he said with a wheeze. "You need to smile more."

Dave looked at his dad, and the longer he looked, the more what he had to do became clear. He needed to visit Otto one more time. He looked at his watch. Otto was never in the office past eight, which meant that Dave would have to go to his loft.

Otto didn't like anyone coming to his home, but with every hour counting, Dave decided to rely on the vintage of their friendship. Fifteen minutes later, he stood in Otto's lobby, which was located in a former bread factory converted into luxury lofts that housed twelve very wealthy, very private owners. He looked straight into the surveillance camera for a beat, took two deep breaths and keyed Otto's number into the buzzer.

"You're late," Otto's voice sounded from the intercom.

Dave looked at the intercom for a moment. "It's Dave."

"Dave? What are you doing here? I thought you were my Thai food."

"I'm sorry to do this to you, but I have to see you."

"Okay. I mean it's you, you're welcome here whenever you want. I'm going to buzz you in, but give it a five count before you pull, or it won't open."

Dave didn't get a thanks out of his mouth before the door buzzed. He waited for five and was opening the door when he noticed a delivery man jogging up the steps behind him.

"Is that going up to the fourth floor?"

The man squinted to examine the bill stapled to the top of the bag. "Four-ten?"

"Perfect, that's me."

He hoped paying for and arriving with Otto's food would put

his friend in a good mood, but with two full bags in his arms as he stepped in the elevator, he began to worry that Otto had company.

Otto was half in the hall as Dave stepped off the elevator, and his face contorted into confusion at the sight of the delivery bags. "You've got my food?"

"I do."

"Did you tip him?"

Dave followed him inside the loft. "I did."

"You shouldn't have. Fucker's late every time. And I mean every time."

He took the bags from Dave's hands and opened them. "Have you eaten?"

"I'm good, thanks."

"Are you sure? Because there's a lot of food here."

"Positive."

Too much adrenaline was speeding through Dave's body for him to eat. Otto pointed a chop stick across the room at a white pool table with blue felt. "What do you think of that?"

"It's amazing, the place looks great."

"Slowly though. Once I decided to stay here for awhile, I started dressing it up."

With fifteen-foot ceilings, one wall of windows, and three thousand square feet of open-space concept, the loft was every bachelor's dream. He had five T.V.s. There was a sixty-inch in front of a horseshoe of leather couches, three twenty-seven inchers by a desk in a far corner and a twenty-two inch in the kitchen. All of them were wall-mounted, and all of them were plasma. A cricket match played on the sixty and three different baseball games on each of the twenty-sevens. Each of them earned flashes of Otto's attention between bites of cashew-nut chicken and glances at Dave.

"So what's up?" he asked, shooing a large hot pepper to the other end of the container.

"Do you ever remember me being lucky as a kid?"

"Lucky?"

"Yeah."

Otto smiled a toothy smile as he leaned back. "No."

"Just like that?"

"Just like that. Because you had to be the most unlucky guy I ever saw around girls."

"I'm serious. Do you remember me winning a lot in games or getting good grades without trying very hard?"

"You did both of those things all the time, but that had nothing to do with luck. You were the best athlete I knew, and you always were smarter than the rest of us." Otto washed a bite of food down with a swig of beer. "Why are you asking me about luck?"

The question shamed him. Put so bluntly, it robbed the recent events of their magic. "I don't know. I've been on a bit of a streak."

Otto smiled again. "Then you came to the wrong place, partner. Because I service people every day who believe they're on a streak or about to turn things around, and if any of them did, I'd be out of business. Now what did you really show up at my place at night for?"

"I need a bankroll."

Otto waved a chop stick as if conducting an orchestra. "You just broke even."

"I've got an opportunity."

"In the market?"

"Better than stocks."

Otto put down the container of chicken to lean back in his seat. His eyes were now fully focussed on Dave. "How much?"

"Fifty."

The number pulled Otto to a standing position. "Fifty? That better be one hell of an opportunity."

"Can you do it?"

Otto returned his attention to the cricket match for a

moment before turning back to Dave. "For you, yeah, I can do it. But that's more than you've taken all year combined."

"I know."

"Fifty's a high-risk number, you know that's going be double the interest."

"You don't have to worry about that."

"I'm not the one who has to."

The team in the dark shirts on the T.V. scored a run, much to Otto's liking, and just like that, he was on to other things. This was Dave's problem now. He had been sponsored, trusted and treated like a friend. What came of the loan was up to him.

Fifteen minutes later, Dave pulled a metal box from the cabinet in his living room, opened it and removed three large stacks of money. The momentum felt natural to him for the first time, and counting the money made him think of winning more. He hailed a cab at the closest corner to his apartment. The new impulse to pursue money felt good, and he didn't need Thorrin or extreme betting for a payoff.

"Hello, my friend," an East Indian man in his late thirties said.

"Hi, the horse betting complex on Queen Street East, please."

"No problem. You like the horses?"

"I don't know. I've never betted before. What about you?"

"I hate horses. A horse trampled me when I was a kid." The cabbie held out his right arm to display a long scar where the bone had broken through the skin many years before.

"I don't blame you."

"My friend, what is jaundish?"

"Jaundice?"

"Yes. Jaundice."

"It's a yellowing of the skin. Babies get it."

"Will they die?"

"No. I don't think so."

"My baby has jaundice."

Dave looked into the mirror at the man's brow contorted into a look of worry that appeared like it could last forever. "That's horrible."

"Very."

"He won't die."

"How do you know this?"

"Because it's common. Lots of babies get it."

"Do me a favour, my friend?"

"Sure."

"Say a prayer for my baby tonight?"

Dave nodded. They didn't say another word during the ride. Dave didn't want to tell him what he thought of prayer.

What he wanted to do was win a million dollars, track the cabbie down and give him half. That would be living a prayer.

Dave walked into the betting complex and stared at the ticker tape listing the day's races. Everywhere he looked, a T.V. hung from the wall playing a horserace. The place surged with anxious energy, which made it difficult for people to hear each other, but Dave was too focussed to be affected. He approached the betting booth and the burned-out looking man in his fifties ready to serve him.

"Evening," the man said.

Dave nodded. "When's the next race?"

"Ten minutes."

"What are the odds for the long shot?"

The man scanned a sheet. With what was left of his hair shaved close to his scalp and a whistle dangling from his neck, he looked more like a gym teacher.

"Little Scamp, lane six. A hundred and fifty to one."

"Good. I'll put fifty thousand on Little Scamp."

The man paused for a moment to see if Dave was serious. "You know something I don't?"

"I don't know anything about horses."

The man broke into the type of hearty laugh people wish

they could will. "Well then, good luck to you."

Dave looked at his ticket while ordering a beer. Seven and a half million dollars.

The bet felt more right than anything he had ever done.

He walked down a set of stairs with the plastic cup of beer and took a seat in anticipation of the race. He scanned the movie-sized screen for his horse in lane six. Sitting among such anxious energy felt weird, but he reminded himself that these people weren't like him; these people were all convinced they knew something about horseracing. The starter's gun fired, the gates opened, and the horses raced down the track. Little Scamp fell behind ten yards in.

Dave told himself to relax, but after a few seconds he couldn't sit any longer, so he stood and moved to the aisle to get a better view of the screen. Little Scamp pulled ahead, and fully caught up in the adrenaline of the moment, Dave exhaled a grunt.

He pumped a fist through the air. "Go, go!"

Little Scamp ran smooth, but a horse two lanes over kicked in down the stretch, causing the room to erupt into an explosion of cheers. Dave waited for Little Scamp to match the challenge, but the horse never did. The room divided into winners and losers before he had time to process a thought. Some people shared high-fives, and others tore their tickets into tiny pieces as if that could erase the reality. Dave sat truly surprised that he'd lost the race.

He'd made his way to the washroom to run cold water over his face when he bumped into a heavy-set man wearing a Leafs hat. "Sorry," Dave said, but the man just brushed past, mumbling something about the lotto. Dave watched as the man tossed a crumpled up ticket against the wall. He stared at the crumpled paper for a second before fishing his own lotto ticket from his wallet and heading for the bar set at the back of the building.

The urge to make up for one loss with another opportunity was what his dad called chasing his losses. He knew there would be a T.V. that didn't broadcast the races in the bar, and he knew he would be able to check the lottery numbers. The corner seat at the bar was open, so he sat down and arched his neck to get a look at the screen.

He ordered a pint to be polite and waited for the ticker tape to reveal the numbers. With his ticket flat on the bar, his eyes darted between the screen and his own numbers until the ticker tape ran the winning combination—thirty-two, seventy-nine, forty-five. Not only hadn't he won, but not one number was correct.

His eyes turned sombre as he stared at the T.V. screen for more than an hour, until he admitted that if luck truly existed, he didn't possess any.

Thirty

Dave didn't take risks, because he feared the complete humility of being a failure. As he sat in the living room with the horse race replaying in his mind, he knew that unlike in the movies and on television, risks are most often not rewarded. Realizing dreams is difficult, and despite what every teacher preaches, a best effort doesn't equal success. For a moment, he wished again that he had died in the crash and that one of his colleagues had lived instead. As much as Todd had annoyed him, there was no denying the man had more ambition, more promise, and more skill. But the moment vanished as fast as it appeared, because no matter how he framed it, he was glad to be alive, and the accompanying guilt made him want to forget everything he knew and start again. Everything except Amy. Before'd he met her, when he'd felt like a failure, he would take a nap, watch T.V., or go out for a drink. Now all he wanted to do was call her. Before the accident, he hadn't known her, and now, along with his dad, she was all that mattered. He remembered Grade Ten, when during a Family Studies class, the teacher had asked everyone to write down the age that they envisioned getting married and having kids. He'd written down twenty-four for both, yet just months away from his thirty-sixth birthday, he had never had a relationship last longer than three months.

He had once attributed that to a combination of a fear of commitment and meeting all of his dates at bars, but as he sat there defeated, he realized that he'd never had a relationship for longer than three months, because he had never been in love. Sure, he'd said it a few times out of obligation, but he had never put any weight on the word. He never cared what happened next, never missed them, and never regretted his actions until that moment, when all he wanted to do was call Amy and tell her how shitty he felt.

The muscles in his forearm twitched as he reached for the phone and keyed in her number as fast as possible, but ten rings later she hadn't answered, and her voice mail didn't activate. Thoughts of Grayson punching her flashed through his head. He tried to steady his mind, but the flashes continued. Yes, the man was her brother, but he'd also watched a man die and showed no reaction, so anything felt possible. Amy could be in danger because he hadn't cooperated with Thorrin. He thought of an article he'd read about a woman who dreamed that her son was on fire every night for three nights. After she woke the third night, the loss felt so real that she had to call her son. Five minutes into the conversation, his dormitory caught on fire, and because he was awake, he was one of only a few to get out of the building alive. Dave told himself his imagination was in control and that these thoughts were nothing more than negative projections based on his own fatigue and despair, but they felt so real, so possible that he needed to see her.

As he drove to her house, he repeated a promise to himself. *Let her be okay, let us be happy, and I'll make our relationship my life's work.*

The steps to Amy's complex were filled with puddles, but there was no time to step around them, so he splashed straight through. Two presses of her buzzer didn't feel like enough, so he leaned his thumb in a third time. After a moment, a light came on, then Amy answered the door wearing a University of Toronto sweater and track pants. She didn't look happy to see him.

"I'm sorry to just show up, but I called you, and your voice mail didn't pick up. I wanted to make sure everything's okay."

"Everything's *not* okay." She turned from the door and Dave followed inside. Her tone conveyed that this was personal.

"What are you talking about?"

"Grayson told me you said you'd leave the city to stop working with them."

"When did you talk to him?"

"I can't leave the city, it's hard enough for me to leave my home. And you know that, which means you don't care about not being around me."

"That's not true. It was just something I said; I'd say anything to get out of this situation."

"I believe that."

"They're not going to let me out of this twisted scenario."

"Who?"

"Thorrin and your brother. They're not going to let me out."

"Are you saying my brother lied to me?"

"They're not going to let me, but if there's one good thing that can come of this, it can be you living without fear."

"What are you talking about?"

"I lost fifty grand betting on horses tonight. Fifty grand in one race."

"What?"

"I was trying to make a hundred times that, and I lost all my money on the first race—that's anything but lucky."

She looked at him like he was the culmination of every bad thing that had ever happened to her. "You're lying."

"I wish I was."

"This is just your way out."

"I'm not finished." He removed the crumpled lottery ticket from his back pocket and tossed it on the table. "The lotto was a bust too."

Her eyes followed the ticket as it bounced and skidded into a stack of mail. She picked it up and began to unravel it to make it readable, then her eyes widened with annoyance.

"This is my phone number."

"That's right."

"You bet my phone number?"

He knew where this was going, so he decided not to respond. She ripped up the ticket and threw the pieces at him. "You have the nerve to come into my home and tell me I'm wrong about your luck when you lost using my telephone number?"

"Your number's special to me."

"I'm a curse."

"Not to me."

"Then why did you lose?"

"Because the odds are in favour of losing."

"You said you'd leave the city."

"I'm having trouble following you right now."

"I believed in you when I didn't think I could believe in anything again, and I had to hear from my brother that you're leaving the city."

"Will you stop talking about leaving the city? It was something I agreed to in order to get out of the situation I'm in. That's it. I came here to tell you I lost, so that you don't have to live afraid. I'm not blessed, and you're not cursed. You've been happy recently because of what we started. You and me, not because I'm a good luck charm."

"Life is too easy for you."

"What?"

"Life is too easy for you."

"You think life's easy for me?"

"You're telling me how to live my life, telling me how I feel, you must know."

"Everyone I worked with died except me. You think that's easy to live with?"

"I want you to leave."

"That's not going to solve this."

"I don't know if I want it solved."

"Slow down for a second."

"It feels like you're making me choose between you and my brother, and I barely know you."

"I'm not asking…"

"He's my brother, Dave. And you keep talking about him like he's some sort of monster."

"Amy…"

"I can't talk any more. Please leave."

They looked at each other for a moment. Amy shook with anger, and Dave looked like he was caught in the mud of his confusion.

"Okay," he whispered. He turned and left the house.

He got into his car to avoid the rain, but he didn't start the ignition for over an hour. His brain was too numb to do any real thinking, yet thoughts flowed through his mind faster than ever. He owed the rent for his dad's care, he owed Otto fifty thousand, and he owed Thorrin his time and inevitably his money. Those thoughts made him gag, but they didn't hurt as much as Amy's look of scorn. The look like it was possible she didn't care about him at all any more, or worse, that she had never cared about him at all. And while reflex told him to throw up his defences and match her anger head on, his mind yearned for the comfort he'd felt whenever he was with her.

When the phone buzzed at seven the next morning, Dave scrambled out of bed as if he'd been waiting for the call. Having dreamed of arguing with Amy, his subconscious tricked him into believe she was calling, but when he answered, the gruff voice on the other end was anything but her. It took him a moment to tune into what the man said.

"Mr. Bolden, there's been an incident with your father."

"Is he okay?"

"He's fine. This has nothing to do with his health. How soon can you be here?"

"Uh, half an hour."

"Very well."

Dave hung up wondering what his dad had done. Had he set up more betting pools? Was he running another card game? Or was he back to proposition betting? Whatever the case, he knew it had something to do with money. They'd never assumed the traditional father-son roles when it came to worrying and the worrier. He always felt a tingle in his stomach when his dad would leave the house, fearing that it was the last time he would see him. The feeling had started when he was a kid, and even the confines of a senior's home couldn't stop that angst.

He signed into 29 Palson, and a new receptionist with close-cropped brown hair escorted him down a hallway to an office he vaguely remembered as the place where he'd signed the contract to have his dad admitted years earlier. The room had no windows, and the director, a man he'd met over the years only in passing, turned down the volume on a jazz station as he entered.

"Thank you for coming, Mr. Bolden. You may not remember me. I'm Daniel Clarry. I'm the director here at 29 Palson."

"It's been awhile, but I do remember you."

Clarry slicked back what was left of his black hair as if he were in the Fifties. His face looked relatively young, but his hair betrayed him by providing a sneak peek into his declining years.

"Mr. Bolden, the reason we asked you to come today is because your father assaulted a staff member during breakfast this morning."

"Assaulted?"

"That's correct."

"How can my dad in his condition assault anyone?"

The director leaned back into storytelling mode. Apparently, for two months Jack and the afternoon attendant, Chris, had been making a series of hockey bets.

Chris had grown up playing hockey, so he wouldn't back down from a rematch each time he lost. Jack had started with double or nothing, moved to triple or nothing and made it to a week's pay or nothing, when eight weeks later Chris found himself down eleven hundred. Pride wouldn't let him stop, and a salary of twenty-four thousand a year before taxes wouldn't allow him to pay.

"You said you needed two weeks, and it's been three, I want my money," Jack said with a firm grip on the cuff of Chris's sweater as he delivered his oatmeal and orange juice.

Chris pulled free with a sneer. "Since when do you know the difference between two weeks and two months, you crusty fuck."

Jack tipped his orange juice and oatmeal to the floor. Neither the glass or bowl broke, but juice and oatmeal splattered across the tiles.

"Jesus Christ," Chris cursed, grabbing a rag from his pocket. "You want to be an asshole? Fine, then you'll be a hungry asshole."

Jack waited until Chris bent over to pick up the food then whacked him over the head with the tray. He hadn't felt that strong in years, but between the adrenaline pumping and his eyes bulging with rage, the swing flowed naturally. Chris wrapped his hands around the bloody point of impact and took a moment to get to his feet. The exertion caused Jack to erupt into a violent cough, which saved him from Chris's retaliation when another attendant entered the room after hearing Jack struggling to breathe.

With the story finished, Clarry leaned forward to get to the matter that concerned him. "Now, Chris is going to be fine, but he did need a few stitches."

Part of Dave wanted to leap out of his chair. That was the dad he remembered. He was thinking of his dad invigorated and full of life when Clarry pulled a folder out of a drawer, which snapped Dave back to the moment.

"No one's interested in pressing charges against your father, but given his history here, and his obvious disregard for the verbal warning, he is no longer welcome here effective the first of the month. And to be fair to you, I'll tell you now that if any other facilities call requesting a reference, I will be thorough and honest in my opinion of your father."

Dave opened the door to his dad's room, and Jack's head snapped towards him. He was anxious about who might enter the room, but Dave decided against sympathy.

"I thought we agreed, no more trouble."

"He was holding out on me."

"You shouldn't have been betting."

"He thought he didn't have to pay me because I'm an old man."

"You promised me you wouldn't bet in here again."

"Get off your high horse will you, for Christ's sake. Who are you to tell me anything?"

"I'm the one who pays the bills."

"Then put me out of my misery."

The words ground the banter to a halt. He'd wanted his dad to feel like a king, yet the tirade had treated him like a high school freshman. "They want you out at the end of the month."

"How many days is that?"

"Six."

"Six too many."

He wished he'd inherited his dad's irreverence. Six days meant little time to find another place for Jack to live, that was if anyone would accept him.

Thirty-One

Dave stepped out of his apartment building, surprised to see Grayson at the wheel of a blue mini-van idling in front. He slid into the passenger seat and turned to see Thorrin in the back with a coffee and newspaper. Grayson wore a black bubble jacket with a fur hood, while Thorrin wore sheepskin that made Dave think of Vikings.

"What's with the mini-van?"

"No one follows mini-vans." Grayson tossed a black toque into Dave's lap. "You're going to need this."

"Why?"

"Because we're heading north."

"Where?"

"Only about an hour outside the city, but it's windy today."

Dave turned to get Thorrin's take, but the man just nodded as he worked on a crossword puzzle. Grayson pressed play on the stereo, and his Japanese lessons poured from the speakers for the next hour. Dave didn't take his eyes off the window, and as the terrain changed from buildings to farmland and from concrete to snow covered fields, a part of him thought again that he was going to be murdered and buried in the woods. But as they passed a frozen bog with the remnants of a yellow canoe sticking up from the ice, a sense of calm flowed through him. They needed him.

He figured they wanted him as a symbol of their life philosophies, as much as for the extreme betting, and to kill him would be paramount to admitting they were insane.

That thought soothed him until the van turned onto the

bumpy road of a farm with a dilapidated barn and a trailer where a house should have been. Thorrin set down his newspaper and tapped Grayson's headrest with excitement.

"What am I going to be doing?" Dave asked.

"Nothing you can't handle," Grayson said, turning the music up.

Dave turned the stereo off. "You should know before we start whatever you have planned, that I have proof that I'm not lucky."

"Proof?" Grayson scoffed as he opened a pack of almonds with his teeth.

Dave ignored Grayson and turned to Thorrin, whose eyes danced with mischief. "I took fifty grand to the racetrack in hopes of working my way up to your buyout price, and I lost on the first race."

Thorrin raised his eyebrows at Grayson. "That just tells me you don't want to leave us."

"Are you listening to me? I lost."

"You wanted to lose."

"No, I want out. You've talked about how I need to have something at stake, well, there's nothing I want more in the world than to get out of this situation, and I lost."

The van hit a hole, and everyone in the car bounced before Grayson steadied the wheel. He turned to Dave with complete disregard for the road. "It's you who isn't listening. If you really did lose, and you're not just saying this to make us doubt you, then you lost because you wanted to."

"You should hear yourself."

"You're afraid of your own success, Dave," Thorrin interjected. "You always have been, or you wouldn't need me to reveal your gift. You hate risks, and your own mind turned on you when you made that bet to protect you from any real challenges."

"*I'm* in my mind, not you. You heard me tell you I lost fifty grand, right?"

"I don't care. Here's the situation. Senthur's waiting with Elango, the man you watched escape the dog that day. A man he claims has phenomenal fortune. Senthur's willing to bet a large amount of money that Elango's luck outweighs yours."

Grayson stopped the car beside the trailer, and for the first time, a large, frozen pond became visible. "You'd be best to focus on the task at hand."

"This is so stupid."

Thorrin stepped out of the van, let out two whistles of excitement and greeted Senthur with a hug. Senthur wore a fur hat with the ears down and a scarf that covered his chin. The temperature was at least ten degrees colder than in the city.

Elango sat on the trailer's steps with a black skull cap and a grey hoodie too thin for the weather.

A man the size of a sumo wrestler stepped out of the trailer and braced himself with the railing until Senthur gestured to him. "Bring the scale." The man returned to the trailer and reappeared a moment later with a scale that looked more like a Frisbee in his massive hand. The stairs creaked from the strain of his weight as he huffed down them and across the thin layer of snow, careful not to slip on hidden ice.

"Gentlemen." Senthur addressed Dave then Elango. "Time to weigh in."

Dave looked at Grayson for a hint about what was going on, but all he got was a shrug. Thorrin walked over to the trailer, back to the van, and paced around. Elango stepped to the scale first, slapping his clearly fit stomach. Even with a hoodie on, the man's taut physique stood out.

"One eighty-two," Senthur announced. Dave was next. He stood on the scale, worried that they were headed for a boxing match. He had never thrown a punch before. "One seventy-four."

"Get the belt." Senthur pointed at the large man leaning on the railing.

The man waddled over to the trailer again only to resurface with a weight belt adjusted to eight pounds. He handed the belt to Dave.

"What's this for?"

"To even the weight. We don't want any advantages." Senthur pointed past Dave to the frozen pond, and everything became clear. They were going to run across the ice. He couldn't help but stare. The pond must have been a hundred yards long and another fifty wide. Directly across, wind-bent evergreens lined the edge, and at the entrance, a stripped maple provided scale. A ripple of fear made Dave's fingers tingle.

Grayson stepped beside him and leaned in close. "Now I know nothing is going to happen to you, but even if you believe you might lose, I want you to understand that falling into freezing water is nothing compared to what can be done to your father if you don't participate."

Dave took a breath so deep the icy air hurt his lungs. "Where am I running to?"

"Just run straight ahead."

He considered that it might be the best moment to strike Grayson for telling Amy that he'd said he would leave the city. If this was the moment before he plunged into freezing water, he figured it should also be the moment of his revenge.

But that would guarantee a slow death for his dad and the end of anything he had with Amy, so instead of swinging at Grayson, he bent down to stretch his tight calf muscles. He'd been the fastest guy on his high school baseball team, but he couldn't remember the last time he'd run full speed, or if he'd ever run on ice.

"Let's do it," Senthur said with a clap.

The large man limped forward to set a briefcase beside Senthur, who waited for Grayson to match it with a duffle bag.

Elango took his position at the pond's lip, and Dave looked at Thorrin before joining him. The weight belt fit snugly around his waist, but the thought of anything slowing him down or increasing his chances of breaking through the ice made him wince. Dave joined Elango at the lip, and they stared straight ahead as if they were at a track meet.

"We start on three," Senthur said. Both men nodded. "One. Two. Three."

The men burst into a full run, and although Elango was faster, he ran like he didn't run often. With his elbows out and arms flailing, no one would mistake him for an athlete. About a quarter of the way across the pond, a loud crack in the ice threw off their strides. Dave didn't know whether to stop or keep running, but he knew he was behind Elango, and that made him push even harder, until three more pops from the ice warned him to stop. His feet skidded across the ice to the cracks beneath him. Elango kept running. He looked over his shoulder to see Dave standing still and broke into a smile, but then his left foot blew through the ice and sank his leg to just above the kneecap. The ice was sharp enough that it tore through his pants.

Elango thrust upward. The gash grated against the jagged ice until he pulled free. Blood was running from a cut that looked like he had just kicked through a glass door. He was shifting his weight to try and touch the wound when his right arm broke through the ice and sent him cheek-first to the frozen ground, where it splintered underneath his face.

Dave wanted to run for Elango, but the water began to bubble beneath his feet, and the ice released primal sounds as it spidered in front of him, so he pivoted and ran for shore.

Elango pulled his hand from the water and was trying to get up when the ice shattered and his body plunged into the water. A series of pops, like firecrackers, followed Dave to shore, where he dove at the maple tree's base.

Expressionless, Thorrin picked up the briefcase and entered the minivan. Grayson stood over Dave until he was ready to stand, and Senthur turned from the pond and went into the trailer. None of them tried to save Elango, and none of them spoke about watching a man die.

Thirty-Two

The Japanese lessons played loud in Grayson's car, too loud for Dave's liking, but he didn't have the resolve to say anything. His body was exhausted. He tried to replay running across the ice, but it had happened so fast that he'd only retained flashes like the cracks under his feet, how heavy his legs felt, and the sound Elango had made just before he submerged. The man had died, yet Grayson listened to the Japanese phrase for "Thank you for your time" as if it were a routine drive.

Grayson took a stack of money from his breast pocket while he drove and placed it on the dashboard. Dave continued to stare out the side window.

"There's your cut."

Dave didn't even look at the money.

"There's twenty grand there. That's half a year's salary for some people. Sweeping floors, losing their souls. You should be more appreciative."

Dave still didn't pick up the money.

Grayson turned down the Japanese lessons. "I'm glad you're with my sister, it's been good for her."

"Glad enough to make her doubt me?"

"What are you talking about?"

"You told her I said I'd leave the city to stop this insanity."

Grayson smiled far too easily, considering what they'd just witnessed. "That's nothing, just more motivation."

"It wasn't nothing. It was enough to have her doubt me."

"You'll make it up to her. Buy her something with this," he said, tapping the stack of money with an index finger.

Dave turned again to the window, causing Grayson to shake his head. "You've got twenty grand on the dash and a screw face, yet you act like it's our fault. When you start embracing our relationship for the opportunity that it is, all these inconveniences you don't like will stop, but until then we'll fuel the business however we have to. It's your choice."

Dave pointed to the next corner. "Right here's fine."

"You sure?"

"Yeah."

Grayson pulled the car over, and Dave got out. He stood outside the car with the passenger door open for a moment until Grayson tossed him the stack of money he'd left on the dash.

"We'll be in touch."

He wanted to throw the money back in the man's face, but between what he owed Otto and the fact that his dad needed a new place to live, he knew he couldn't afford to be so rash. Before he could give it a second thought, Grayson drove off. Dave stood for a moment on the corner and looked at the stack of money before walking along to an intersection, where he crossed. He had crossed that intersection thousands of times in his life, but now it felt like visiting a gravestone. He stopped and stood in front of what had once been his place of work. Plywood filled all the windowpanes. The metal frames and concrete were bent and chipped from the crash, but the site was otherwise clean.

It already looked more like another store gone out of business than the site of a bizarre tragedy.

A woman in her fifties with short hair and thin-rimmed glasses looked hard at the crash site before turning to Dave. "Do you know what happened here?"

"I'm sorry?"

"I live in Barrie now, but my husband and I lived in this neighbourhood for fifteen years, and he always had his accounting done here. It looks like some sort of accident, maybe a fire."

He wanted to tell her about the truck. He wanted to tell her how horrible it felt to be the only survivor, and that part of him felt so guilty, it was hard to live naturally, but another part of him felt so grateful that it was impossible to forget. He wanted to tell her all of this, but he said nothing.

"I don't know," he said, just dismissively enough to stop the conversation.

He remembered how nervous he'd felt on the first day of work. Four coffees before eight didn't help, but he wanted to be early, so he got up at six, then he found himself there at seven with the doors locked. He waited outside sipping coffees for half an hour until Mr. Richter showed up. Most bosses would have opened the door, given him a quick tour of the office and wished him best of luck, but Mr. Richter had insisted that they go for breakfast. And not once during breakfast had he mentioned accounting or business.

He wanted to know if Dave had siblings, where he went to school, what part of the city he lived in, and he told Dave about his four-year-old golden retriever and the new fence he was building in his backyard. Within ten minutes, he had Dave so relaxed that he wanted to work for Richter for the rest of his life.

A homeless man stumbled out from the alley beside the building, and Dave snapped into the moment.

"Spare some change?" the man asked. His teeth were crooked and purple.

Dave fished in his pockets for all the change he could find and put it in the man's hands.

"Can you see them too?" he asked with a finger pointed at the boarded-up storefront.

"See what?"

"The ghosts. They're everywhere in there."

Dave looked at the way the man's eyes bobbed in his head. What should have been the whites were veiled by thick, blood-shot vessels. Spittle stained the front of his shirt, and he smelled strongly of some sort of cleaning fluid. Dave gave him five more dollars and ushered him back down the alley. When he came back out to the street, two teenagers were stapling promotional posters for a rapper on the plywood. They had no idea what had happened to the property, and they didn't care. The plywood made a nice frame for the posters.

"Don't do that," Dave said, stepping towards them.

"What?" the one with a backwards baseball cap asked.

"Don't put these up here."

"Why not?"

"There was an accident here. People died. This shouldn't be advertising space."

The teen looked at him for a moment then over to his friend, who was too into the music pumping from his headphones to notice the conversation. "Sorry, I didn't know." The teen tapped his friend on the arm. "Not here, man."

"What? Why not?"

"There was an accident here, people died."

They moved on, and Dave stepped closer to the building, then regret hit him hard enough that he had to steady his legs. He missed the place. He'd complained about it daily, considered leaving regularly, called it boring, a waste of his life and lame, but with it gone, he wanted nothing more than to have it back so he could live just one of those days over again. He missed reading the paper on the bus ride every morning, the smells from the dessert shop on the corner, the Korean woman who had served him coffee every day, who always had a kind word despite not knowing his name, and the Jamaican food across the street that he ate every Wednesday. He missed the birthday cakes that people at work took turns buying once a month, whether it was somebody's birthday or not, he missed Shannon's acerbic rants about her neighbours' complaints and poor taste in flowers, Irene's running fashion commentary and how she'd teased Todd for his terrible taste in clothing, and Mr. Richter's steady smile and easy-going nature that made every moment with him as unthreatening and pleasant as listening to music from the Fifties. He even missed Todd. Because despite their dislike of each other and despite his piggish eating habits, Dave had always known that Todd was the best accountant at the firm.

He'd learned more about accounting from working with Todd than he ever had at school, and he missed that very much. He regretted not appreciating the place more, and the shame of disrespecting his colleagues that way made his eyes sting. Then a hand touched Dave's shoulder and startled him.

"Dave Bolden?"

"Yeah."

"My name's Phil Bryer, I'm Mr. Richter's attorney."

The name made Dave wince. Phil Bryer, the man who'd left him a message a week since the accident. From Dave's perspective, the man was a shark turning tragedy into business. Phil was in his forties. No taller than five-seven, his heavy frame made him bull-legged, but he had a smile that was disarming. He extended his hand, which Dave shook.

"I could have used you here a half-hour ago. Those vultures from the insurance company are low-balling us, and it would've been nice for them to hear an employee's perspective."

Dave's eyes didn't leave the storefront.

"Have you received any of my messages?"

"I got them."

"Well, I don't blame you for not calling back. I'm sure you've got a lot on your mind, but we really do have some things we need to discuss. Why don't I take you out for a quick beer, and we can seize the moment?"

Resigned to the situation, Dave nodded and led the way to the Saunders pub on the corner.

"Do you mind if we take a booth at the back?" Dave asked, hoping to go as far into the shadows as possible.

"Not at all."

Dave was relieved to see that the waitress was new, and no more than twenty. She could care less about the history of neighbouring businesses.

"Stella fine?" Phil asked.

Dave nodded and kept his head down.

"A pitcher of Stella, please."

The waitress smiled and walked away without looking at Dave.

"Is this your first time back to the building?" Phil asked.

"No, I need to come back sometimes."

"I understand. The press really didn't want to leave this one alone. You would have thought it was a conspiracy murder with how many calls we received about Mr. Richter's history. They really wanted to run with it, but we held our ground. You must have got a few calls."

"I ignored them."

"Good man."

The waitress delivered the pitcher and two pint glasses, and Phil paid before Dave could reach for his wallet.

"Thank you," she said as if he'd given her a two hundred dollar tip instead of five.

"You're welcome."

The waitress moved to the next table while they both sipped their pints, until Phil broke the silence. "What would you say she is, nineteen, twenty?"

"About that."

"It's a great age. Everything in front of you."

Dave took a longer drink from his pint and glanced at the bar to make sure the bartender wasn't staring.

Phil leaned forward like it was time to talk seriously. "I'm not sure if you're aware of this or not," he said, pointing at Dave with his pint glass, "but Mr. Richter didn't have any living relatives."

"I didn't know that."

"Mr. Richter's love was his business. As he says in his will, 'The smell of the office, the importance of the work, and most

of all, the employees.' His business was his life, and he thought
of anyone he worked with as his family. This may come as a
shock to you, Dave, but it was Mr. Richter's wish that in the
event of his death that his assets would be divided equally
among his employees. But as a result of the extraordinary
circumstances, you become the sole beneficiary. The sole
beneficiary to ten million dollars."

"What?"

"Mr. Richter left you his inheritance. Which means all of his
personal assets, his life insurance policy and the insurance claim
on the business."

"That can't be."

Phil put a folder on the table and turned it so that Dave
could see the paperwork. "It's all right here for you to digest as
the shock wears off. I'll leave it with you, and of course I'll be
in touch to sort out some of the administrative bureaucracy.
Until then, my only advice is this, do the man justice, you just
inherited his life's work."

"I don't understand."

"It's a lot to process, and being the man Mr. Richter was, he
knew it would be, so he included this letter." He slid a sealed
envelope along the table. "It's not addressed to you personally,
because he assumed the money would be divided, but you'll get
a feel for the spirit it's written in."

"I can't take his money."

Phil finished his beer. "This isn't an offer, Dave. All this
paperwork makes his wishes official once he's dead, and his
wishes were for you to have the money. Now, if you want to
speak to someone about how to manage the money or how to
invest it, I've got a number of people you can call. And if you
decide you want to give it away, I've got some opinions about
where to give, but if you ask me, and I knew the man for over
thirty years, he didn't leave it for you to give away. He could've
done that himself."

Thirty-Three

Home was not home any more, so Dave didn't want to open the letter there. After leaving Phil Bryer, he walked a few blocks. His thirty-five years in the city had conditioned him to respond to the word "millionaire" with euphoria, but his mind told him that the inheritance made things worse. He didn't want to profit from anyone's death, let alone Mr. Richter's. A coffee shop with a rusty sign reading DINER felt private enough, so he went to the back of the place, ordered a coffee from an obese man with a moustache and set the envelope on the table. Circumstance overwhelmed him. If Mr. Richter'd had a wife or children, the envelope wouldn't have been in front of him; if he had decided to apply to any of the larger accounting firms his dad had wanted him to, the envelope wouldn't have been in front of him, and if he hadn't slept in because of a hangover that fateful morning, the envelope wouldn't have been in front of him. He opened the envelope from corner to corner. If he didn't embrace the moment, he'd risk throwing it in the garbage. The paper smelled like a cologne Dave didn't know the name of, but he was sure was reserved for understated people over fifty. He held the paper close to his nose and inhaled. He hoped to be half that gentle one day. With the letter spread out on the counter, he began to read, and as he read, he couldn't help but adopt Mr. Richter's voice.

> *Good morning, afternoon or evening,*
> *You are all probably more than a little confused right now. Why would the boss that never gave you more than a three per cent raise leave you all the money he had in the world? Was he*

that alone, disconnected or pathetic? Those would all be fair questions, seeing as people don't leave ten million dollars to their employees everyday, but none of them are the right questions.

The right question would be: Did he really care that much about his business? And the answer to that is a heartfelt yes. You were the remaining people that drove the business I dreamed of, and as a result I want to leave my money to you. Nothing came close in life to making me as happy as my business, and as my love, soul and passion, it wouldn't have happened without you. Many people left the business as their careers grew over the years, but you are the ones that kept it running until my end. I do ask, however, that you embrace the spirit that just made you rich. Go out and spend, make your loved ones happy, then decide how you can use this money to start your own legacy. Start your own business, pour your soul into it and live the dream. Each of you helped me to live out my dream every day, and for that you should be rewarded with the opportunity to live your own. Thank you for your diligence, care and passion in making Richter Accounting my one and only home.

Sincerely,

Terrence James Richter

Dave read the letter again to be sure of every word: *My love, my soul, my passion; embrace the spirit; start your own legacy; live the dream.* Ten million dollars. He didn't know where to begin. Just as the moment the truck crashed through the front of Richter Accounting had, and the moment Grayson had approached him, reading the letter changed everything forever.

He hailed a cab back to his place and went straight to the landlord's apartment. The man answered the door without a shirt on, and Dave could see a hockey game playing on the television in the background.

"What's the trouble?"

"No trouble. I just want to give you notice."

The man sighed as his fingers picked at thick chest hair. "Are you buying a home?"

Dave thought about the question. He could buy twenty homes. "I am."

"Fucking interest rates. They don't think about the landlords when the banks do this, you know."

"No, I guess they don't."

Dave went up to his apartment and bee-lined to his desk. He'd kept every photo he had in a shoebox, and there was one burning a spot on his mind. He sifted past photos of his dad, a few women he'd dated and one from a bachelor party, then he found a picture of him with all of his colleagues the day Mr. Richter had the sign outside the office replaced. He sealed the picture in a zip-lock bag and headed for a collectables store three blocks away. The owner looked like a giant. He had to be at least six-eight and well over two hundred and fifty pounds, with black hair that looked like he'd put his finger in a light socket and a long beard he twisted into a point. He would have stood out in any crowd.

"I need a plastic case that would protect my cards outside in the winter if I wanted to leave them there."

The owner smiled and revealed a large gap between his two front teeth. "Then you want the tomb," he said in a Russian accent.

"That's the best you have?"

The man's eyebrows rose, and it was clear he took it more as a challenge than a question. His back cracked as he bent over, then his knees, but he resurfaced from under the counter with a plastic container the size of his forearm in one hand and a hammer in the other. He placed the container on the counter for Dave to inspect.

"This is the tomb. My Mickey Mantle is in a tomb. My Babe Ruth is in a tomb. My Gordie Howe is in a tomb. And my Johnny Unitis is in a tomb. Here's how much I trust the tomb." He raised the hammer over his head with two hands and brought it crashing down onto the top of the tomb. The table shook hard enough that a stapler fell to the floor, and the impact caused Dave to step back, but the tomb looked the same as it had before the blow. The owner wiped a drop of sweat from his brow.

"You see, not a scratch."

Dave bought the tomb and hailed another cab back to what remained of his old office. A hot dog vendor had positioned himself in front of the store, so Dave had to work around him, but he took two pieces of concrete and a shard of broken tile and placed them in the tomb. He then added the picture of the office looking pristine and sealed it shut. He decided that would be his last visit to his old workplace. He didn't want to see it turned into a video store or a dry cleaners, he didn't want to see the faces of people walking by in droves, none of them aware of the tragedy, and he didn't want to remind himself of a time when he hadn't appreciated what passed him every day. He hailed another cab.

"Deer Park cemetery, please."

He tipped the driver a twenty and walked up the path to the north end, where, despite all his money, Mr. Richter had insisted on a modest gravestone. Two bouquets of flowers rested at the base of his plot.

The flower proved people remembered the man, and that made Dave smile. He set the tomb, with its picture of the business and the concrete and tile that formed it, beside the flowers and crouched down. *Thank you.* He tapped the tomb. *Thank you.*

Thirty-Four

A drop of rain hit Dave's nose, spilling over each side equally. It occurred to him that he needed to see Otto and be around someone that understood him the way only a life-long friend could.

Dave stepped into the crowded internet café , walked to the back and approached Otto's office like he was the owner. Otto was squinting at a computer screen when Dave tapped on the door. "Do you have time for a beer?"

An hour and three pints later, Dave sat back in his living room, where he surfed the Net for the city's most desirable homes. It felt good to imagine another life. He'd saved a housing site in his favourites when the phone buzzed.

"Hello?"

"Are you ready to change your life?" Grayson's tone was more excited than usual.

"I am."

"Good. Because Thorrin just got a proposition from a kindred spirit, a proposition that will earn you half a million dollars."

Dave did the math. His cut was twenty per cent, which meant Thorrin stood to make ten million dollars.

"Can Thorrin afford that kind of a bet?"

"He won't have to."

"What's the challenge?"

"You'll see when we get there. I'll pick you up in an hour."

"I'll be ready."

"You don't even need a pep talk this time?"

"The mention of five hundred thousand did that for you."

Dave decided the word "odds" had lost its weight. With all the outrageous stories people are exposed to on television, the movies and the internet, he acknowledged it felt like anything was possible. Going from a one-bedroom apartment in government housing to a mansion with an indoor pool felt as feasible as falling in love in a foreign country or starting a company that earns a billion dollars. These stories are so common, the extraordinary doesn't just seem possible, it feels probable. But Dave knew better. Years of watching odds toy with his father had forced him to respect them, to appreciate the variables that contribute to success and failure, and to fear the power of risk. The last month had made him embrace the wonder of odds. To calculate the odds of conception, you need to multiply the fact that a man releases millions of sperm with every ejaculation by the number of orgasms prior to conception and multiply that by the chances of finding your partner in a world with billions of people, and multiply that by the possibility of your partner releasing an egg at the time of sex, then multiply the total by the odds of a miscarriage. From that perspective, odds are everything. From that perspective, beating the odds *is* life.

He stepped outside to a dark sky and pulled his collar up over the sides of his face. He'd started to bounce on his toes when Thorrin's limo appeared in the distance. For the first time, he noticed the headlights were oversized and centred on a shiny grill. The vehicle looked like something from the future.

Dave opened the side door expecting to see Thorrin, but only Grayson was there to greet him. "I hope you're well rested, because this is a whole new level of money," he said, swirling a fresh scotch so the ice cubes tinkled against the side of the glass.

"I'm ready."

"So you believe in luck now?"

"I'm agnostic and I'm stubborn, but even I can see a pattern."

Grayson finished his drink and looked at Dave for a moment with a furrowed brow before reaching for the scotch bottle and raising it to eye level. "Good man."

They didn't speak for the rest of the drive. Grayson watched a business show on a screen so beautiful that it didn't belong in a car, and Dave stared out the window as drops of rain splattered against the pane, leaving streaks that blurred his vision.

The vehicle turned into Thorrin's driveway, and Dave snapped into the moment.

"It's going down here?"

Grayson raised his eyebrows with a wry smile that made Dave wonder how it was possible for the man to be Amy's brother.

They stepped out of the car, and Grayson led the way to a garage adjacent to the house. With Italian tiles, restored brick and an eighteen-foot arched ceiling, the structure was better than most homes. The inside, however, was eerily sparse. Other than exercise mats hanging from a rack on the south wall and a metal trunk in the corner below them, the cement floor and white walls dominated the space.

"Do you want me to take off my shoes?" Dave asked.

Grayson shook his head as the door opened. A gust of cold air sent a chill through the room as Thorrin entered the garage, followed by Otto and a muscular man Dave had never seen before. The man had orange stubble on his shaved head and a thick goatee on his pale face. Otto carried a metal briefcase.

Neither Otto nor Dave acknowledged each other. After setting the briefcase down beside Grayson, Thorrin headed for Dave and massaged his shoulders.

"Today's our day," he said in a whisper. "This is the biggest day of our lives."

The man with the shaved head looked at Dave, and Dave dropped his eyes to the floor.

Grayson walked to the metal trunk under the exercise

mats, and the sway at the bottom of his overcoat gave him the swagger of a sheriff from the Wild West. He removed a small key from his breast pocket, put it in the thick silver lock and opened the lid. The room watched as he put his hands in the trunk and removed a python as thick as his head.

Dave was imagining the snake constricting his waist when Thorrin raised a hand. He removed a quarter from his pocket and extended it to Otto.

"Is it okay with you if we leave it to chance?"

Otto looked at Dave, whose eyes told him to proceed, before offering Thorrin a nod. Thorrin lived for chance, and the addition of an hors d'oeuvre made his bottom lip quiver.

"The honour is yours," he said, passing Otto the quarter.

"What are we flipping for?"

"Heads we go with the snake, tails we go with another thought."

The coin looked small between Otto's fingers, and he held it a moment before flipping it into the air and taking a step back. The metal echoed through the garage when it hit the floor, bounced twice and landed tails up.

Thorrin clapped his hands as he hovered above the coin. "Another thought it is. Grayson, can you give our participants their tools?" He bent down and tapped a metal case at his feet.

The python's tongue flicked incessantly as Grayson lowered it back into the trunk. He took the case from Thorrin, opened it and removed two silver revolvers from their casings. He passed one gun to the man with the shaved head, who looked at it as if he had never seen a weapon before. Dave stepped forward and reached for his gun. The metal felt heavier than he expected, and it smelled like silver polish.

Grayson moved to the centre of the room, measured five feet on each side and marked the measurement with strips of duct tape. Everything about his movement was efficient. He was enjoying being a step ahead of their guests.

Dave took his position at the tape closest to him and looked at Otto, who rubbed the nape of his neck. Dave let the gun's weight stretch his arm to his knee and straightened his back.

"Real simple, gentlemen," Grayson said. "Spin your cylinders, raise your weapons and pull the trigger on three."

Dave looked at the open cylinder to see one bullet and five empty slots. He flicked the cylinder, let it spin for a few seconds and pushed it into the gun's centre. He tightened his grip on the handle and pointed it at the man with the shaved head.

From his perspective, the gun pointing at him appeared fake, and for a moment he thought about the time Grayson had pointed a starter's pistol at him in Thorrin's office.

"One." Grayson held up a finger, but Dave stared straight ahead. "Two."

Dave could see Otto out of the corner of his eye, the look of disbelief, and the worry in his eyes. Otto hadn't expected Dave to be in danger when Dave told him about inheriting ten million dollars. And he hadn't expected to see a gun pointed at Dave when Dave had given him Thorrin's number and asked him to arrange an extreme bet. But Dave didn't worry, because he knew something Otto didn't know. He knew luck was on his side.

"Three."

The word wasn't fully pronounced when both men pulled their triggers. Dave's released the impotent click of an empty chamber, while the gun pointing at him fired. The sound that only a gun can make filled the garage, and Dave didn't blink before the bullet tore through his left shoulder, just a fingerprint away from the clavicle. The bullet's power took him off his feet, and he landed on the floor hard. The back of his head bounced off the cement before he looked up groggily to see blood seeping through his shirt.

Shock washed over Thorrin's face. He'd lost millions of dollars in a second, and everything about his reality changed. He felt his momentum grind to a halt, witnessed chance making its rounds, and it crushed his faith in an instant.

Otto looked at Dave, nodded. Otto whispered to Thorrin. "I'll wait outside for my money."

Otto left the garage, and the man with the shaved head followed him.

The pain in Dave's shoulder numbed his left side, but a smile still filled his face. He made his way to his feet and stumbled toward Thorrin.

"You lost," Thorrin said, as if this was a dream or something that could not possibly be real. And then his face contorted into disgust.

He looked at Dave the way an agent looks at leading actresses when their faces begin to age. The fondness he'd developed for Dave over the course of his victories blurred into contempt for being yet another false hope in search of someone immune to life's inevitability. "Get the man his money," he said to Grayson with a gesture to the door. He turned from Dave, promised himself he would never look at the man again and left the room determined to forget they ever met.

Dave pivoted to look at Grayson, and for a moment he was convinced the man offered a smile of approval. He left the garage just behind Grayson with blood running down his arm. Otto helped him into the car, where he watched his friend wince before passing him a towel.

With his head back, Dave arched his neck on the headrest. If the man Otto brought had experience with guns, Dave would have died. If the man's wrist had been stronger, Dave would have died. But it wasn't, and instead, the bullet went clean through his flesh from one side of his shoulder to the other as if a minor annoyance on its way to somewhere more important.

Dave locked eyes with Otto. "What do you look so stressed for? You just made five million dollars."

Otto shook his head. "You are a lucky son of a bitch."

Dave put the towel over his face and smiled the smile of a man with fifteen million dollars and his freedom.

Thirty-Five

Dave called Amy ten times, but she didn't answer, and her voice mail didn't pick up, so he went to her house. Enjoying the possibilities that the money brought wasn't an option without making amends with her. He tried to tell himself to relax, that she would answer the phone eventually, but the compulsion to see her shunned reason. He wanted to hear the perfect note of her voice, to smell the sweetness of her skin, and to see a look that cared when he stared into her eyes. He hailed a cab on the corner and stepped inside to see the first female cabbie of his life. She looked more feminine than he expected. With a dirty-blonde ponytail, green eyes, and a black jump-suit hoodie, the exhaustion under her eyes was the only thing tough about her. He gave her Amy's address, but she didn't drive right away. Instead she examined him through the mirror before holding up a cigarette.

"Is it a problem if I smoke?"

"No."

She pulled onto the road, and just the motion of moving made Dave feel less anxious.

The cabbie looked at his arm in sling. "What happened?"

"Skiing."

"Uh-huh. When she leave you?" she asked and exhaled a thick stream of smoke.

"I'm sorry?"

"You've got eyes like mine, and my husband left me two months ago. When did she leave you?"

"She didn't leave me."

"Okay, when did you fight?"

Dave rubbed at his face without responding. She took another drag. He had never seen anyone smoke that hard.

"I've got a piece of advice for you," she said. He didn't respond the way she wanted, so she waited for the next red light and turned to face him. "I'm just saying, I've been in your situation, and I know what men don't do that they could do to make everything better."

"What's that?"

"Tell her you're sorry you upset her. Saying you're sorry about whatever you fought about is obvious. You both are. Tell her you're sorry you upset her."

Dave nodded. The cabbie pulled up in front of Amy's, and he tipped her forty dollars.

"A forty dollar tip?" she asked, stunned.

"For the advice."

He pressed Amy's buzzer and waited for her to answer the door. Just before he pressed the buzzer again, he heard footsteps approaching. He took two deep breaths and the door opened. He wanted to hug her, but the look on her face warned that she didn't feel the same, until the sling finally caught her attention, and the anger in her face turned to concern.

"What happened to you?"

"I'm free."

"I don't understand."

"You don't need to, and you don't need to be angry. I just want to see you. I'm sorry I upset you. Everything we talked about needed to be discussed, and a lot of it still does, but it didn't have to stress you, and I'm sorry for that."

They looked at each other for a moment.

"Something amazing happened to me, and there's no one I want to share it with more than you. Can I come in?"

Amy turned, and he followed her inside. A small battery-powered lamp was the only light on in the house. The temperature was as cool as outside, and all of the drapes were shut tight.

"I can prove you're not unlucky."

Her eyes stuck on him like he couldn't have said anything more annoying. "You've already told me how you feel about that, Dave."

"Yeah, but I think you'll like this example."

"Why?"

"Because you deserve it."

"I'm pregnant."

The words stopped his flow, and flashes of responsibility, miracles and lineage flashed through his mind. "Pregnant?"

"The condom didn't work."

A smile filled Dave's face as he thought of odds, chance and the creation of life. "That's the best news I've ever heard."

"I thought you'd be upset." Amy's lips began to move so fast, the words left her mouth with the rhythm of an Uzi. "I've had four miscarriages, and we've only know each other for…"

"I think it's amazing. And the timing couldn't be better."

"Really? Because it doesn't seem like perfect timing."

He extended an envelope, and she stared at it for a moment before taking it from his hand.

"Go ahead, open it."

She tore one corner and removed a cheque. "I don't get it."

"Read it."

"It's a fake cheque for a million dollars."

"There's nothing fake about it."

"I don't understand."

"I inherited money. The man I worked for left his money to his employees, and I'm the only one alive."

"What?"

"You're right about me. Something is working in my favour, and while I'd trade it in a second to bring my colleagues back, I can't. So the best way to honour them is to live."

"Why would you give me money?"

"Because now you can't ever say again that you're unlucky, and because I want you to be happy. I've been thinking about how much you believe you're destined to have bad things happen to you, and it drives me crazy, because I'm proof that you aren't unlucky. How can you possibly be cursed with anything negative when you're able to make me feel better than I've ever felt in my life?"

"I don't know what to say."

Dave smiled, and Amy locked eyes with him.

"What about my brother?"

"He's not interested any more."

"Just like that?"

Dave nodded. "I don't know how he'll feel about seeing me, but it's not about me or him, it's about you, so we'll figure something out."

She held up the cheque. "This is real?"

He nodded. "We can bring the concerts to you now."

She smiled and let out a primal squeal of happiness. If he believed he was lucky, then she could believe *she* wasn't unlucky, and it felt great to react without thinking.

"Try to tell me you're not lucky now."

He considered the statement. He couldn't tell her he wasn't lucky, because he *knew* he was, and he knew that it took taking risks to discover luck's power.

Dave walked into 29 Palson with an empty suitcase in each hand.

"Sign in here please, sir," the receptionist said and spun a clipboard towards him.

"Actually, I'm signing out. Jack Bolden is scheduled to leave by the first of the month, and we're going to do it today."

Jack didn't notice that Dave was carrying suitcases as he entered the room. "Did you bring today's line?" he asked without taking his eyes from a billiards match on television.

Dave removed a photo from the side pocket of his jacket and held it at eye level.

"What I brought is better than the line."

"Don't be an ass."

Dave put the photo in dad's closest hand.

"What's this?"

"It's the new cottage."

"I want the old cottage."

Dave smiled. "So do I, but we'll have to settle for a new one."

"Is there bird shit at this cottage?"

"Not that I know of."

Jack inspected the photo. "This isn't the old cottage."

"No, it isn't. But it's a long way from here."

He began to pack his dad's belongings, and it occurred to him that he was his dad's payoff. After sixty years of hustling, calculating odds, and playing the systems, the man could finally have whatever he wanted. Ten million dollars. Dave didn't know what money meant to his dad any more, but he knew that he could buy him the freedom to do whatever he wanted with the years he had left, and that peace of mind made the whole journey make sense.

Acknowledgements

My thanks to Matthew Stone for placing the book with DarkStar Fiction, for your rare insight and invaluable notes. To Benjamin Gilbert for reading everything I've ever written long before it was worth reading, and for making all of it better. Christopher Sandy for your passion for knowledge and attention to detail; Mark Adriaans for your irreverence and Matthew Deslippe for your understanding of character. Thank you to the encyclopedia of music, Steve Dalrymple, for giving the book its rhythm. My respect to Simon Gilbert for making being smart cool as a kid, and to Eddie and Debbie Gilbert for introducing me to the arts. To Skye Bjarnason for our late night literary discussions. My appreciation and thanks to my editor Allister Thomson for your passion and precision; to Sylvia McConnell for your support of the project and for your guidance during the process; and to Emma Dolan for designing a groovy cover.

Scott Carter was born in Toronto and raised in the Beach neighbourhood. He has worked in the book publishing industry and is now a high school English teacher.

Scott is also a screenwriter who has worked on numerous feature films and short films with various companies, including his own Sad But True Entertainment, founded in 2007.

He lives in Toronto's Riverdale district with his family.